MW01200410

Our Last Year

Sincerity itself is the railway track. [It is a] beginningless and endless track. There is no starting point, no goal, nothing to attain. Just to run on the track is our way … But when you become curious about the track, danger is there. You should not see the railway track. If you look at the track you will become dizzy. Just appreciate the sights you see from the train … There is no secret. Everyone has the same nature as the railway track.

Shunryū Suzuki, *Zen Mind, Beginner's Mind*

Fall

If you wish to know the truth
don't think for or against.
Likes and dislikes
are the disease of the mind.
    Sengcan

In the kitchen sometime before seven in the morning, after waking before sunrise to the figure of his three-year-old-daughter, their youngest daughter, pulling him out of bed by grabbing his arm and saying pull, pull, pull, he was standing in the dark, having forgotten to turn on the light, preparing to take their youngest daughter to school, thinking that he needed to put grass-fed, organic mac and cheese in a Tupperware container, then organic strawberries in a smaller Tupperware container, then organic, non-GMO veggie chips in a small, brown, compostable sandwich bag, all things he had done the morning before and the morning before that, with small variations, and which, he thought, he was about to do again now, and which he would do – feeling the almost effortless stupidity of it – for many more days after this one, disliking that he was doing it, until, most likely, he didn't have to do it anymore, until both his daughters were grown and there was no longer any need to prepare their lunches in the morning. Now, thinking of that future moment when he no longer had to make his daughters' lunches, rather than feeling relief that he would not have to devote time mindlessly to doing the same mundane thing every morning, he knew he would miss it, and not only miss it but nostalgically want that time back, want the doing of it back if not the thinking about the doing of it, and so he told himself to appreciate what he was doing, to be grateful for it. Though he wasn't. He knew he wasn't.

While he was pulling with his hands – he didn't bother to get a spoon – some refrigerated mac and cheese from a large Tupperware container and putting it into a smaller Tupperware container, his youngest daughter was running around the kitchen, yelling, Daddy, Daddy, pink yoghurt, pink yoghurt, and he told her to hold on, he was finishing making her lunch, and when he finished putting everything in the appropriate containers, as soon as he found the pink yoghurt in the refrigerator, opened it, got a spoon from the drawer for her and handed it to her, she stopped running and looked at him plainly and directly and said, No. Veggie chips, please. He said okay, re-covering the organic Greek yoghurt with plastic wrap. He quickly rinsed his hands at the sink. Then he went to the pantry and surveyed it, boxes and boxes of non-GMO, organic, processed food. The types of snacks that he and his wife bought for their daughters had caused them to slip into a vaguely sarcastic form of joking about their own supposedly sustainable practices: they called their daughters the non-GMO-daughters because they tried to feed them organic foods, which included all of the processed foods they bought, like Cheetos and tortilla chips and gummy bears and breakfast bars. He thought of being at the grocery store one day with his wife, and while she placed ten boxes of organic, non-GMO macaroni and cheese in their cart – it was on sale – he had loudly said just as another mother and father were entering the aisle that he was really glad both of their daughters were one-hundred-percent-organic humans. I'm proud, he had said in a serious, politician's voice, that our daughters are all-natural, organic beings. Not only that, his wife had said, her face stricken with seriousness, they're certified non-GMO. They're delicious, he had said, looking vaguely in the other parents' direction and into their cart as they'd passed, smiling at their cart in mock judgement.

He smiled while he recalled this as he once again re-trieved veggie chips for his daughter. He'd already packed them in her lunch and now they were out again as her breakfast. He'd given some to their older daughter as well. She'd caught the bus, it was her first year of doing that, and he already missed her needing him, or her mother, for everything. She could get to school on her own. Though, now that she was nearly six, she often told him that she needed an extra bag of veggie chips for the ride home, which he knew she traded for candy. Now he put some veggie chips, again, in a small, compostable brown bag and handed the bag to his youngest daughter, who said, Thank you Daddy, and began running in a small circle in the middle of the galley kitchen. His thinking, he saw in this moment, was barely thinking: he understood he was barely awake and didn't want to be doing right now what he was doing but he was doing it, though he was barely awake, and was trying to be okay with doing it, and he further understood that he woke up in an awful mood, feeling pointless and confused and frustrated that he had to do this day – a day he had done over and over again – again, now, once again, but none of that felt like actual thinking, he thought. It felt like his reactive response to a situation he didn't feel like being in and to doing something he didn't feel like doing, and so his thinking felt more programmed than actual, more reactive than active, as though he wasn't really living his life but was on sleep mode and was only observing the programmed responses his mind and attention and consciousness were all making from some distant place deep behind his eyes. His patience with his youngest daughter while she ran in circles around the kitchen – sort of in his way – therefore, was not actual patience, just basic, semi-annoyed responsiveness to what was before him, an unengaged boredom, which he hated and wished he wasn't feeling. It was the same way, he thought, that he and his wife had been interacting lately. With a kind of basic disinterest, the same unengaged boredom, which he thought was just a phase, and which he thought was because she was in one of her depressive modes, in which she ate less, was often quiet, and seemed to view him as an annoyance in her life, and which he knew there was no real remedy for. It would pass or go away or whatever. She had told him recently, apropos nothing, that they needed to stop being robots. He'd looked at her and pretended to move his head mechanically and inquisitively, like he was an android who didn't understand her statement. But she'd said, Seriously, we're on autopilot, it sucks. Standing in the kitchen, he could barely even see the real thought beneath all this, but it was there, a small creature in the grasslands of his mind, with this moment in the kitchen packing his youngest daughter's lunch as evidence: he was bored with life, and what was worse, what made him feel worse, was that he didn't think he was a person who should be bored with life, and at the same time, he had no idea how that feeling had begun nor how to stop that feeling, how to feel something else.

Above the sink, the sky was just lightening, the trees and leaves and misty morning seeming to come into existence as though some great being were undimming the inner light of all things, those things becoming more and more real, as though in the dark out the window only moments ago the things of the phenomenal world hadn't been there at all. It was the sun rising. He didn't notice this. Though of course, that was not an accurate description of what was actually occurring: the sun was rising only in relation to certain beings on the surface of the planet at this particular moment in time, and in reality the sun was neither rising nor descending, though it was moving, moving around the centre of the galaxy, orbiting the centre of the galaxy in the same way the earth was orbiting it, and the sun, in the same way the earth spins on its axis, was also rotating on its axis. What it was doing was only what it was doing, not rising, not falling, but moving, being what it was, sending energy to the surface of the planet unwittingly, just doing what it did, and while momentarily, in this particular city in this particular part of North America, the sun was not obscured by cloud and the day would be clear for a while, to the east of the city a large storm system was moving, itself caused by the sun and many other factors, and would arrive in some hours, the start of two weeks of steady rain that arrived each year and signalled the end of summer.

In the kitchen, putting a Tupperware lid on the container with the organic strawberries, he didn't see the morning, didn't notice the light out the window, but he heard the girl's mother doing something in the bathroom. She was putting on makeup, combing her hair, and was, he knew, late for work again. She yelled something, then he realised she was talking to him, she was asking where her keys were. There was a clear frustration in her voice, an almost easy-going annoyance, like clearly it was his fault that her keys were missing, though she never put them in the same place, and he yelled back that he was getting lunch ready, and her coffee, and he didn't know where her keys were. Maybe she should try putting them in the same place, though he said the last part quietly so that she couldn't hear, because he knew that if he said something like this to her directly, though it was the truth, it would prompt an argument in which she accused him of always pointing out her flaws, accused him of looking for ways to blame her, which he sometimes did, and after which she would refuse to engage with him for the rest of the day and night and possibly for the next day or so as well. It was like this, he thought: they could make jokes, watch movies, smoke pot, but they could not talk seriously about what they saw as each other's shortcomings without devolving into some sort of soap opera-ish argument. Even the world, he thought, would suddenly become melodramatic in those moments, with a Vaseline haze blurring the edges of their lives, and as they began arguing he'd so feel he was in some role that he didn't want to be in that it was almost as though he could perceive his hair becoming lacquered in the style of a narcissistic banker while her jeans and T-shirt would be replaced with a gaudy pink dress suit and pearls, and they'd yell stupidly at each other's faces, only to come out of it hours or days later, apologising but never knowing what the actual problem was. Not only this, but lately he had located some irritated narrator in his unconscious mind taking control of the track of his thinking, whispering to him almost without him knowing: the thing about her is that she can't take responsibility for certain things, this voice would say, she can't take responsibility for her mistakes, her mistakes aren't mistakes in her mind, see, they're things she uses to blame you for, which means that she uses her own feelings to blame you for how she's feeling or failing to be feeling, which of course means that she uses her feelings as weapons to defeat your feelings, that is, she uses her feelings to show you how wrong you are not only about her, not only about yourself, not only about your daughters but about everything, everything. Not only this, but she can't clean up after herself, can't decide anything on her own, you live with another child, that's what's occurring here, you live with another child, and, like a child, she's incapable of considering anyone else's feelings unless that other person's feelings are positive, and if something occurs that she doesn't like, especially if you've done it, then her anger is both beyond reasonable and, for her, justified, which makes you angry, and yet your anger is then your fault and just another thing that is frustrating to her, like a child. This little hum of thought occurred in the background of his mind, running right below his more obvious conscious thought and lived experience, like it was now: of course she was once again annoyed at him to start the day, of course there was something that he had nothing to do with that she was finding a way to make his mistake, finding a way to blame him for: he'd lost her keys, was what she was saying. He stood blankly at the sink, drinking his coffee, noticing the way he was thinking. He had been noticing it more and more. Standing in the kitchen with his coffee, he thought that thinking in this way had become so rote in the last month that he would almost not notice it, and then suddenly, as he just had, he would take note of it and feel awful that it was a part of him. He took a sip of coffee and thought that he didn't even really believe these were *his* thoughts: he didn't want to think them, he didn't like them, and he didn't actually feel this way about her. It was almost as though he'd feel some frustration from her – as he just had with the keys thing – and this annoyed dialogue would bloom into life of its own accord, his think-ing thinking itself, rather than him being in control of it. Though he knew that wasn't true. He knew that was an excuse of some kind. These *were* his thoughts, he thought in the dim kitchen. He knew what was true was that his own frustration engendered the thoughts, that his frustration brought the thoughts into being, and whenever he noticed he was having them, as he was now, he tried to silence them with other things he felt about her, in order in some way to take control of his thinking: she gave him time, he thought now, she gave him time to work, and over the past six months in particular, when he'd begun the new series of paintings for his first large gallery opening, she'd given him time for the quiet and silence he needed to create, a much more important kind of time, which she understood he needed, which meant, he tried to think on these occasions, that she was understanding, that not only was she under-standing, she understood, and what she understood was *him*, and she supported him and his painting – she took the kids to the pool or the park or the museum while he painted, and in turn he made them all dinner and cleaned up afterwards, and then he was back at it while they watched a movie late into the summer night – and he knew, he tried to think on such occasions, as he was thinking now, that she was not trying to annoy him by being messy or by seeming to outsource all of the housework to him, she wasn't trying to frustrate him, she was just messy and that was nothing to be annoyed about, and additionally, he tried to make himself think, she was a caring mother but also busy, two kids were not easy, and also, he thought, she was the only person he could openly talk to, be fully him-self with, and she accepted everything about him, or almost everything, mostly everything, though she could get resent-ful that he needed to be alone to work, that he needed to be alone, that he had always needed it, it was a part of him she refused, though she tried, he thought. Also, she could get upset that they didn't have much money, that, even with two children, they were living paycheck-to-paycheck, on teachers' salaries, that he had never done what she'd thought he'd do, which was become a teacher who was paid well, an artist whose art was actually sought after, and so they constantly felt the pressure of not having enough money, of always barely having enough, though she didn't blame him, except when she got very angry. In actual fact, she supported him, had supported him for years while he was paid much less than her, and he needed to consider that, needed to consider that she did these things for him, things that were not easy – he was not easy, he knew, and his lifestyle did not make things easy for them, and there was the constant worrying in the back of their minds that they were not putting nearly enough away for their daughters, that they weren't providing for them in the right way, not providing for their children's futures let alone their own – and yet she was there for him, she had been there for him, he needed to be aware of that. He washed his hands at the sink, though as he did so he realised he had just done it a few moments earlier after putting his youngest daughter's lunch together.

He picked up his coffee and took another sip. It was warm, steam rising out of the blue glazed mug that a student had made him as a gift. The student had made one for his wife as well, though his wife had at first been jealous rather than grateful, and she rarely used the mug. He thought that the reason this attempt at a shift in thinking towards something less negative didn't really work, and why he always ended up thinking in the other way, was that the shift itself had become boring and rote, as though he were seeking some antidote but didn't know what the poison was. In his mind, he just saw two opposing things:

the things he liked about his wife and those he disliked.
He saw these same things about himself. He saw the way
he wanted to be, but he couldn't embody it. He saw some
place that his life should be, but it was like the landscape
as portrayed in a barely glimpsed Polaroid from years ago:
he didn't know how to get there and stay there. Where was
that place? A place where he was present, available, able
to work on his paintings, taught well and diligently, made
between ten and fifteen thousand dollars more a year, put
money away for his daughters and him and his wife and was
an attentive, caring father and husband, was playful, fun,
not moody, not depressed, didn't look at society in despair,
though saw it needed work and so volunteered in a soup
kitchen or donated his time and energy to Habitat for
Humanity, bought a hybrid car, and saw things both inside
himself and out in the world as manageable, and thus didn't
internalise things he didn't like about the outside world,
and accepted himself for who he was. It seemed like some
impossible place to get to, he thought. Even worse, people
had it so much harder than he did that he felt bad even
thinking in this way. What about the poor, the disenfran-
chised, the marginalised? He was a white male, he told
himself, a straight white male, he had everything he could
possibly need, and yet he was still lost. How could that be?
He took another sip from the mug, considering the mug,
feeling suddenly more awake due to the coffee, and then,
as he considered the mug, he realised that he didn't remember even pouring himself a cup of coffee, let alone adding
cream and sugar, which felt portentous in a remarkably
banal way: if he hadn't noticed that, what else was he not
paying attention to, and suddenly this question felt like
a metaphor for his life. This was the failing, he told himself:

his lack of attention. He felt like chastising himself for it or possibly being self-pitying all day, but then he thought that this was nothing new. This was nothing new at all, he thought, like a chant. This is not new. He didn't like it, but it wasn't unique. He already knew this, he already knew he disliked these things about himself and the world, and yet there was no way out. It was just how things were, how he was.

From the dining room of their small bungalow, running into the kitchen, their youngest daughter yelled, Baby cat outside, and then slowed to a walk and, smiling, said, Hi Daddy. He said hello to her and looked out the window above the kitchen sink to see if he could see a baby cat outside, not seeing the cat but seeing the late summer day, momentarily, the sun rising above the houses across the street, the trees still and unmoving, their deep green just beginning to shift shade, and not seeing a cat, he looked away, told his daughter there wasn't a cat outside, and she said, No, baby cat outside, as though it was as obvious as the rising sun, and he said, Yes, okay, conceding a reality that wasn't real, and then he paused a moment and wondered what exactly it was he was supposed to be doing instead of thinking, and then saw that he had yet to put all the various Tupperware containers in their youngest daughter's lunchbox, and then did and zipped the lunchbox closed and handed the lunchbox to her. Their older daughter, he thought, had her lunch with her as she rode the bus to school. Their youngest daughter grabbed the lunchbox and playfully swung it, walking towards the family room swinging the lunchbox, talking to herself about a baby cat. He watched her go, feeling amused, then he watched his feeling of amusement. He thought again about their older daughter, who was already gone, who had already caught the bus and who now existed in his mind only as an abstraction – she was floating in the blackness of space in his mind, getting older, receding from him – and in the same way, when he dropped their youngest daughter off at school, she would only exist for him in his mind as an image, a concept, and though her physical body would be somewhere in the world doing things, both of their daughters would be on pause in his mind, which was necessary, he thought, which he needed and which lately he had begun to crave, and which was another example, he thought, of a way he didn't want to feel: he didn't want to see his daughters as jobs he wanted to finish with as soon as possible each morning. When had that happened? It wasn't always like that, he thought. There were months and years of purely enjoying them, and before that there were months and years during which he and his wife were completely free and purely enjoyed one another, or mostly did. The story seemed so simple and clear: they met in grad school, they struggled to make enough at menial jobs – she worked at Best Buy, he at a bookstore – and he painted and failed and painted and failed and they drank too much and argued, and then they got older, or they just got tired of drinking and feeling shitty every other day. She got a teaching job in a high school, then another, while he got a fellowship, then an adjunct position. They stopped drinking almost completely, hiked more, went out to eat, felt healthy, went to movies, became environmentally conscious though still sort of did the same things, and made more money, but having two kids sort of cancelled things out. They grew up together, but how had they arrived here, he wondered. It was impossible to see. He didn't know why things felt so shitty now, why he was constantly looking for an escape, a way to get away, into the studio, to be alone.

His youngest daughter returned to the kitchen. He told her to put on her shoes please, and before she did, she held up her lunchbox and said, You did it, Daddy, you did it, which he laughed at, a line from her favourite TV show, and which also suddenly reminded him that he didn't have to be annoyed, that he didn't have to see this moment as work he had to complete, as though he were employed by his life rather than living it, and, thinking this, he suddenly no longer felt like an employee and felt himself become cheerful – like a small candle lighted in his mind, illuminating some dusty, forgotten neural pathways – and said, I did it, which just the saying of felt good and made him wonder what exactly he had been irritated about a moment ago, and as his daughter ran into the family room again with her lunchbox, swinging her lunchbox, singing some nameless and joyful song, he remembered why he had been irritated, it was just having to do all this again, and it was also the feeling of being annoyed at his wife pointlessly, which in turn made him more annoyed, so that he so easily followed his annoyance towards ever-increasing annoyance and told himself stories about it, as though he had downloaded some virus that would eventually overrun all of the principal emotional reactions of his operating system with either frustration or anger and then rewrite the entirety of his life in the same way. He felt himself survey the physical reality of his life: the mostly white kitchen with stainless steel appliances from an overstock store, the old hardwood floors, one side of the house pine and the other side oak, the red oak kitchen table he and his wife had built one summer before the birth of their second daughter, along with the bench. Then he looked at the family room with the grey-blue sofa from a sustainable furniture company and a coffee table his grandfather had made from a fallen tree, the tabletop a cross-section of that very tree. His wife liked that table, she had refinished it, and said that his grandfather would want it taken care of, which he agreed with, though he hadn't thought of it that way before. He looked at all of it, the room, the floors, the furniture, the coffee table, as though seeing it after not seeing it at all for a very long time, as though it belonged to someone else and he was just a stranger here, homeless in his own home. He watched his daughter put her lunchbox on the coffee table, sit on the floor and pull her shoes on. All of it was exactly as it was, and yet he himself was, or had been, deeply annoyed about it all, like it had been doing something to him, like it was not his life but the myriad obstacles in the way of his life that he wanted to get away from, as though he were experiencing some kind of obstruction in his being, like it was choking on itself. Now he thought that if he could restrain his mind, rein it in and pay attention to what was actually happening – to his daughter playfully running around the family room, saying, I fast, I fast – maybe doing it all again tomorrow didn't have to feel bad, maybe it could feel pleasant, he knew it could, but he felt at the same time that it was so difficult to direct his awareness in this way, though he tried, this bit of cheerfulness and attention allowed him to try, he knew, and he said, in a pleasant half-yell to his wife in the bedroom, that their youngest was ready. But I don't know where your keys are, he added, and in so doing he felt both pleased with himself and as though he wasn't being completely earnest. After all, he was still annoyed, it was still there, somewhere down there, waiting.

And then he remembered what his wife had told him last night: that she needed to talk to him today, they needed to have a serious talk, and could he please make some time tomorrow night, which was today, and that was another thing he didn't want to do, and it made him tired and annoyed all over again because he knew this would be about him, something he had done wrong, another way he was behaving wrongly, another thing about him she disliked, another thing he probably wouldn't like about himself, and he was tired of being wrong, he was tired of her explaining to him the wrong way he was being, though he knew she was often correct in her assessment of the way he was being, so he had to prepare himself for it, to hear this thing she was going to tell him about himself, another thing about himself he'd have to correct, fix, another thing he wouldn't want to do but which he was always having to do.

To the east of their small city the rainstorm was moving, pushing northeast along the eastern seaboard of the country. It would arrive in their city after lingering in the mountains for two days, moving swiftly over the lowlands, where it would eventually sweep out to the sea and dissipate. But now it was preceded in their city, in their neighbourhood, by wind, which was pulling the leaves from the trees. They were green now, but soon, after the fall rains, they would be yellow maples, brown and red oaks, orange crepe myrtles. It should have been fall now, but the rains were late, and there was the late push of a warm summer, with temperatures in early October still rising into the eighties but cooling more and more each night as the days got shorter. The burned-out grass in the neighbourhood was wet in the mornings as rainfall returned, the two weeks at the end of every summer in which rain brought cooler temperatures and drowned browned lawns. The movement from summer to fall was apparent over a certain period of days and weeks, but the exact moment of its arrival was impossible to pinpoint. Fall hid inside summer, summer inside fall. The days began to shorten, the sun's rays became less direct, the axis of the planet shifting the western hemisphere away from the path of the sun's energy, causing the plants and trees in the various regions of the western hemisphere to make their slow move towards dormancy, and in the same way, many of the animals would begin their process of hibernation: first the gathering process, plant and animal gathering for winter, plants storing nutrients and forming a protective layer around their fruit, the last push of the energy accumulated during summer, and animals hiding nuts, storing fat, flying to warmer climates. At the same time, all that was naturally occurring had now been irrevocably altered by the minds on the planet. Consciousness had caused a change. For the first time in millennia, something ancient, which was always changing, which was composed of change and return and change, changed in a new way: burnt coal and oil and methane and exhausts of all kinds, in order to make power, created something new, the heat of a near ninety-degree day and the drought from summer carrying on into late September and early October. The changing light, softer and more diffuse at this time of year, worked now in tandem with the changing atmosphere of increased carbon and methane gasses. Record high temperatures. While the insects' electric noise was fading, it had lasted longer than in any other year, and yet the insects themselves seemed to make that noise less urgently, as though nature itself had become neurotic and confused. No one noticed this in the neighbourhood, that it was still summer, still summer, and then, just barely, fall. No one really saw it, though they complained about it and made assertions about hybrid vehicles, composting, vegetarianism, recycling. What they really did was prepare for the day as they always did, inside their minds, which they understood to be their own, which they held to be different from the changing world around them, more permanent, more real, and not in any way related to the old, old thing around them, which they saw, occasionally, as scenery.

From the bathroom, his wife heard the annoyance and frustration in her husband's voice, the accusatory tone – *he* hadn't lost her keys, he seemed to be saying, *she* had – and her jaw clenched momentarily because he'd already expressed this annoyance not a few moments earlier, and now, apparently, he felt the need to do it again, he felt the need, she thought, to really let her know just how annoyed he was. At her. Always at her. And right then she decided she wouldn't speak to him today. Just for fun. Just to see what would happen. Would he care if she didn't talk to him all day today, she wondered. She recognised the thought as a mean one, a cruelty. She didn't like that she was having it. She didn't like that she was angry. She didn't want to be a person who was angry, and while she sort of generally agreed with the outrage culture that she read about online – women were angry and they had a right to be, and men had to deal with it, learn to deal with it – she didn't feel like being angry herself. Who wanted to be angry all the time, she often thought. She knew a lot of women who were angry, and it was exhausting to her. She felt somehow out of the tribe, like if she wasn't outraged all the time she was letting all women down somehow, and yet she also felt that, despite the many horrible things that had been done to her by men throughout her life, she no longer wanted to be angry. She'd done it and was done with it. She understood these other women, she got where they were coming from, but also, now, at this point in her life, there were other things to feel. Or, she wanted there to be other things to feel. She wanted to feel her life, herself, not her husband's frustration and then her reactive anger, which wasn't hers, and also not what the internet told her she should be feeling, just another reaction, another way in which she wasn't being and feeling for herself. So now she tried to ignore it, this anger she felt at her husband, though at the same time that she tried to ignore it, it lingered there, a puddle of oil in the sea of her mind, and she wanted to look at it again, wanted to touch it, wanted to hurt him. Part of her was annoyed that he was annoyed again, and part of her was happy she'd found something to do to him that might communicate how annoying it was that he was always annoyed.

She went through the house looking for her keys, while at the same time thinking that he was almost always irritated, frustrated, like a child who constantly wasn't getting what it wanted, so that now it felt like she was living with three children, which was of course frustrating to her. And she was tired of it. Literally. It made her tired. It drained her. His annoyance, she thought, which caused her annoyance and anger, made her unable to have room to feel or think other things, and fuck that. It so crowded out other things, she thought, that she barely registered that she was tossing a pillow off the sofa, lifting seat cushions, leaving them out of place, all done dramatically with overlong sighs of annoyance so that he could hear. Hear me, she thought. Then I'll ignore you. She went into their youngest daughter's room, picking toys off the floor, putting blocks into the cylindrical container. After a moment in their youngest daughter's room, she almost said aloud, what am I doing again? Then she remembered, and she thought that she'd almost forgotten she was looking for her keys because she'd been thinking that she knew why he was so easily irritable right now, which was in turn causing this shitty mood for her. It was the series of paintings he was working on that wasn't working, as he'd said to her many times, without any specifics. Then she felt even more pissed off because what she was supposed to be doing was something for herself – finding her keys, though that was only sort of for herself, as she was finding them in order to go to work – and she was thinking of *him*. Him and his paintings that were not working and which he wouldn't explain to her why they weren't working. He just moped. Though what he would do along with mope was tacitly blame her: he had no time, as he said, because of the girls, because of his job, because of making dinner, cleaning the house, walking their dog, many other things, the things that he deemed kept him from his freedom, which was necessary for his creativity. She hated how he talked about these things like they were things he owned. Not only that, she was tired of the way he talked about things as though he saw what was wrong with the world and no one else did, which just meant to her that he was constantly complaining. He hadn't always been like this, but now it was almost all she heard. And she'd heard the story so many times, despite the time she tried to give him on the weekends, taking the girls to museums in the morning or to the pool so that he'd have a quiet house to work in, and he was ungrateful, or not ungrateful, she thought, but he didn't see that when he complained to her about all the papers he had to grade, all the annoyances and interruptions in his life, the miserable state of politics, the disgusting, oppressive system of capitalism, the unfixable environmental crisis, to say nothing of systemic bigotry and racism, all things, he explained, that made it difficult to do any work, he didn't take into account that *she* was *giving* him all this time. That it was *her*. That *she* was the one who made any of it possible. And rather than shoulder it this time, his frustration at his art and his life and the world, rather than shoulder his frustration – which was to some degree her fault, she knew, because she'd done it for him, she'd spent years, while he was getting his degree, while they worked menial jobs, giving him time to create, giving him time to disappear, while she waited, waited, and what did she wait for? Him. She waited for *him*, and, well, sure, maybe some money too, but mostly him, and so she knew she too was to blame, but no more – she thought, I'm going to ignore it, ignore him. Let's see how he does when I'm not the one constantly shouldering his life for him, she thought. Like now, like just now, he could be helping me, he could be doing something, but he isn't and instead is being irritable and blaming me for losing my keys. Which, fine, is probably right, but still.

She went to the bedroom and grabbed her purse. She looked under pillows on the bed, the clothes from the laundry she'd wanted to fold but instead had just tossed on the bed and from which she'd chosen a clean shirt and pair of pants. She looked again in the family room, under more pillows, pillows she'd already looked under, then went to the bathroom. Nowhere. She looked at herself in the mirror and briefly thought that she looked good, that maybe she'd see him at work today, then felt guilty for thinking that thought with her husband in the other room, but also noticed that she looked very good. If she saw him at lunch today, he'd probably appreciate her and what she was wearing. She hoped she'd see him, though she shouldn't be thinking that, it was wrong to think that, she thought, despite liking thinking it. She picked up some mascara and leaned into the bathroom mirror and began applying it. She liked to think about him, and she liked to think about the fact that she was thinking about him, and she liked even more the thought that he was thinking about her. She allowed herself to do it now, just for a minute, and another life bloomed: a concert, some show she hadn't been to in years, too many drinks, dancing, a hotel room, his blue eyes drawing her in, and then, beyond that, an apartment in a medium-sized city, him attending to her, time opening up for her, the languidness of days, going on a walk hand in hand, a park, a field. She thought there was something deeply enticing about those images that would rush in – it didn't feel like she was creating them – like if she just allowed herself, she could live another life. Or, if not with him, then just alone, maybe starting some kind of no-kill shelter for dogs and running that. Doing an actual thing with her life, helping in some real way. Making her life matter. Showing her daughters that what one did mattered, that there were actions one could take in the world that could actually improve it. A saved mutt, a saved pit bull. It made her smile to think this, and at the same time it was so depressing because it exposed what she felt was missing in her own life. She wanted her teaching to matter. But it didn't, or she thought it didn't, and this other life was intangible, a kind of fairy tale, and yet he was real. She saw him every day. And so that life seemed more possible because he was there, really there.

So that other life seemed to be right there, too, like a word one can't remember but whose meaning, the image, the thing itself, was just there, but the word itself out of reach, and she felt it through him: his blue eyes and quiet demeanour, his jeans and button-down shirts, not unlike her husband's, and his attention to her, his quiet laugh. She thought she hadn't thought about anybody this much in a long time. It felt so nice, like finding a little piece of land, some place of quiet and calm, where in her mind she could go and attentively give and receive affection, even if it wasn't real. Mommy, Mommy, she heard her daughter yelling from the hallway. Baby cat outside, her daughter said.

She realised she hadn't even been looking for her keys and now sighed, annoyed again, first that she was back in her house, her life, and second that she hadn't fully been doing what she should've been doing and instead was putting on more makeup while thinking of a boy, like a teenager. She hated that she was thinking of a man as some way out. It disgusted her a little that this was the way she thought. A man, really? But she couldn't help it. She put the eyeliner down and then walked down the hall to the bedroom to get her shoes and socks. She knew it was such a stupid thing to think about, this other man. What about the fact that he was also friends with her husband? What about their daughters? Where were they in this life she was imagining? And yet, she thought, maybe they were with their father for a weekend, or hell, even a week. Though could she do that, live without them? She didn't know. She didn't even know if she could really live without her husband, whom, she had to admit, when she wasn't annoyed at him for being annoyed at her, she liked. She shook her head in the mirror to stop herself. She had to go, get on the road. She had to ask him. Before actually doing it, she first thought that she had to go to the kitchen to say goodbye to her husband and tell him that she'd have to use the spare car key, which was in his car. She had to ask him for help. Had to make him pay attention, if just for a minute, when he should've just been doing it, should've just been helping, paying attention. She didn't want to ask him for help, but she had to. She found herself vaguely rehearsing it, as she found herself vaguely rehearsing her entire life: Hey, I know you're busy, but I need to get the spare out of your car; Hey, thanks for getting the kid ready, but I need the spare key; Sorry to bother you but I need the spare; I need the spare from your car; Get me the spare key. Then, just as quickly, as she was rehearsing for her husband, as she put on shoes and socks, she found herself rehearsing seeing the other man later in the day, sticking her head into the room he taught in: Hey, just seeing how your day's going; Hey, what're you planning on for lunch today; Hey, are you having trouble with Lizzie Grainger? Yeah, she can be so inattentive. She pulled on her left shoe, then her right, and knew this would devolve into the fantasy of a full-on conversation, or, if a conversation with her husband, a full-on argument. She was having arguments with her husband in her head before having arguments with him in real life, as though she were practising for it. It was so dumb. Stop, she told herself. She took a breath and composed herself and told herself not to be stupid, just ask him for the keys, and when she was about to leave the bedroom, he was there, coming down the hallway, holding their youngest daughter's hand. Hey, he said, this little monkey has something to tell you. We found your keys, Mommy, the girl said, smile huge, holding the keys. You left them on the bookshelf, he said.

For a moment, she didn't know what to say. Great, she said. She stepped around him, around them both, in order to get out of the room. She understood that she didn't know what to say because she hadn't expected him to be looking for her keys and had wanted to follow through on what she'd thought earlier, that she was going to ignore him today in the same way he was constantly ignoring her, but instead, surprised, she now heard herself saying, suddenly remembering it was maybe something she should say, Thank you, and then saying that she had to go, she was so late, and he told her goodbye, and she said, Really, thanks, feeling mean now, that maybe she'd just been in a bad mood this morning and that she shouldn't have been so hard on him, though she also thought that she hadn't said any of this to him. So what did it matter, these thoughts? She quickly said goodbye to their youngest daughter and went out the front door, and when outside, walking to her car, she breathed out as though she'd been holding her breath all morning, as though there was no oxygen at all in the house, only toxic fumes, and she felt both relieved and depressed that she was relieved to be leaving.

She got in the car, started it, backed out of the driveway, and was then moving quickly down the tree-lined street, leaves whipping up around the car as she drove, not seeing any of it – the early morning fall light, the still green leaves, the squirrels darting across the neighbourhood roads, a black cat trotting down the sidewalk and then into the trees – but thinking a thought that seemed to arise, as it had before, from the darkest ocean of her mind, different from the way she had been thinking just minutes earlier: she no longer knew if she loved him. It was a thought that kept surfacing from the depths of her like some impossibly buoyant stone, and which she then pulled towards her, each time holding it longer and longer, then polishing it, like she was trying to see if it was real or not or what it was made of. The thought took on a force she could feel. She didn't know if she was shaping it or if it was shaping her, but it was real, as real as anything, as real as the steering wheel in her hands. And this real thing, this thought, was here again: she felt it. She held it. She didn't know if she loved him. Was that the same as not loving him? If she was completely honest, she didn't think she loved him anymore, though she didn't know for sure. It was as though she were peering around something to get a glimpse of him, and when she finally got him in view, he'd slip behind another rock or tree or door. He had taken so much, she thought. He was always taking, and even in the moments when he wasn't, he was still somehow thinking of himself: rubbing her back was not simply rubbing her back, it was, she knew, making her feel better so that he could feel there was nothing he had to worry about while he painted; making her dinner was so that he felt he had done his duty of taking care of her so that, again, he could spend hours in his studio; playing with the children was, well, okay, she thought, that was actually playing with the children, and yes, she told herself in the car, he also just seemed to play with her, too, they still liked to play, but nonetheless, the other stuff stood, she told herself. And she *was* tired. That was real. She *was* tired of him making her tired and all the various ways he made her tired. She tried to understand that not all of this was his fault. Her tiredness wasn't entirely his fault. She knew that what she felt couldn't be *all* his fault. She knew that this feeling of freedom in the car always gave way to the same thing, which she told herself was partly, maybe even mainly, her fault: she didn't know who she was. She was a worker, a wife, a mother. And his selfishness had something to do with it, but it was irrefutably her fault, too. She had to acknowledge that. Her life, she said to herself while turning out of their neighbourhood, hitting the light on Spring Street and now waiting behind SUVs, BMWs and various hybrids, was her responsibility. She'd chosen it. And how depressing, the choices she'd made. She'd made choices that had led her to not know who she was. How had she done that to herself? It made her hate herself, hate him, and look out at the world with bitterness and resentment. She resented him and resented herself. She didn't like that this was the way she was seeing things. The light turned green, the procession of cars lurched forwards, then moved more quickly. And yet, she thought, exiting the neighbourhood and passing through the small downtown of their southern city, for the first time in so long, amidst this sadness, she felt some opening to something else: she wanted to know, she wanted to have the chance to discover who she was. Not in the sense that she wanted to go find herself, but in the very simple, mundane sense that she wanted to do what *she wanted* to do, now. It was her turn to get to do what she wanted, and she simply wanted to know what it was she wanted to do, and he had taken that from her.

The downtown was still, quiet, empty, and she passed through it like passing through a dream, remembering when in college she woke early and went on runs. Those years of anonymity, carefree, the empty morning streets, the undimming grey sky, the wind pulling down leaves. That was how that time felt to her: images that accumulated into a feeling of freeness, or maybe carefreeness, but even that feeling, she knew, wasn't real – she had longed for a

different life then, too; those images, also, were handpicked,
images not of reality but of some highly curated version
of reality, which in turn led to some highly curated version
of herself. And yet despite that knowing, in the car, she felt
that former self inside her, real or not, something long
buried and dreaming, wanting to wake up. Now her life was
scripted for her, or she had scripted it, which was sadder,
she thought. She looked out the passenger side window
– a cardinal on a fence – feeling more in the world. It would
be another hour before cars were parked and people walked
to get coffee, scones, croissants. She envied them. She had
nearly an hour's drive to work, and she'd had it for nearly
three years, despite the fact that he'd told her she would
be done with this job in a year or two. She couldn't be done.
They needed the money. They always needed the money
and they never had any of it. She again tried to remind
herself that she knew this wasn't all his fault, but she also
knew that some of it was, and, driving towards the highway,
she knew she would have to tell him. She left the downtown behind and glanced in the rear-view, their small city
framed there, grey and flat, like it was a city long abandoned, lifeless and lonely. The main road out of town, lined
with gas stations and chain restaurants and home repair
stores, stretched towards the highway and receded from
her mind, and she thought that telling him meant so many
different things. For one, it meant something for their
daughters, which she didn't want to think about. Though
she had thought about it. She'd been thinking about it.
Moving them to a small apartment. Half their toys there,
with her, half with him. Half their clothes, their books, their
cups and plates. Her daughters would be halved, but she
wouldn't be. She'd be whole. She thought that it was so

weird to understand that, whenever she thought about this and examined it, however briefly – she didn't know if she loved him anymore, that it was time for her to be away from him to discover what sort of person she was and if she really loved him – she would also experience the impossibility of it for their daughters, who loved him. How could she separate them? After all, he was a good father, and thinking that made her now acknowledge that in fact there were good things about him, namely, that he was, a fair majority of the time, a good, attentive father. Not only that, he loved their daughters, taught and played and disciplined them in an easy way, effortlessly, rarely annoyed. His annoyance he saved for her, she thought. Though she couldn't help but note that despite his distance and annoyance towards her, when he wasn't that way, there were still things she liked about him. How funny he was, or how he could be attuned to her needs and wishes, if not frequently, then certainly in a way that no one else was. He could look right through her to what was bothering her – though not about this, this she kept hidden – and it made her afraid to lose him. She had to admit part of her was afraid to lose him. Though maybe that was just fear of change. She didn't know. Thinking that she was afraid to lose him made her want to pull up the stone that she kept buried in her in order to examine it again, to see if maybe it wasn't that she didn't know if she loved him but that she was somehow being unfair or that her love was simply changing. She did it again now, hands on the steering wheel. Examined it. It wasn't there, was what she felt. What she felt should be there was not there. In its place was another feeling entirely, that was both a feeling and not, something more physical, the sense that her body was being drained of energy. In this draining, it wasn't that she felt she hated him or hated her life, it was that she felt it was all empty, a great void where she should be feeling something. When she tried to visualise this, which was a thing a therapist had told her to do in the past, she felt flat and white as a sheet of paper, as though her life, which she had lived now for thirty-six years, was empty of meaning and that in fact her story was blank, un-begun, and then, creepingly, she'd begin to feel that it was subordinated to his. Her life was an asterisk to his, the artist. That was gross, she thought. An asterisk. She was an asterisk. It was almost funny, but it wasn't, and then she thought, when had she become so unfunny? My god, she used to be funny. So did he. Now, she wasn't, he wasn't, they weren't. She tried to will herself to think a funny thought just to prove to herself she could still do it, that there was levity in her, but nothing. It was like trying to conjure a fart by an act of will, she thought. Eh, no good. She turned on her blinker to get into the left-hand lane so that she could get onto the on-ramp and enter the flow of cars, moving at eighty miles an hour, everyone hurrying, it seemed to her, pointlessly. The sun wrapped around the front of the car as she completed the hard turn on the ramp and joined the traffic on the highway. She flipped the sun visor down and put on her sunglasses. She thought that she hated that she would have to tell him soon, though she would have to tell him soon, and although she had told him last night that she wanted to talk to him this evening, to please make some time, so that he wasn't surprised when she came into his studio, it made her tired to even think about talking to him this evening because she was unsure she could really say what needed to be said. She didn't want to hurt him, after all.

The rain still twenty miles to the east of their small city had moved across the continent of North America, forming on the western part of the continent in California. It was so easy to view a rainstorm moving towards one's house or apartment and believe it had risen into being moments before, and that once passed it would dissipate, but this was not the case. This rain system had travelled two thousand miles, slowly gathering, losing, reaccumulating force: in the San Joaquin Valley the sun had risen two days earlier without cloud cover or wind, and had heated the surface of the earth unrelentingly, which caused the air in the San Joaquin Valley, which stagnated for a day, to be incredibly hot, one of the hottest September days on record in the state. The earth in that valley shimmered with heat, and a mirage emerged, where, across the flat plain of the valley, the earth itself was broken and sharded by the heat rising from the surface of the planet. This hot, relatively wet air was pushed eastward a day later, after wind from the Pacific moved it, and that air, caused first by the sun's energy and lack of any atmospheric coverage, then by the earth itself, moved along with the wind and met the Sierra Nevada mountains. Having nowhere else to go, the hot air rose, where it met with the cooler air above the mountains, and the relatively wetter and considerably warmer air from the San Joaquin Valley mixed with the cooler, drier air above the Sierra Nevadas, causing a further rising motion, and the hot, warm air ascended into the upper atmosphere of the planet over the western part of the continent, where the convection necessary for cloud formation began: water vapour conveyed by the warm, wet air cooled and released heat and then condensed, forming grey cumulus clouds over the mountains of California.

He grabbed his keys out of the little wicker basket, the place he always kept them, where his wife never kept them, which was just like her: she didn't keep her keys in a certain place so that she might find them when needed, and because of this she had to search frantically for them in the mornings, getting annoyed at him for something he had no part in. It was a general carelessness, he thought. She was a careless person. Then he quickly recognised that this was the exact sort of thought that he'd been having just moments ago, which allowed him to see just how inaccurate the thought was. She was careless sometimes, with some things, he told himself, but she was also a deeply caring person, he reminded himself, when it came to animals, people, their children. She was, in fact, probably the most caring person he knew when it came to strangers, so much so that he often worried about her because she'd arrive home late from school with a story about helping someone. Not two weeks ago she'd explained how she'd seen a woman walking on the side of the road carrying a toddler, and explained to him that she just couldn't let them walk, not in this heat, so she'd given them a ride – the woman was dropping her little girl off at her sister's house and then had to hoof it back to work, and she just couldn't let that happen. It was ninety out with nearly eighty per cent humidity. The woman was soaked in sweat and the toddler's hair was matted against her face. He'd listened to this story, and others like it, in admiration, a low-level anxiety growing in his chest, and in scepticism: she just did this for another person? Really? But she had, and there was no reason not to believe that what she was saying was true, that she just did this thing because it needed doing, and yet it was difficult for him to believe because he passed people walking on the side of the road every day and had never once stopped, or he had once, when he was younger, but had learned his lesson when a woman told him she needed a ride to bail her husband out of jail, but didn't have a car because her husband had got a DUI, see. The car had been impounded, this woman had explained. And so he'd given the woman a ride, only to have her direct him to a crack house, outside which, while he was waiting for the woman to return, he was threatened with a gun, asked what the fuck he was doing in this neighbourhood, and told to get his dumb ass gone. He hadn't been able to move for a moment, he had been so terrified. When the woman returned, she threw a crumpled five-dollar bill into his car and then disappeared into the house. He'd let the bill sit there the entire ride home and never touched it after that. His wife, at the time his girlfriend, had thrown it away, and from then on he never picked anyone up again. He'd see people by the side of the road, see people standing by a broken-down car, and he'd let them pass, or he'd pass them on to whatever was coming for them. But even after similar incidents, his wife wasn't deterred: she stopped, she helped. It was as though there was some openly compassionate part in her that just responded of its own accord, a thing that the rest of the world didn't have, that he certainly didn't have, and yet, he reminded himself – as though trying to be as accurate as possible in his mind, as though that would reveal what exactly the problem was between them – she was the most defensive person he knew about lost keys: frustrated, annoyed, closed, blaming. He sometimes wished, like he was now, that she saw him as a stranger, and then he thought that he wished he saw her as a stranger, too.

Barely registering that he was saying it, he told their youngest daughter it was time to go. She grabbed her lunchbox from the coffee table and then ran towards him with her lunchbox sort of pulling her off-balance, smiling and saying, Let's go. They went out, he locked the door, he picked her up off the front porch and got her into the little car. He strapped his daughter into the car seat and then got in himself, feeling his mind withdrawing once again from the outside world – knowing that he would soon be in the vacuum of his office, an office he shared with other adjuncts at the local college, and that he wouldn't have to interact with anyone else for hours – in a way that he disliked: there was a part of him that constantly thought that what he actually wanted to be doing was being fully present with his wife and daughter in the morning before work, presently engaged, or, if not that, then to be present driving south to the national forest in order to go hiking. He saw himself moving along the trail, his body and legs working, the trail winding first through the deciduous trees and then, as he made his way up, through rhododendron, then higher still into conifer trees. He backed out of the driveway, waited for a car to pass and then pulled into the street and started towards the school. This way, his daughter said from her car seat, and then coughed, her voice scratchy. Are you a little hoarse today? he asked her mindlessly, and she replied, No, Daddy. I'm not a little horse. He looked at her in the rear-view mirror and she was smiling, and then she said, Daddy funny. He laughed and said, You're right, my bad. It was a small moment of joy, which he felt himself receding from already; he could no longer seem to hold these moments, stay in them. He'd been able to once, but not anymore, and he didn't know why. He turned onto Spring Street, leaves coming down on the windshield, and he imagined being on this trail, one he preferred to all the others in the area because a stream ran alongside it almost the entire way. The stream was rushing and wide at the bottom of the mountain, almost a river, but as he ascended it became shallower, just a small stream, and then it would widen out at points, with little falls as the trail grew steeper, and then it would thin out and become shallow again, though always making a sound. Eventually, the stream became barely that: just a trickle of water through stones, and he continued following the trail until he located, as he liked to do, the stream's source, which was merely a small patch of wet, muddy, rocky ground at the top of the mountain. It didn't look like a spring. It didn't seem like it would be the source of the quick-moving stream miles below, but it was. He didn't particularly like it, that this patch of muddy ground was the source. He thought it should look more like a granite fissure, maybe, a rocky hole in the mountainside from which poured clear, pure spring water. The source was not what he expected it to be. It was not what he thought it should be. It was ugly, muddy, almost primeval, with a kind of bubbling of water and what appeared to be various fungi growing on the fallen trees around it. It smelled like shit, almost. It made him think about the source of his own life – what would that be, and would it look anything like he expected? Would it be ugly, too? It made him consider that maybe the reason he felt like this was not his life was simply that he wasn't in touch with the source of his life, and in the same way, it made him feel that maybe everyone was like this, that everyone was secretly unhappy or dissatisfied in some way because they didn't know their own life – not only did they not know the source of it, but they didn't know what it itself was. You could look at a stream and understand: it was water moving down from some higher part of the mountain. You could look here and see clearly that this part of the stream was deep, rushing, the stones old and rounded, and that there were fish, it was maybe a place to fish for trout, and then you could move higher, see the way the stream bent higher up, the pebbles and stones smaller, some more jagged, and the stream shallower, with slower water, and you could see that the ugly, muddy source was not its own thing, not separate from the lovely stream further below, they were not two. The beautiful, wild parts were the same as the ugly, stinking parts. They were one. Though they were also not one. They were different, too, somehow, and it was easy to see, so obvious. But it was not possible to do that with one's life.

This way now Daddy, she said from her car seat. He slowed as he approached the stop sign, looked left, down the hill, waited to see if a car was coming, then turned, continuing on, his thoughts also now continuing on. You could look at the stream and make the metaphor, he thought, but you could not look at your life and really see anything about it. You couldn't see it because you were the one trying to look, like a stream trying to look at its whole self, and you could imagine that you understood the ugly birth of your life, the source, but that was not really where you began, was it? Just as the source of the stream was not merely the muddy spring at the top of the mountain, he thought – it had formed over centuries, land colliding with land, snow and ice etching the earth, some water deposited there, an endless beginning, now polluted with chemicals and plastics and whatever else – you began when your parents met, he thought, or you began when they were born, or with your grandparents, with the food they ingested, with the thoughts they engendered, and you also began when everything else began. But when did it begin – the source was impossible to know, and your own life was so confused, he thought, it was all confused with so many other lives, and yet you couldn't see beyond your immediate waves and ripplings: should he be painting and creating or making more money and finding a better job, or should he be a better father? Should he focus on being a better teacher, forget the money, just do the job correctly, or should he be a better husband? What did better mean? What was a better self, a worse one? The stream didn't wonder this. Why did he? What did he have to improve? He didn't go out drinking or doing drugs; he had no desire to cheat on his wife; he wanted his daughters to grow up to be whatever they wished for themselves and to do this with care for others. But what were his own intentions? To understand why he had slowly become so dissatisfied with his life and to eradicate that dissatisfaction for himself. But how to get back to a time prior when he had felt an easy-going freedom, an effortlessness in the world? And there was also the dissatisfaction of others to consider, namely his wife, who was clearly dissatisfied, and he couldn't pinpoint why, and not only that, he seemed to be unable to do anything to help her. Or maybe he was unwilling, he thought. Or unwilling to really do the hard work of it. He didn't know. When he'd asked her weeks ago why she was so down, she'd responded by saying that she didn't know who she was, and he'd told her that that didn't make sense, he could see who she was, and then she wouldn't say anything more, or she'd say that this was just one of her down periods, he knew she got them, which he did, and he also knew there was nothing he could do for her unhappiness, she alone could do something, he'd told her, though now he thought that couldn't be right, that would mean that everyone is a distinct, separated stream and that streams didn't converge, but that wasn't true, they did, everyone converged, wasn't that true and real? Wasn't it true and real that they were separate and alone, but also together? And yet, even if that were true, he couldn't see his own confusion and dissatisfaction clearly, so how could he possibly see and help her with hers? Was it even really hers? Was his even really his? Or was it just easier to divide things in that way because that's what everyone did with everything: this is mine, this is not, this suffering is mine, that suffering over there is sad, but it is not mine.

From the back seat his daughter said, Fast, fast, meaning that she wanted him to drive the car faster, a thing she liked. He drove the car faster and went over a speed bump, hitting it fairly hard, which made his daughter say, Whoa, big bump, and he said, Yeah, that was a big one. He turned and briefly looked at her smiling in her car seat. He didn't want her or his older daughter to be the type of person he was: the type of person who couldn't stop thinking about everything. He projected himself out the front of the car. There were trees along the street here, changing colour slowly – some still green, some a blazing orange, some in between – a blue sky, thin strands of cirrus clouds, and yet he'd just been thinking about hiking and had turned that simple desire into a convoluted explanation of his dissatisfaction. The simple thing of hiking, of being in the woods, was turned into a metaphorical narrative about his unhappiness. Why did he do that? He didn't know, and he feared this way of being for his daughters because it wasn't really a way of being: it was a way of avoiding being, he thought, which was yet another thing that disappointed him about himself, that he didn't like about himself, and this thought now was also that same avoidance, thinking about the avoidance itself was also the avoidance, he thought. That he attempted to really *be*, and to not be afraid of his being, and yet he was constantly finding a way around it, to think himself out of having to be. It was just how he was, though, and there was no changing it. Yet what he could try to do was make sure that didn't happen for either of his daughters, and especially his younger daughter, who seemed the more sensitive of the two, though, he then thought, his hands gripping the steering wheel harder, he had no idea how to make sure that didn't happen.

From the back seat his daughter said, Mommy's car, while pointing out the window, and he said, No, that isn't Mommy's car. That looks like Mommy's car, but it's not her car. Not Mommy's car? his daughter said with a little uptilt of a question in her voice, and then said, Okay. He watched the car that looked like his wife's car pass and thought of where she was, somewhere on the highway, maybe stuck in traffic as she so often was on her way to work. He thought of her reaction earlier to his finding her keys, a reaction that had been so weird, like she was addressing a friend rather than him, like she didn't want to thank him, didn't want him to have found the keys, and wanted to remain frustrated with him. It felt symptomatic of how things had been between them lately, though he knew that this wasn't a big deal, just a small thing to work through, it was just that he was having a hard time seeing how to work through it, since the small things had been occurring with more frequency, and he was becoming more and more confused about what she was feeling at any one time. What she had said this morning was not what she had expressed with her body, her eyes, he thought. She'd thanked him, but she hadn't really thanked him, he thought. She'd said the words, but what she'd really done was say the words and slowly back away from him. She hadn't looked him in the eyes. She hadn't touched him, hadn't given him a hug or kiss goodbye, not even a hand on the arm, and then she'd left, like she'd wanted to be away from him as soon as she could. Maybe he was making that up, he thought. Maybe she hadn't really felt that way and what he was feeling was self-imposed, somehow, a projection, due to his own frustration and annoyance earlier in the morning. From the back seat, their daughter said that it was sunny out, interrupting his thinking, and he looked at her in the rear-view mirror, then looked out the windshield, as though he hadn't been doing that, as though he hadn't been driving or seeing the world before him, and he saw now in the rear-view that the sun was shining into the car and right into his daughter's face, and she was squinting. Her announcement that it was sunny was not positive but an indictment of the day. He said that it was a sunny day. He asked her if the sun was in her eyes, and she said, in an exaggeratedly painful way, Yeeesh. He told her that was okay, it would be out of her eyes in a minute, when they turned again, and he further explained that it was a little cooler out today, to which his daughter said, Cold, cold, and made a shivering sound. He had the feeling that he was ready to get her to school so that he could fully invest in thinking about what he thought he needed to think about, so that he could figure out what went wrong between him and his wife, all the little arguments, the accruing distance, the lack of conversation between them in the evenings, to mention nothing of the lack of sex, though he knew they were both just busy, that

47

this was just a particularly stressful time, a busy and difficult time. He thought of what had happened that morning and of why his wife was ignoring him. Then he wondered if that was what she was doing, was she ignoring him, that's what it felt like had happened, and he told himself to trust himself on this, that yes, she was, and so fine, he thought, if that's what she wanted to do, he could do that too, he could easily ignore her as well.

Nearly fifteen miles away, on the highway, driving through heavy morning traffic, moving at eighty miles an hour in the middle lane of the three-lane highway, a corridor between two cities, she sat in her car with her coffee and with the radio on, not actually listening to the radio. A newswoman on NPR was talking about a shooting that had occurred at a synagogue, and while she felt as though she should be paying attention to this story, and while it made her feel like her problems were petty, she couldn't focus. What she was attempting to feel was the same thing she attempted to feel every morning. A sense of freedom. A sense that her life was not the rote and scripted life she felt herself to be living. In order to do this, she'd tried, recently, to see her commute to work in a new way, though it was difficult because she disliked the commute so much. She turned off the radio because she didn't want to feel guilty for not paying attention, she didn't want to dislike herself. And yet, now paying attention to the road, she found herself just disliking the drive, the other drivers, the aggressiveness of it all. She especially disliked the idea that when someone was aggressive with her, cutting her off or riding her too closely, she then became aggressive, which was the opposite of what she thought she should do. She wanted to be feeling free to drive to work while listening to music she liked. She didn't want to have to think about her daughters or work or her husband for forty-five minutes. She just wanted to have a pleasant, relaxing drive, but lately there was something reminding her that this was not what she wanted to be doing, which, she'd begun to think recently, was really because this was not really the life she wanted to be living. The thought had begun like a seed in her mind. Over the summer it had grown, and when school had begun, she'd felt as though she were watching the ugly weed of it wriggling before her: this was not her life. It was someone else's! It was like a great discovery, like discovering a new, grotesque flower blooming in her own back yard, and it momentarily felt freeing, but over the next few weeks she'd begun to feel trapped. If this wasn't her life, where was it? Who was she? And then what had dawned on her, and which was the closed loop of her thinking, what she began to feel every day, was that she was no one: she was a wife, a mother, a worker. Nothing else. And then she would die. She was, she'd decided, wasting her life. She had wilfully, eagerly, done it, been complicit in it, an accomplice to the meditation and murder of her own self, had seemingly signed the papers, like a moron, had looked everything over, thought about it, made the choice and said, Yeah, sounds great, I'll be nobody, an asterisk in this man's life. She smiled at herself and, after smiling, thought that at the very least what this realisation had done was allow her to be amused again by herself. She'd been disliking her life for so long, all spring and summer, and she was tired of it. She knew it wasn't fair to blame her husband. She knew she had made these choices, too, but when he commanded so much time, when his life and his work took precedence, and when her things, things that were important to her, were subordinated to his important work, to his artistic friends, to the art events he needed to attend, it was difficult not to see him as the problem because so much of her life was edited out: her friends were unimportant or uninteresting, though they were interested in her, unlike his friends, her interest in volunteering, with animals at the shelter or at the soup kitchen, and in the harsh realities of the community were overridden for artistic events, and so much of her time at home was spent as if in a kind of limbo, waiting. Not to mention he could be a real dick, she thought, considering the frustration in his voice that morning, his easy-going annoyance with her. Though, she thought, he had found her keys, too.

Another car, an SUV of course, was right on her tail, and she hit the gas and changed lanes and moved her car through traffic like a knife, cutting down the right-hand lane and passing a line of five freight trucks, and then slipping back into the middle lane skilfully, effortlessly, feeling pleased. In the rear-view mirror she saw the SUV she'd left behind, stuck behind the trucks, and felt free to return to the problem at hand: this feeling that her life was not her life and had never been, or hadn't been for a long time. She'd tried to talk with her husband about this some weeks ago. Both of their daughters were asleep, they were in the family room on the sofa, and the windows of the house were all open, a summer storm, beginning in the late afternoon and continuing through the evening, had come through the piedmont, and they listened to the rain on the big trees in their old neighbourhood, oaks and cottonwoods, rain on the pavement and windows, steady and static now that the front had passed. It brought an earthy smell, a smell of woods and streams, that she had missed that summer. Typically, they hiked, went into the woods, camped for a few days and, as her husband said, touched what was real. The last time they were planning to go, he'd asked her, Hey, let's go touch something real, huh? What, a tree? she'd said to him. You know what I mean, he said. What is this touch-what's-real stuff, she'd said. Okay, he'd said, it's this. We need to go out into nature in order to realise what we've forgotten, which is that we're a part of nature, and in remembering we're a part of nature, we'll understand that we're also one with nature and thus sense our smallness and insignificance in relation to the natural world, the cosmos, which is vast and wild, and, in doing so, touch what is real, our humanness and animalness at once. Or, like, camp in the woods? she'd said. That, too, yeah, but now that I think about it, he said, I guess just saying it has done the job. I feel significantly more universal now. What do you think? Yeah, screw camping, she'd said to him. She liked talking like that, playing like that with him, but they hadn't done it much this summer, not the talking or the camping.

She didn't know why they hadn't, but it's how she had begun the conversation a few weeks ago when she tried to explain to him how she'd been feeling, which was not a feeling she herself understood. If she was being completely honest, part of the reason she had tried to tell him was so that he could help her define it. Though of course she hadn't said that to him. She hadn't said that she was needing help. She'd just begun the conversation by saying that she wondered why they hadn't gone into the woods this summer at all, that was a thing they usually did. She missed it. He'd looked at her and said that yeah, he guessed that was right, and then had gone back to his book. She recalled feeling herself manipulating the conversation, not knowing how to say what she wanted to say. So she had continued by saying that it felt like something was missing from their summer. Didn't he feel that way? This was a thing they normally did, a kind of resetting, but they hadn't done it this summer and she wondered now if he missed it, it was such a part of them. He'd put the book down and said that he hadn't really thought about it at all, but if she wanted to take a weekend and go to the woods, they should, they could easily do that. She remembered how, when she didn't respond, he'd looked at her and asked if everything was all right, if something else was bothering her, and she'd said no, nothing else was bothering her. She'd felt him looking at her and heard him say, Okay, but it feels like something's bothering you and you're not telling me. She again told him that nothing was bothering her. She was just tired tonight and was talking, wanting to talk with him specifically, and he was being distant, as usual. That's passive aggressive, he'd said. As usual? She said that it wasn't passive aggressive and wasn't meant as an attack, it was just the truth. He didn't say anything, had just continued reading. After a moment, she said that she wasn't feeling like herself, that this summer she wasn't feeling like herself. He'd put his book down then and listened as she talked. She explained that she was feeling a little stuck, a little depressed. He'd asked if she could explain why she was feeling this way, and she'd said it was just a feeling, that was all. Now, in the car, she was deeply ashamed of this lack of honesty, this lack of directness, this fear that if she said what she really felt she'd hurt him. At the time, it had seemed like a kindness, but now, in the car, she wasn't so sure. It felt more like cowardice. It's probably just one of your little lulls, he'd said. You get them, especially before school begins again. You're just missing the summer, I think. Your freedom. I bet it'll pass when you're back in a routine and not dreading what's coming, he'd explained, like he explained everything, like he explained her life to her so that she'd understand it, but implicitly, so that it wasn't an inconvenience for him, making it seem that his understanding of her life was more important than her life. This was the way it had been with her and men, she thought. Though he was better, or he could be better at times.

She thought of the men in her life, almost as though visiting some remote corner of her mind upon which she viewed a tableau of selfish and ugly beings, though not, she had to admit as she mentally viewed their faces, without their good points. Her father had disowned her twice, once in college for losing a family heirloom, a gun, which really he had lost, and then again in graduate school, for not visiting one summer while he was moving and needed her help. She had taken care of him – he had terrible gastrointestinal problems – for much of her life, even when she was a young girl, and in turn he had used her, abandoned her and treated her with kindness only when it was convenient. She had been called home on countless weekends in college, during spring break, during the summer, to help him as he got over a bout of ulcerative colitis. She had cleaned his house, made him meals, cleaned the shit off the bathroom floor when he couldn't get to the toilet in time, washed his jeans and underwear which had shit in them. She had taken care of him. And she had wanted to be there for him, but on her terms, and it hadn't been. He'd ask her home even when he didn't really need her, wasn't really sick, and then, when he was, instead of being completely grateful, he threatened her: you should move back when you're done with college, you only really have me. If anything happens to me when you're away, you won't have me anymore. She'd almost hated him then. Other men had done similar things. When she was young, only twelve, her mother's boyfriend had given her massages. It always felt wrong, made her feel disgusting, but her mother loved the man, and the man told her that if she told, she'd ruin everything for her mother. In high school, she dated an older boy who constantly broke up with her and then took her back, like she was some pet, some stray, that he had to deal with. He made her do things, sexual things, yes, but also things like steal money from her mother, steal things from her friends. She'd lost so much throughout her adolescence. She'd lost her adolescence, she now thought in the car, mentally viewing the faces of these men, and she'd lost her sense of self. It all started then. All of this had made her feel small, like only the smallest spot in the world was reserved for her, and now she saw that while her husband was not like any of these men, was not abusive or unkind, he was selfish. And his selfishness made her feel small in its own way. She wished it wasn't this way. She wanted him to be how he could be, uplifting her, seeing her, hearing her, but in these last months, in particular this last year when he was so fervently working on this gallery opening, he wasn't the way she knew he could be. And she now saw that this was because he didn't care enough about her. She thought of telling him all this. She'd had the conversation with him in her mind many times. This was nothing new. She would say that his focus on himself, well, it lessened her. It took some substance out of her life and made it seem not like hers at all. You did this, she inwardly told him. You've made me feel like this.

And yet, she thought in the car, not far from school now, she hadn't come close to telling him the full truth. Each time she'd had a chance that summer, she hadn't told him the full truth. She had almost asked him to guess what was in her mind, as if she were testing how well he really knew her. And that was so unfair. Could she really blame him if he sort of wrote off her feelings, if she didn't fully tell him what she was feeling? Of course not, she thought. Of course this was her fault too, which was maddening. She was so stupid, and so he was he, but she'd allowed it, allowed it all, and in some very real way, she'd done this all to herself.

She pulled into the school parking lot, found her usual spot and went inside. At least this was a place where she could be who she wanted to be. Then she remembered that he was here today, that maybe she would get to eat lunch with him, hang out, joke and flirt some. It made her excited. He wasn't always there, because he taught a college class only twice a week to the seniors, and otherwise he was at the campus as a teaching assistant, still finishing his dissertation, but today was one of the days. She walked through the lot, the air warmer, and waved to another teacher, the basketball coach, then an assistant principal, who was struggling with his briefcase. He was leaning over in his back seat, trying to close the briefcase, but it was too full. She went in a side door. She thought of going to her classroom to get some work done before the day began, maybe grade a few quizzes, but felt a strong pull to see him. She wanted to see how he might react to seeing her first thing in the morning, to see if he might notice what she was wearing, if his eyes might go a little wide and he'd smile and say something to her. Then she thought she really needed to get some quizzes marked, but as she got to her door she immediately passed it, didn't even open it, and went up the steps to the first floor, down the hall, towards the room he taught in, which she could see was open. It made some energy in her chest and stomach seem to charge up, but when she went into his room, he wasn't there. She stood a moment, waited, then thought he must be in the teachers' lounge, so she left their little code on his board, just a note that said, Dude, which meant text her or call her or stop by sometime during the day to talk. She went back down, the little charge of electricity through her body dissipating, a slight disappointment, and then she turned into her hall, where she found him leaving a note on her door, which caused that bit of charge to ramp back up, and she felt herself smiling. I was just looking for you, she said. He said that he was doing the same thing, obviously. He gave her a small hug and said good morning to her and then said that she looked great, how was she doing? She told him she was doing great, now that she'd seen him. She knew it was a comment that would make him look at her, and it did, it made him look at her, and he said, Great, me too. She unlocked her classroom and they went in. He asked her what she'd done that weekend and she said not much, really, she and her kids went to a museum, they went out to dinner, they watched a movie one night. He nodded and said that sounded pretty good. She was aware that she was calculatedly leaving any mention of her husband out of the conversation. But then he was asking how was her husband doing. He needed to get in contact with him. She said he was fine. Then he asked if things were better between them, and she shook her head, said that they were fine, not very good, and she didn't really feel like talking about it today. She thought that she had decided to ignore him today, and that's exactly what she was doing, ignoring him. She quickly asked the other man what about him? She said that he didn't have kids and was free to do whatever he wanted, so what'd he do, go to a show, something fun like that? He nodded and smiled and said that yes, he actually went up to the mountains and saw a band, made much too late a night of it, but it had been a lot of fun. She asked what band – she held eye contact with him, then looked away. It was fun. She liked how his eyes followed her. She was removing things from her bag, books and notebooks, papers. She'd find his eyes, then release him. He said something she couldn't hear and then continued by saying that the band was fine, not all that good, but he'd just enjoyed doing it, being there. She said it sounded fun. She asked him if he made such a late night of it, where'd he stay, with one of his girlfriends? He said, Oh come on, that isn't fair. She said that he didn't have to tell her if he didn't want to, and he said, I wouldn't call it one of my girlfriends, and she said, *Her*. You wouldn't call *her* one of your girlfriends. Right, he said.

There were now footsteps in the hallway, the first students beginning to arrive, the ones who were dropped off by their parents. She walked from behind her desk to the door and shut it. We've got ten minutes, she said. I don't want to see any of them longer than I have to. They're all sick, he said, it's insane. It's like you get them together and then *bam*, all of them get sick, and then you get sick and feel like shit, and they can go home, but you really can't, you still have to teach them. And the sickness, she said, seems to adapt. You just pass it on, and they get it again because it's changed, and all the symptoms are the same, except for one little difference: it's not just a sore throat and headache, now, it's aches in the legs and fever. Exactly, he said. And they get it again, and by the time you're healthy, they've all passed it around again, and so it's something different again, which you have no immunity to, and you're sick once again. I hate it, she said.

They talked like this for a while, and she was able to observe them doing it. She was doing it. This little banter, this slightly amusing conversation, and right below it there was something else. Was it only attraction? she wondered. Was it something more, something bigger? She didn't know, but she liked it. She liked it more than she'd liked anything in a long time. She knew that didn't make it right, though she also knew that didn't make it wrong. She also felt that it made her feel important, his clear attraction to her. She wanted him to notice her. He did. In everything he did, he noticed her, she could feel it. Him trying to get closer to her. His body. Herself allowing him to do it. It made her feel different than she felt at home. Bigger, fuller. As though she were a completely new person, someone she wanted to explore further, alive and wild and dangerous and willing to take what she wanted, to get what she wanted and deserved. After a few minutes, he said he probably needed to get back to his room. She said, Yep, and then thought she might ask him about lunch, but decided not to, and then he said, Hey, I wanted to see if you could grab lunch, but I have to be back on campus. Maybe we could do Wednesday? She said that sounded good. As he was going out, right before he opened the door, he said maybe instead of lunch today she could send him a picture like she had last week, he'd really liked that. She looked stunning today, he said. She felt that energy in her chest flush over her body and mind like the wave of a drug hitting her and she said maybe, if he was good. When he left the room, she repeated the phrase to herself like a little chant or prayer, although, she knew, it was neither, and she knew that it was actually power, that she liked the way she said the words and the way the words changed something in the room, namely his face, wide-eyed, glowing almost. If he was good if he was good if he was good if he was good.

In the distance, beyond the town and the fuzzy mountains, which were hazed over in humidity, the storm front lingered, seemingly motionless, brief flickers of lightning beyond and above the mountains, lighting the horizon. It was raining and windy up in the mountains, but in the piedmont there was stillness and heat. The line of clouds above the mountains seemed to be more mountains, as though the mountains themselves had, overnight, been infected with cancerous cells and had now blossomed in an ugly way. It looked like a bad storm. Those viewing it in town said that it looked like a big one. They viewed it with excitement, with disinterest, or they didn't view it at all, didn't even really look. The storm itself, which had travelled all this way, across the entire country, was a natural phenomenon, a fact of existence, was languageless and banal, beautiful and ordinary, unrelated to any of the lives in the town below, full of powerful energy and energy that would dissipate, change into something else, just as it began, just as the sun's energy heated the earth, which heated the air, which rose into the atmosphere.

After dropping his daughter off, he drove to the community college, which was less than five minutes away. He parked in the parking lot and went to his office, all seemingly without experiencing what he was doing, thinking only that he was glad he had some classes to teach today because he didn't feel like sitting in his office pointlessly, though he would do some of that before teaching, he would sit in his office for a couple hours for his office hours, though he was never particularly sure why he had office hours because none of his students ever came to them. They could only ever meet at other times, and yet the school demanded it. So each Tuesday morning, before teaching, he sat there, pointlessly, he thought, until two hours were gone, feeling wasteful and vaguely imprisoned, sitting in his office pointlessly, feeling he could be painting, reading, running, hiking, meditating, doing literally anything else, thinking all this on his way into his office, which of course made sitting there that much worse, and which he knew was making it worse. He was aware. He was aware that he was in some way constructing the problem, that if he just didn't wish he wasn't there, he'd be okay, but it was too true, too real: he didn't *want* to be there.

Making his way to his office through the hallways of the art department, he knew that he could be productive in his office if he wanted to be. He had a clear awareness of this, and there had been plenty of days in the past five years at this job when he had been productive in this office, but something had changed this year, and he couldn't focus. His concentration, it seemed, had diminished over the summer, like one of the summer storms that passes through town, drops an enormous amount of rain, and then you can watch as the streets steam, the water cycling back into the atmosphere, gone. His concentration felt like that, vaporous and aloft, something he was constantly grabbing at but couldn't hold, just air. He'd been thinking of why, after such a productive period, nearly a year, he had stalled not only with his work and creativity but with his concentration. Sitting at his desk, his bag unopened, his computer on a news website, his hand on the mouse, clicking through articles he was skimming, he wondered if it had to do with the feeling he was now getting more and more often from his wife. This morning she had been distant and frustrated with him, and that seemed to be the way they were operating in regard to each other almost all the time now, and now she wanted to have this discussion with him, she wanted, as she said, to talk with him, and he knew what that meant. It meant that she was unhappy with something he was doing, or, more accurately, he thought, with something he was not doing, or some way he was failing to be, she always thought he was failing to be some certain way, and she had a list of these failings that she would sort of pull out during their worst arguments, like a laminated checklist, a list that made him look like a selfish asshole, which, admittedly, he knew he could be. But it was wearing him down.

He stood and went to the window. The blinds were closed, and he opened them, revealing the campus, students with bags on their backs, many of them still wearing pyjamas, cars parking and searching for spots, coffees in many hands. From his window on the second floor, it was like watching a silent film: things were happening, action was occurring, but there were no words, there was no language, and he liked the languagelessness of it all. He felt something move down in his bowels and realised he would have to shit soon and felt, momentarily, pleased. He continued looking out the window, the silent movie passing before him. Viewed in this way, no one walking on the sidewalks across campus was happy or sad, no one was in emotional distress, no one was a genius or a moron, no one

even was black or white or brown because that was just
a further designation created by language, and no one was
male or female, no one was anything except what they were
doing, and how much simpler that would be, he thought.
It would be so much easier if everyone were completely
empty inside, if everyone were just an acting body, emotion-
less and thoughtless. Eating and defecating, fornicating
and giving birth, all the same. Of course, what he was doing
was eradicating personality, he knew that. But everyone
took their personality so seriously. It was codified online,
in avatars, on social media, in photos, all things speaking
to identity, the importance of identity, the importance of
being a unique individual with an interesting personality,
sometimes a public personality (a thing that seemed like
the worst vanity, and he was an artist), and constantly
refreshing to make sure that one's personality or public
personality was unique among the sea of other unique personalities. Maybe if everyone had a little less personality,
cared about it a little less, people wouldn't be so shitty to
each other. The real problem with personality, he thought,
was that it was linked to social and cultural views that were
fucked. That's all a war is, anyway, that's all racism is anyway, he thought. Personalities disagreeing, and the ones
with power win. Self-interest, and the self-interested with
power, like him, he thought, that was where all the problems of the world stemmed from. One set of beliefs, hier-
archically organised, against another. Protecting one's
personal views, one's personal beliefs, wasn't really protecting those beliefs at all, it was protecting power. He wanted
to look out the window and see what he saw as complete
and real, just beings living their lives freely. But that wasn't
true. Some were more free, some were less so. Eradicate

personal self-interest, eradicate individual or group self-interest, thus eradicating the need to empower certain groups and disempower others, and instead focus on the larger body of the world, maybe then things would be better. But he was a white male, a straight white male, it was easy for him to think this way, he thought. There was no consequence for him. It was just a thought experiment, from the safety of his office, in order not to think about his own petty problems. And additionally, no amount of thinking about it could make him any less involved in the ugliness of it all. At first he'd thought art would get him out, but it hadn't. Art was even worse, another way to divide, another thing to like or dislike, another form of self-interest and power.

He saw a flicker of lightning above the mountains. It would be better, he thought, if everyone could just agree on one thing, that they were a body and that was all they were. That was all that was provable, after all. And for everyone to agree on it. But he also thought that what he sensed when he looked out the window in this way was that there was something that levelled everyone, that equalised, that dissolved all distances and separateness – was it death? – that connected everything, because what he really saw when he looked out the window was not trees and grass and people walking and mountains in the distance and clouds and highway and cars, but something that was containing it all. Like a mind gently holding everything in it. It wasn't death then. It wasn't birth either. It wasn't the world, it wasn't existence. It was something else. Though maybe that was just a feeling, an idea he had. Maybe that mind wasn't real at all, maybe that mind wasn't really there. Maybe that thought was just part of his personality. Just something he held to be true, and he knew that if it was in his mind, if he was thinking it, then it was most likely another one of the thoughts in the world, a thing that was there and gone. It was a fantasy he made up to make himself feel better, he told himself, that there was something that connected all beings. Really, it was probably more true that everyone, everything, was separate and distinct, and there was no reason, really, to do one thing rather than another except if you liked it and it gave you pleasure or if you didn't and it gave you pain. There was no reason, for instance, for him to stay with his wife, for him not to flirt with, say, one of his colleagues, Colleen maybe, who was attractive and sort of funny. There was no reason really for anyone to stay together when things got difficult, he thought, because there was no actual order to the world, there was only what people made up, the constructed contracts of society and culture, and the hierarchies therein. And if he chose to make up that the world was one interconnected thing when he watched it out the window, even that did not give him a reason for not being with someone else. It may, in fact, give him a reason to. If everything was interconnected and one thing, if all bodies were just one body, as the Buddhists said, then why stay with any one person? Feelings, thoughts, ideas, self-interest, that's why, he thought. The feeling that this person was the person, or the emotion that this was love and that wasn't, or the idea that this was real with this person and that wasn't with that person, that was why people stayed. Until those things began to break, he thought, and then you weren't in love with this person, though maybe you could be in love with that one, and maybe you didn't think this was the person for you any-more, but maybe that one over there could be the person for you, and maybe if this was no longer real with this person then perhaps something real could be found with that person. All of that is thinking, though, he thought. None of it will lead anywhere. Staying is a choice, leaving is a choice, that is all. And believing that people are separate and alone is no different from believing all things are connected. Believing that there is something beyond the world one can see and taste and smell and touch and think about is the same as believing everything means nothing, he thought – it is all in the mind, all belief. There is nothing that is real. Then he felt it, down in his bowels, that distinct tumbling feeling. He had to go to the bathroom. He walked down the hall, entered the bathroom, entered a stall, pulled down his pants, sat on the toilet and defecated. It took a minute, and his mind went blank. It felt like a reprieve, a rest. He was just there, a body on the toilet, shitting. He wiped and was finished. Then he washed his hands and walked back to his office and wondered what it was she wanted to talk to him about today and felt exhausted thinking about it. He sat at his desk, where he decided to grade some essays to stop thinking, to stop thinking until class began, and he knew that doing something mindless would be the best way to do it.

*

The storm moved northeast, following the descending mountains, and then seemed to break free from the mountains entirely, as though the invisible hand that had been holding it finally and suddenly released, allowing the storm to push towards the piedmont and coast, the lower land.

He moved through his lessons with an easy annoyance at having to do them and doing them mechanically, while in the background of his mind he was constantly thinking of his wife and what was wrong with her and what was wrong with him and what was wrong with the world, and though he couldn't say what, he knew it was something, feeling this something all day. Everything, it seemed to him, was a hindrance. The bored students in his class were a hindrance to living a fuller life, the domestic duties he had to perform every day were a hindrance to his creativity, his wife's melancholy was a hindrance to his relationship with her, his melancholy was a hindrance to his happiness or maybe his contentment, the other cars on the drive home were in the way of him getting home quicker, and despite understanding that he didn't have to think this way, he also understood that he himself was somehow a hindrance to himself, and it was only when he was finally alone in the studio, after work, that he felt better, though then, when trying to do something with this new series that was going nowhere, which he felt no inspiration or interest or passion for, he had been experiencing only a dull boredom with what he was doing – photorealistic depictions of art, people, sex, women, himself. What he once loved and had once freed him he had also somehow ruined. He knew that there needed to be a shift in his mind, that he was in some way in the way of himself, here, but he had no idea how, he knew only that he was alienated, alienated from his work, his life at home, his art and, in the end, he knew, alienated from himself, and there was no way out, he thought. It was a thing he had realised over and over again about himself, and no amount of realisation was going to do anything now. Things would get worse or they'd get better, or they'd remain the same, no amount of understanding himself would make for change.

She poured herself into her classroom, giving herself up to it, fully there, and the students engaged with her and argued with her, and she felt their engagement as a physical sensation in her body. She moved around the room, wrote on the board, made direct eye contact with them, an energy moving in the room, through her, to them, and back again. A feedback loop of intensity, positivity. They were discussing factory farming, they were discussing antibiotics and growth hormones. They were writing a rhetorical analysis and using the food industry in the United States as fodder for argument and insight. She pushed them up against their limits and they pushed back. She was charged, alive, gesturing with her hands, pulling more out of them. This was something real, important, she thought, and she was able to use it, to take it from one class to the next, and though not all her classes were as engaged as the first, she brought them to it, pressed them, challenged them to do it, and they did. And then at lunch, after the rush of it all, she felt accomplished, her body tired in a good way, her legs a little rubbery from standing for several hours, tired in a way that was not the tired she felt at home. She saw a text from the other man: Wish we were hanging together. And she remembered the gift she had planned for him, and her tiredness evaporated, another burst of energy inside her, this one different from teaching, centred right in the middle of her chest and going into her stomach. She ate her lunch in anticipation, then went to the bathroom, checked that no one was around and used the full-length mirror. Pulled her dress up playfully, one leg exposed, posed, and clicked the phone. She looked at herself looking good.

She took two more. The lace of her panties in one. She sent it and then turned off her phone. She wanted to anticipate what he would say, wanted to read his response at the right time, wanted to make him wait, so she made him wait. And the day, charged with this anticipation, went differently for her, her afternoon class a little more rote. She felt herself focusing elsewhere, on him, on his imagined response. When she was done, she looked at her phone in the car, turned it on. Whoa, you are something else entirely, with a heart, a kissy face. She sent the same face back. Something else entirely, she thought. Yes, something else entirely. That was so perfect, she thought. It was exactly what she was and what she longed for. She took it as a sign and then drove home, feeling all the good feeling going away, like a wind scattering seed, being replaced by a low-level guilt that she didn't feel like feeling guilty about. She didn't want to see her husband. She didn't want to have this talk with him, but with everything that happened that day, she knew it was time. She'd got the sign.

*

The leaves of trees were upturned and white-looking in a wind that had begun on the west coast of the continent and arrived here, a wind that began as energy from the sun heating the surface of the earth, rocks in a valley and the pavement of a highway and rising into the atmosphere, creating clouds and the storm. The storm had gathered force as the jet stream across the country moved it, hot air colliding with cooler, wetter air, the jet stream moving the storm and the convection created by the storm itself generating an energy of its own, now here first as wind, not the same wind or even the same energy that began in the San Bernardino Valley, but also not a completely different wind or energy, both the same and different, not two. The sky darkened to the east of the small city on the east coast in the piedmont of the Blue Ridge Mountains, and bulbous cumulus clouds hung above the houses of their neighbourhood, clouds a grey-blue that appeared almost to be generating their own electric blue light. Lightning brightened trees and pavements and historic homes that had been restored, gentrified, plantation homes, bungalows, colonials, all lighted briefly then gone, no trace, until it happened again. The rush of wind in trees. Cooler air suddenly, the hot September day replaced by something else. Cicadas went quiet. Birdsong ended. Two cats in their neighbourhood sped across the street to their home or a hiding place. There would be a moment of stillness, like energy itself was waiting in some distant place to come into being, and then wind rushed in and the trees made their wavelike sound, leaves falling and small branches coming down. The first drops began. There was thunder. And then it was here, just this rain, this wind. It was nothing ceremonious, nothing special, just an early fall rainstorm, begun far away and now present here. It was the start of the week-long period of rain that occurred every fall, the beacon of a new season.

Out of the family room window he saw two cats run across the street and wondered, vaguely, if they'd be let inside, and then asked her where their daughters were and she said they were at a friend's for a few hours. He said okay and tried to prepare himself, told himself to be gentle and open, told himself to listen and address directly what she might have to say, not to be defensive. He said okay, so what was it she wanted to tell him or were they waiting or what.

She immediately sighed and said that something about the way he said what he said felt like it undercut the importance of what she wanted to say. Like she was just another part of the world that was in his way. He glanced at her and immediately said that he was sorry, he didn't mean to imply anything, he was just asking a question here, and she said it was fine. He asked her what exactly was wrong, what was she thinking here.

She watched him watching the rain and thought that she didn't want to make him defensive. She said that she didn't know exactly what was wrong, she wanted to talk it out, and what she wanted most of all right now was to be heard, that was all, she said. She just wanted him to listen to her, really hear her, that was all. Though, that wasn't true, she thought, that wasn't *all* she wanted. Though it wasn't possible, she thought, to say all that she wanted because even she didn't know what that was. She knew she had to be careful, because he could get defensive quickly and then the whole thing would devolve into an argument that she just didn't have the heart for. She didn't have the heart for a lot of things anymore, she thought. And that was the problem, that was what she wanted to be away from, and she was beginning to understand that being away meant being away from him. There was the gentle sound of the rain against windowpanes and the roof, dripping from their porch, padding softly on the grass in the yard, a metallic, echoing sound of water hitting one of their cars in the drive, the many different sounds of rain creating this one humming sound. She thought of that. How the rain, if you weren't paying attention, sounded just like one thing, just rain, but if you were really listening, it was so many different sounds. This was the beginning of the fall rains, and it sounded different on the leaves of the magnolia tree than it did on the grass, and different coming down from the eaves of the porch than it did on their cars, the windows, the roof, all these sounds making one sound, which was rain. It made her want to cry but she didn't know why. Something in her seemed to rise up, some tangled knot she'd been keeping down in a hidden place, it was just suddenly there. It made her chest hurt, and she rubbed it like she had indigestion. She watched him come sit at the table and ask her what was wrong, really, she could tell him. And she said she didn't know, but she didn't think she was supposed to feel this way. Feel what way? he wanted to know. I don't know how to say it, she said, it just feels wrong. Something just feels wrong. What felt wrong was that he spent all of his extra time in his studio, working on his paintings, working on things that were not bettering their situation, that were doing nothing for them, not for their daughters, not for their relationship or for the family itself, but which he seemed to think took precedence and which she had come to resent. She said that he painted many different things, but lately it was explicit pictures of women that were not her, and this hurt her, and while it was true that he painted her too, it bothered her. Maybe she was old-fashioned or just narrow-minded, but it bothered her. She'd read her Wyeth. She knew painters got off on that, it wasn't just art, and – she stopped. He said he painted all kinds of things, not just women, men too, and many other things, and she said she hadn't meant to start there, that wasn't even that big a thing, it was just a thing. It was just one of a lot of things. He had felt like calling her a prude or saying that she confined him artistically, but what she'd said had been right, and frankly, he didn't even like making those nudes anymore, photorealistic portraits of women he'd found on-line, which had at first been exciting, voyeuristic, sure, but also commentary on what the internet was, the sad, strange, maybe beautiful lives of these women and men. But it had become boring. He liked sex, but he didn't like it that much, to make a whole series about it. He didn't even know what he'd been doing now, why he'd been doing it. It had seemed so interesting, but now he was bothered by what was inter-esting, and after all it seemed so clichéd, an artist painting sexuality that he'd witnessed on the internet, reproducing a reproduction of sexuality. Was it art or pornography? He was annoyed at his own attempt at cleverness and wanted now to make paintings about people and things just for the joy of doing it. But he didn't know where that was anymore. He thought about saying this, but instead of saying any of what he felt, he thought that what he was really doing was thinking of himself when she was trying to tell him something here, so he didn't say a thing.

After a moment, she said that while that other stuff she'd said was true, what she really felt, what was more important, was that she felt she was just a wife. She was just a mother. A worker. And that was it, that was all that her life was. Just this servant. She said to him that that felt wrong, that she didn't want to feel that way anymore. That there had to be something other than this to her life. He quickly said that he thought she was just depressed, work was difficult, she was always busy, she'd feel better if she had a break, and she shook her head. She said that he didn't understand. She felt low, she felt like a slug, like some in-sect that didn't deserve anything good, that was pointless, that could be stepped on and smeared on concrete without a thought. There had to be something more to her than those simple, stupid things, than being the artist's wife. There is, he said. You're so much more than that. She looked at him and said, Please don't give me some motivational speech here. She felt herself looking at him in a way that was unkind, and he closed his mouth and sat back, and she said, That right there. That shit where you cut me off and try to explain me out of feeling what I'm feeling, that is maddening. I wasn't cutting you off, he said, and she immediately said, Right as I'm saying you're cutting me off, you cut me off again. That makes me feel like you don't really want to hear anything that I have to say. That makes it seem like you don't want me to have any feelings about anything unless they are feelings that fit the narrative of how you think things should be. She pushed back from the table, sitting in a way that communicated distance, her whole body going away from him, like she was taking it from him. She crossed her arms. She could feel herself pulling inwards and almost sensed him decreasing in size, as though she were pulling herself into some other dimension of reality where she could watch him in this world, small, uncaring, losing something. She didn't want to hurt him and at the same time she wanted him to see what it was he was losing. Where a moment ago there had been tears, this feeling of great sadness, now she felt a hot anger in her chest, rising up and moving into her face.

He watched her cross her arms and sit back, which made him sort of involuntarily sit back as well and look at her face, which still had tears on it but which was red now, her face which was not looking at him, her eyes narrowed, looking down. He wanted to say that what she was saying didn't make sense, but he told himself not to say it, that that wasn't what needed saying right now, that he needed to listen, but then he couldn't help himself and he was saying that sure, okay, her feelings were valid, but that didn't mean they made any sense or that he was the sole cause of them. In fact, what he thought was that she was using him, unconsciously, unconsciously, as a scapegoat for what was wrong in her life. She needed somebody to blame, and he was who was around, so she was blaming him. I mean, think about it, he said. You don't like your job, you don't like how busy you are, you feel pointless and as though your life is pointless, this is what I'm hearing, and I'm wondering how I'm connected to any of it. Because all of this, all of it, seems like *your* shit, not mine. If you don't want me to paint nudes, I won't do that, but I thought you were okay with it, that's the one thing I can see here that's an actual problem, though of course that doesn't have to be a problem if you don't want it to be, but all the rest of it is your own shit you have to figure out.

She watched him while he was talking and thought that she didn't know who he was, maybe had never known. She felt that that was an unnecessarily mean thought, but when he was talking like this, it did feel like he was some alien being. He was getting angry now, she saw, which was where he usually went. He was telling her that what he thought the actual problem was was that he had something that made his life meaningful, and see, what she did was she made it in her mind so that he was the problem, so that he was in the way of her making her life meaningful because she didn't have anything that was meaningful to her in the same way painting was to him, and so she found all these elaborate ways to blame him, but there was no one to blame for the way she felt except herself. Look, he said. I take care of the kids, the house, I try to take care of you, and yes, I do paint too, I work, but that's for me so that I can do these other things. She was not looking at him now and was shaking her head and was so removed from engagement with him that he felt she was two-dimensional in the dim light of the dining room. There were no lights on in the bungalow and it was raining and she seemed barely there, curled into herself, as though she could collapse inwards into a singularity before him and then hiccup out of existence, and as he was talking, he felt himself barely there as well, just a person saying words which he had no idea whether they were true or not, he couldn't tell if the words were true and real or if they were only words meant to defend himself.

When she didn't say anything to what he'd said, he sat back in his seat and said, Look, I'm sorry about all this. If I've fucked up, I'm willing to own it. I'm listening to you. Are you? she said. Because it only seems like you're listening to me when it has to do with you so that you can then counter-argue whatever I'm saying. Like you think you can defeat me and convince me of what I'm *really* feeling. That's not what I'm doing, he said. I hear you. She sat forward in her chair, brought a leg up, her knee to her chest. She looked away seemingly at nothing, at the dinner table, without actually seeing it. It was still raining out, but he barely heard it, like a kind of static in his mind. He had wanted to pay attention to this storm as he seemed to have missed all the good ones this summer, and now he had to do this instead. He had never viewed rain as melancholy or sad. He hated that convention in films and books. Rain was just rain, a beautiful thing that occurred, and he was annoyed now that he was missing this rain and equally annoyed that it was the backdrop of their argument. He didn't want to do this at all, but it was more important than he'd realised. He looked at the wood grain of the table and said, I feel like you're not saying all that you want to say. She said that she was. She was trying. It wasn't easy saying any of this. He told her that of course it was, she could say anything to him, and what he was hearing was that she didn't feel like she was a whole person, but she was, she was an incredible mother, that was true, but she was also a wonderful teacher, a disciplined, compassionate teacher, and she had many, many students who sincerely thanked her every year for what she did, she was one of the kindest, most compassionate people he knew, so this little story about not knowing who she was was not really fair to her, he said, or even really to him, because it took the person he cared about and was interested in and admired and reduced her to something he didn't recognise. She shook her head and said that he didn't understand, and that he didn't understand partly because he was not listening and partly because she hadn't known how to say to him aloud that something had turned off in her like a switch, but she could say it now. She said that she didn't know when it had happened exactly and yet at the same time it felt like a switch had been turned off. There was a pause in the conversation. Then he began talking. What had turned off? he wanted to know. And when she didn't say anything he asked again what had turned off, and again after she didn't reply he asked if what she was saying was that she didn't love him anymore, was that what she was trying to say here? She didn't let him see it, but she felt an enormous relief, a relief that he had said it, and it somehow felt real, even though she hadn't formulated it like that yet, and she said she didn't know, but she thought so. She said that her love for him was not something she could locate, was not something she could feel, it was simply gone, turned off, and he said so this didn't really have anything to do with her not feeling like a she was a whole person, a real self, or the nudes he painted or the girls or her job or that he didn't make enough money for 'their situation', or any of the bullshit she'd been telling him, and she said, No, no, all of that applies as well. But it's this, he said. This is the real thing you've been wanting to say. You don't love me anymore and you just made me say it. I didn't make you do anything, she said. You made me decode all of this shit, he said. You can't say anything directly, forthrightly. I didn't make you say anything, she said. He said, I wish, if that's what you feel, that you'd just say it now. You have to say it.

Her phone began to vibrate with a text message. It was the woman who had their girls over for a playdate. She was asking about acceptable dinners. They both looked at the message, which reminded each of them of some significant information. This conversation had been between them and now there were other people to think about. For a moment, he thought of bringing up their daughters. He could use them, he thought. But he didn't. Where is this coming from? he said. I don't understand. She put her phone face down and said that all she knew was that it had begun sometime during the summer. When you were so absent, she said. Always in the studio, and I began to feel alone not just in the house but in my life. I was there to support you and nothing else, is what it felt like, and I began to really examine our relationship, and there have been so many times you've acted selfishly. When my grandmother was dying and I was with her in another state, you went to a party. You did something similar when my grandfather was dying. He looked at her and said that that was nearly ten years ago, he was still a kid. Not with my grandfather, she said. I went to a reading and a welcome for a new artist in town, he said. You weren't there for *me*, she said. That is so unreasonable, he said. I can't believe how unreasonable that is. What did you want me to do? Wait by the phone? How about drive me to the airport? she said. How about tell me you'd be there for me? These were the people who raised me. I realise it's not the same for everyone with grandparents, but you know my story, and you ignored it for your own, so you could go mingle and flirt. He said that this was so unfair he didn't even know what to say, that was years ago, and she then said that he told her he wanted to know and she was telling him, this was it, this was her version of the story, he couldn't change it, this was real to her. She told him she had been hiding all this shit for so long, she was tired of hiding it. She resented him. She resented how he'd subordinated her. She was saying this without anger, with a kind of detached amusement, as though it was something she'd watched in her life rather than lived. Outside it was still raining, the thunder and lightning already passed. No great storm, no great event. Just another moment of weather. It had begun across the country, all conditions lining up to create this weather system, and now it was here, signalling the beginning of fall. The rain would linger in the piedmont, stuck against warmer air rising from the coastal waters, and it would shift the temperatures in early October towards cooler ones, and in doing so the leaves would also begin to change their colours. The rain was saying something, but it was not saying anything about them – it was only speaking a language of change, of cause and effect, of relationships between things. It was not speaking to them, nor was it a metaphor for their life, but it did have something to offer: a reflection of how things came to be.

Sitting at the kitchen table, he asked her what he could do, and she said that she wasn't sure there was anything he could do. She was sorry that for so long she'd hidden this from him but she hadn't known how she'd felt, and now she thought she knew. She momentarily thought of telling him about the man at work, but she decided against it. What would be the point? That would make it seem like there was some other motivation for her, and there wasn't, not really. She then said that maybe there was something he could do. He could be honest with her for once. He didn't like her, did he? How long had he not liked her? He looked at her quizzically and said, What do you mean I don't like you? I love you, I don't love anyone else. Okay, yes, she said. That may be true, or you may think that's true, but really, you don't like me, and I think you haven't liked me for a long time, and I wish you could just say that to me now. I'm being completely open with you about everything, and I really wish you'd be completely open with me as well. He put both of his hands on the dinner table, palms down, sort of feeling the table and remembering when they had decided to build it themselves some years ago, in order to save some money and because they thought it would be fun, it was something to do together, they'd planned to build other things too, and he thought that this was a kind of sentimentalism now, like by laying his hands on the table he could somehow make some point about what they'd built together and that right now they were jeopardising what they'd built together, the table could be a metaphor for their life, but then he looked up and saw her looking at him and he knew he had to address what she was saying to him and so he said that it wasn't that he didn't like her, he liked her a lot, she was his best friend, it was just that he was having a difficult time right now and he was easily annoyed, and he realised that wasn't right. Maybe he had taken that annoyance, that basic frustration with how his life was going, out on her on occasion. If so, he hadn't meant to do that. As he was saying it, he was thinking that he should also be saying that he had certain complaints as well, for instance he cooked her food, cleaned up after her and the girls, waited for when she wanted to have sex, which was infrequently and on her terms, and which was probably a pretty clear reason why he was painting sexually explicit photorealistic images. She said that she wondered then what he had meant to do. What did you mean to do? she said. What were your intentions? Because it's clear to me that you no longer like me. If you can't explain this, at least explain why I might be feeling this way. Why I feel like you don't like me. She looked away from him, his hands on the dining room table. She said if he couldn't tell her why she constantly sensed he disliked her, then there was no way forward for them, and really, she didn't know if there was a way forward for them now anyway, so much was irrevocably broken, it was all such a mess, she didn't feel like she had a voice in her own life, she felt like he didn't like her and so he either couldn't admit that he didn't like her or was trying to make her feel insane, and he said that that was just the thing, he was trying to explain, he had been through a very difficult, stressful period, he had been paid to paint all of these paintings based on just two others, he had been given a commission, a fee, and he had to honour that, and also that was a way forward for them, he was thinking about them, about her, about their daughters, about all of them,

and he had been frustrated, yes, because he no longer
believed in what he was making, there was something hol-
low about it, and yes, he knew he had made things difficult
for her and had maybe put his life before hers occasionally
– he seemed to be speaking from somewhere deep in the
caves of his mind, barely registering her existence – but it's
not as though things had always been this way, there had
been plenty of time, days and weeks and years, that he had
devoted to her and their daughters, when he hadn't been
painting, and it was as though things he had done, good
things, hadn't accumulated any merit all these years – how
could that be? – and she now said, louder, that he wasn't
paying attention to what she was saying, and he said of
course he was paying attention to what she was saying, he
was addressing exactly what she was saying, she was saying
that her life, that he made her life somehow less meaningful
than his own, and he wasn't disputing that he had done
that, he had done that, for a certain period of time, he had
done that the last six months, yes, he had done that, but to
say that the previous ten years he had done that was deeply
unfair and frankly untrue. She said that from the beginning
this was true, from the very beginning. So what do you
want, then? he said without looking at her. Without looking
at her, he waited, and then she said she didn't know what
she wanted, she couldn't imagine being without him, she
really couldn't, but something was wrong and it wouldn't go
away. So something's wrong, but you don't know what you
want to do to fix it? he said. When she didn't say anything
after a moment, he said that it seemed like what she wanted
was some kind of freedom. Did she want to see other people? She told him she didn't know what she wanted, she
just knew something was wrong, and after another moment,

waiting for her to say more, but nothing more coming, he said, Okay, maybe what we should do is open the relationship. Do you want to do that? Is that something that would help? I mean, I don't want to be just pushed out of the house so suddenly. That isn't what I implied, she said. Yes, but I don't know what you're implying or even really saying except that maybe you don't love me anymore or you feel like you don't love me, but you're uncertain because you keep saying also that you can't imagine living without me, and you won't say it yourself. You've made me say it. I haven't made you say anything, she said. We've already gone over this. I didn't make you do anything. Okay, okay, yes, you didn't make me, but so, I guess what I'm saying is that it feels to me that maybe if we open the relationship it will give you some breathing room. Some time to yourself, to be yourself, as you say you want. It'll maybe give you a chance to see something about me again, too. Maybe, she said. I don't know. I mean, is this something that is a possibility? he said. I'm asking.

She felt bad for the flutter she felt in herself, for the luck of it all. Somehow she'd got what she'd wanted and she hadn't had to say a thing, and she hadn't even known this was what she'd wanted. He watched her again and perceived a small smile on her face and then saw that she was kind of exhaling and smiling and crying a little and saying that she really couldn't imagine being without him, maybe this was the solution, and he said, he felt stupidly, Wow, thank Jesus for modern marriage. He took a deep breath and smiled weakly. Fall rains are here, he said for no real reason. She looked out the window. It'll probably rain for a week, she said. They seem later this year. He nodded, glad that they were talking about something else. They hugged briefly, and he felt a simple relief for the chance to figure out all that had gone wrong and all that he had done that had hurt her and how they had got here, and she was barely even feeling him at all, and, released from the hug, she felt herself to be back in a world of possibilities, and she thought that when they went to bed tonight, once he was asleep, she would text him and tell him that her husband had opened their relationship, would he like to meet?

Winter

Lord Liu Yuduan asked Yunju, 'Where does the rain come from?'
Yunju replied, 'It comes from your question.' Lord Yuduan was
delighted and thanked him. Yunju asked back, 'Where does
your question come from?' The Lord could say nothing.

Book of Serenity, Case 857

She told the man who was not her husband that one day she felt she was just done with her husband. Just finished with him somehow. Like the computer that was her life had one day shut down, rebooted, updated and then started up again. But when it restarted, it was without him as part of her life's operating system. All the past, the memories, even the good ones that had been sitting there for so long, all of it was just gone, like some album of her life that'd been erased. I had this terrible feeling of freedom, she told the man who was not her husband. Like, here I am, finally, and at the same time, I was terrified, you know. I finally get to be me, and I'm not even sure what that is. And not only that, I had to tell him. It took me weeks to really understand what I had to say.

The man who was not her husband was leaning towards her with a beer between his hands, listening intently in order to show her that he was listening intently. He had his ski goggles on top of his head, his ski jacket open a little, his face still a little red from the last slope. He said he was thinking of doing his own update, but sometimes those things were glitchy and he didn't want to forget his dog's name or not have his left hand work anymore or something. She said, Okay, yeah, the computer metaphor's dumb. No, no, he said, I was kidding. I like the computer metaphor. We are computers. We text, we email, we look at the internet, we listen to music, we watch videos. I mean, we're basically this close to living inside a computer. The metaphor is to- tally apt. Do you even have a dog? she said. No, total plot device, he said. She reached for her beer with her left hand and pretended to be unable to use her fingers, her limp hand hitting the glass. He laughed.

She looked out beyond the veranda where they were

having drinks and appetizers, towards the slopes and the peaks looming over them. She was here ostensibly for a conference, satisfying one of her professional development goals for her school. He was here because he came here once a year to ski with friends. That their trips had occurred on the same weekend was fortuitous, she thought. Sign-like. She was meant to be here. Looking at the slopes, she could see that it was not snowing out, though occasional gusts of wind made the snow, which was produced by snow machines, swirl in the air, as though it was snowing from the ground up, and except for the horizon, which was clouding the setting sun, the sky was clear and deeply, late-afternoon, early-evening blue, making the mountains and slopes and snow all appear a very light whitish-blue as well. The mountain was sculpted, trees cleared for the chair lifts and the gondola, wide openings for the greens and blues and blacks, or sometimes narrow runs, gently rolling curves around slopes, moving through trees, and then there were mounds for the moguls, which could've been geometric, alien snow drifts on some distant planet. Beyond the mountain they were on, which she thought seemed somehow to exist in another realm of reality, were wild forest and pines and peaks, deep winter.

She watched the man she was sitting with, the man who was not her husband but whom her husband knew well, whom her husband was actually friends with. She saw that he was alternately watching her and the slopes beyond the veranda, upon which skiers and snowboarders were descending, the day ending. When she and her husband had opened their marriage, there had been several discussions about rules and regulations. We should lay down some guidelines, her husband had said. Some rules and regulations. This is the rules and regulations talk, she'd said. It was playful, until it wasn't. As they spoke, he had asked her if she was interested in someone else at the moment. It was like he had some kind of radar that had detected her sexual interest was directed elsewhere. She had hesitated and then had told him that there was some-one, yes, and he said okay, and that as long as it was no one he knew, that was fine. As long as it wasn't one of his friends. Though, he'd added, he didn't think one of his friends would want to be involved in, he sort of stammered, whatever. This. But still, he'd said. That's my one rule. That would be, you know, hurtful. She had thought that if she were in his position, it would've been a good rule, but she wasn't, so she just quietly agreed and said she knew such a thing would be hurtful. She watched this other man now, both her friend and her husband's friend. She'd felt so fortunate when her husband had opened the relationship – she could explore this other person – but then the rules and regulations. She watched him take a sip of his beer and tried not to feel guilty. He put a hand in one of his pockets and seemed to be feeling around for his phone, and then she saw it, the hand, come back out again, just a hand. It made her want to check her own phone, but the only reason she ever checked her phone was to see if her husband was asking about their kids or groceries or something, or, alternatively, to see if the man who was not her husband was texting her, and he was sitting right here and she didn't want to see if her husband had texted. It was weird, she thought, that in her life at home with her husband, all she wanted was to be away. She understood now that being with this person was her way of being away, that being on the phone with him was her way of being away, and yet even now, here with him, she had the desire to check her phone, the strange desire to be away. She was away, she thought. She was finally away from all that was unreal and false in her life. She was with the person who made her feel what she wanted to feel, and yet still there was the feeling of wanting to be away. It was like she'd trained herself to want it, this escape, and now that she'd escaped into what she wanted, it was interesting and somewhat thrilling, but also a little more ordinary than she'd expected. She felt her own phone in her pocket and felt herself pulling it out, just to see if her husband had texted about their girls, but she made herself stop.

She cleared her throat and said that she really was sorry about the computer metaphor, she was thinking of taking a coding class, but that's also how it felt. At one time she and her husband were a single operating system making a certain life work, or trying to make it work, but honestly she felt like it, their life, had become infected with viruses and spyware and malware, and really and truly it was *not* working anymore, *they* were not working anymore, and she'd just shut it all down. Not even that *she* did it. She'd had no choice. She didn't choose. It shut down on its *own*. That's what was so strange about it, she told him. It just happened on its own. And now I feel that I'm my own self again, and, you know, to complete the metaphor, I should operate my life in the way I see fit. Like today, I could never have done this, could never have got away, could never feel this way if it wasn't for feeling that I can be my own person again and not be tied to this other person. If that makes sense. The man who was not her husband leaned forward and took a sip of his beer and said it made total and complete sense. You're updated, he said. You're a new you.

She took a drink of her beer. She observed the ski jacket he was wearing, a grey one with a sort of fake fur collar. He looked handsome in it, she thought. He had strong shoulders. He was in shape but not thin, and the well-fitting ski jacket with the ski suit beneath, or bib thing, whatever it was called, made the thought of removing the jacket and suit all the more appealing. She thought of being in a hotel room with him, of watching him take off the suit and get into the shower. Would he have hair on his chest? A lot, a little? What would it be like to touch his chest, his shoulders? She didn't have a jacket on but a full snow-boarding suit. The suit was white with black accents, all neoprene and very warm and comfortable and form-fitting, which was why she'd bought it, because of how good she looked in it and not only because it was warm and comfortable. He'd told her when they first met on the mountain how good it looked on her. Now, thinking of his body beneath his jacket and bib thing, she unzipped part of hers a little, hoping that he'd notice her neck and the tight-fitting black thermal she'd worn underneath that emphasised her breasts. This small action made what she felt was feeling ordinary feel less so, a moment filled with potential. She noticed his eyes trail along the unzipped portion of her suit and she looked away, knowing he was looking. Let's take a photo, he said. Catalogue the day. She nodded and moved closer to him, and he waited for a second, looking at her. It'll have to be your phone, she said. Right, he said. He pulled his phone out, they smiled, shoulders touching. She felt herself trying to smile just for this moment, trying to make this moment with him complete and unspoiled, though she was aware that there was another moment that she was claiming to be a part of,

and then his hand was around her – she felt her body
relax into it, a warm electricity – and then the brief flash,
fixed in place. They moved back to their places at the table,
his hand trailing across her back. She felt the tracing of
his hand linger on her back. A warmth filled her chest. She
wanted to see the photo but she also didn't want to see,
didn't want to see what she might look like at this moment.
She swirled her glass of beer and noticed that the sun created a strange effect when she moved the glass, intertwined
ringlets of amber light surrounded both their glasses, and
her rings, while she was swirling the glass, swung on the
tabletop like small tossed hoops made of light.

Every year, the winter arrived earlier in the mountains
than in the piedmont: cold weather, rain, snow became
trapped, and because of the higher elevation – 6,000 feet
above sea level at the highest altitudes, the mountains older
than the Rockies, than the Alps, which are taller but which
will one day erode in the same way the Blue Ridge has – and
the thinner air, temperatures dropped quicker, and as the
earth's axis rotated the northern hemisphere away from the
sun, the rays of sunlight became less direct, more diffuse.
In the piedmont and Blue Ridge, the land cooled, the leaves
changed colour and fell away, and then, in the mountains
in November, snow fell. Temperatures dropped below
freezing more than half the nights of winter, but the Blue
Ridge was also shielded by the Great Smoky Mountains to
the east, blocking or slowing some of the cold air that
moved down from Canada, which then stagnated, warmed
in the great valley between the Smokies and Blue Ridge,
and allowed warmer temperatures during the day. Animals
that had stored food or fat completed their changes,
their bodies modifying for the cold: the groundhog's

or chipmunk's heart rate dropped, their body temperature decreased, their metabolism slowed, and they hibernated, with stored food in their small dens or tree holes as sustenance; honeybees clustered together in their hives, generating a collective heat and surviving on stored foods; all bumblebees died except for the queens, whose eggs would hatch in the spring; many species of bird, millions of birds that most people don't even notice, left the forests completely, flying south at night to warmer weather and more easily accessed food; black bears hibernated in dens and gave birth in the winter, so that cubs would be ready for spring; elk moulted and grew a thick winter coat and continued to forage with a lower metabolism. Winter was most difficult for the scavengers and predators, because prey was so scarce. Foxes, coyotes, bobcats sought out rabbits or squirrels or deer they might come upon. Many died. And with the roads, the new houses, the new developments, prey became even more scarce, and what was once hunting ground was now an ever-expanding ski resort. Scientists claimed that certain animals were extinct in this region of North America because of the encroachment of people on these habitats, but these supposedly extinct animals had been spotted by locals, like ghosts haunting the landscape: now, just beyond the resort, a mountain lion crouched in the snow and waited for a foraging Appalachian cottontail.

The man sat back, looked at the photo he had just taken. She observed him looking. Was he admiring her, happy they were both in a photo, or something else? He was smiling, she saw. He looked at her and said she looked really gorgeous today. It was a good photo. She had known this, that this was what he was seeing, but she had wanted the confirmation. It had been the same on the slopes today.

She'd snowboarded in front of him and she knew he was
watching her, maybe watching the curve of her thighs as
they sat in position, shifted with the slopes, manoeuvred
the snowboard. She was a very good snowboarder, probably
a better snowboarder than he was a skier, and she enjoyed
feeling watched, sensing he was seeing her movements,
noticing her athletic body. He put the phone away and she
wondered if her unzipping of the suit that revealed her very
tight kind of spandex shirt thing, which made her breasts
appear full and almost as if presented to be massaged or
kissed by him or something, was a message he was receiv-
ing. She thought it must be. You look different here, he said.
I guess, yes, like you said earlier. New. She said she felt new.
Saying this made her think of how she'd described, once,
briefly, the problem with her husband, how the relationship, the connection between them, had become negative,
yes, but also distant, cold. Or maybe, she'd corrected,
she'd gone cold to it. Or maybe it was that she knew it too
well. Either way, she'd told him, what was old was over.
There was no more warmth there, no more joy, there was
only frustration, a constant, low-level anger and negativity,
though she also explained that it wasn't like that all the
time, and her husband, for his part, didn't think this was
the case. But she knew it to be true. He just hasn't admitted
it in his own mind yet, she'd told him. And that's what
I like about being around you, she'd said. That what's
between us is simple, warm. She stretched her neck side
to side and watched him observe her, then look away
towards the slopes.

He drank a mouthful of his beer and put a hand on the
table, as though he were placing some important document
there. More seriously, he added, and he didn't mean to be

seeming to make a suggestion here, he wasn't doing that, it's just what he saw, he knew because he'd experienced it, that over time it was hard for people to see whether they were still good for each other. It's hard for people to see if one of them is messing things up or if one side of the relationship doesn't care for the other side, he said. I was in a relationship for nearly ten years, and after a certain amount of time it just became impossible to see anything clearly. There was nothing between us anymore, and it took us a long time to admit that to ourselves, let alone each other. We weren't connected anymore, which meant we didn't really care for one another. It was like we stayed in a bad situation because we thought we were supposed to be together. Or because we were afraid of being lonely. It was crazy-making. He removed his hand from the table and picked up his beer and took a small sip. And sad, he said. On the slopes, she watched a family of four skiing down a wide, easy green, the children herded between the parents, moving in S-curves. Then she turned her attention back to him. What he was saying, he said, was that he'd been there, he knew the feeling of being totally disconnected from a lover, and his advice, not that she was asking, but his suggestion was that she needed to trust what she felt and go with that.

She sat back a little and moved her beer in a circle, rotating it on the table, swinging the rings of light. She tried to decide what she felt about this last comment and wondered if she felt that he was closing the subject down. Before she could say anything, he said that he felt like that last comment might sound like he was attempting to move the conversation beyond what they were talking about, and that if it felt like he was attempting, in some way, to close down the current topic of discussion by suggesting she just needed to trust herself, end of story, he was sorry about that, he didn't mean that, and additionally, he explained, he didn't like that he was sort of adjudicating here, as though he could possibly know what she was going through. What you two are going through, he said. Though of course I do know to some degree. It all sounds a lot like what happened in my last relationship, and possibly what you need now, though you don't realise it, is help realising the position you're in. He took a drink of his beer in what she felt was a way to compose himself. That's what he'd needed, he said, and fortunately he'd had a friend to help him through it all.

She told him she was fortunate, too, because he was helping her and being a good friend to her. And she appreciated it. She took a drink of her beer and checked her phone. He said that one of the things he wanted her to know was that when he was with her, she helped him feel less lonely. He hadn't said this to her before, but it was the case. I'm saying it now, he said. He'd been alone for a long time, he went on, after his last relationship fell apart, and while it was a little awful that things were now working out like this, that he was interested in the wife of his friend, while he felt bad about it, it was also true that he felt less alone with her, that it was her who alleviated his loneliness. No one else does that, he said. And just, he liked being around her. And that's what he wanted now, to just be around her, her alone. Are you saying that you don't want to be talking about my husband? she said. No, no, he said. I didn't mean it like that. It makes sense, she said. He was shaking his head. All I'm saying is that so many things make me feel distanced from my life. Far away from it. Lack of money, working on this dissertation, my previous relationship even, working as a part-time high school teacher and an adjunct, the fact that I'm living with my folks while I finish this PhD, all of it makes me feel as though I'm stuck in this lonely, isolating place. Until you, he said. He just wanted her to know that. You sort of pull me into the world again. She told him thank you. She said that he didn't need to say that. He told her he wanted to. He wanted her to know, and he also understood that this must all be a bit confusing for her. He got that. I think just trust what you feel, he said. She watched him as he drank his beer and wondered about what he'd just said. He must feel that this day was meant to be a little box of a day in which they could live just as themselves, she thought. He probably didn't mind being there for her, but at the same time, he was most likely ready for them to talk about something other than her husband, for them to be there fully, with each other and just each other. He'd left all of his stuff at home, and she'd brought hers with her.

She swirled her glass with her left hand, and he watched the ringlets of light dance on the table. They looked like a necklace made of hoops. Then she picked up the glass, causing the ringed light to disappear momentarily, took a long drink, then replaced the glass and, unwittingly, the light rings. With her right hand she was texting on her phone, and he waited for her, watching her hands move – was he annoyed? He added now, as she was texting, I mean, that's really it. You need to trust what you're feeling. That's really all I'm saying. I denied what I was really feeling in my last relationship because I thought we were supposed to work it out. Who wouldn't? We'd been together eight years. But in the end, I had to admit to myself that we just didn't care anymore.

The sun had gone behind some clouds, and the forest beyond the slopes darkened. There was snow there, but it was of a different quality from the snow on the slopes. When people on the ski lift looked out into the forest, they saw stillness. Nothing moved. The trees – spruces and firs and loblolly pines – appeared frozen in place, a dusting of snow on their branches. But further in, on the back side of a slope, where wild nature was still wild nature, a supposedly extinct mountain lion was crouched. A man who had skied out west into the backcountry had made his way up to this part of the mountain, beyond the resort areas, and was preparing to go down. He adjusted his pack and zipped his jacket closed all the way. He looked down the slope and saw his route, through the trees. A quiet wind blew a dusting of snow across his path, which made him go still, and then he saw it, about a hundred yards off, just in the brush. A small, light brown rabbit. It moved skittishly, foraging around the underbrush. It occasionally lifted its head, smelled the air.

She put her phone upside down on the table, then quickly picked up her beer, took a quick sip and put the glass down. She took a deep breath, as if preparing herself to give a speech at the conference she was supposed to be at, and said she was sorry about texting like that, she just got a message from a colleague and needed to send something back. Anyway, she said, and shook her head a little. She said it was something about the care part of his comment that she didn't like, though she also understood that he was just trying to be helpful, but she thought she at least owed it to her husband to clarify something here. She said that she didn't want to keep talking about her husband, but she felt she could at least be considerate given the nature of the conversation, which, after all, she'd started. She watched him sort of put up his hands, nod his head and quietly say, Oh, I understand. Please go ahead. She liked how patient he was, a cool and refreshing patience, how it came effortlessly to him, seemed to flow from him like a mountain stream, not like the way her husband got frustrated even at little things. Sitting with him at this table, she felt free to say anything, to be open. She leaned back and said that it wasn't that she didn't care for her husband, she wanted to make that clear. It wasn't that she didn't consider him a friend, and certainly not that she didn't consider him a good father. He was a good father and, if she was being completely honest, a good friend – her best friend, if she was really being completely honest – but it was just that she was done with their arguing, the coldness between them after an argument. She was done feeling like shit. For arguing with him about their youngest daughter's sleep habits, or whose turn it was to pick up their older daughter from a friend's house, or why their older daughter wasn't reading well yet, or who was keeping up with household chores. All that shit. Additionally, she was sick of her life being secondary to his. She was tired of him explaining everything to her, or, not everything, but explaining her feelings to her, her psychology, like he knew it better than her, and really, she just wasn't attracted to him anymore, which was strange because she could see that he was handsome, moderately successful, and a moderately talented artist, but it was just so weird, she wasn't attracted to him at all anymore. So it's not exactly about care, she said. I want him to be okay. I want him to be well. I know he's feeling bad because he wants us to work out, and I feel shitty about that, too, because in some way I've caused it. I mean, we've both caused it, but I feel bad that he's feeling bad. So it's not about care. No, no, I didn't mean to insinuate, he said. Oh, you're fine, she said. I would never, he said. It's really okay. Suggest. You're fine. Okay, good. You're fine. They both laughed. It felt good, she thought, there was nothing else to be upset about. She had clarified something, and now it was over. This was not an argument, it was an understanding.

The Appalachian cottontail doesn't build its own burrow. It uses an abandoned burrow made by another animal or finds a hole in a tree or some low-lying, brush-covered area to make its home. Typically, the rabbit leaves its burrow twice a day in winter, once at dawn, once at dusk, to forage for food – the bark of certain trees, birch or white oak, or sumac bushes, or in desperation it will eat its own faeces, which are full of bacteria that can help fend off disease. Or it will find a place near a human habitation – a farm or school – and eat any scrapped grain that may come to it. It spends almost its entire life in a three-to-five-acre range. With little food and freezing temperatures, most do not survive the winter. A human looking at a cottontail, like the man at the top of the slope, might anthropomorphise it, see it as a victim, as prey for a predator, or feel it was lost. But this rabbit was not lost, it was not a metaphor, nature was not a metaphor, it was exactly as it was. The rabbit on the trail had once eaten one of its own after a hawk killed and dropped it in the snow. It was, like all things on the mountain, wildly alive and attempting only to survive until the planet again shifted on its axis. It was, in this way, no different from the mountain lion some two hundred yards off, crouched in the forest, in the brush, where the man couldn't see it and where it couldn't see the rabbit. It was hunting opportunistically.

You're kind to be talking to me like this, she said. For listening to my shit. He told her it wasn't a problem, he was glad to be here, glad to help her, though he felt that he'd messed up by saying that one side didn't care, and he was sorry about that. Maybe he'd been talking too much in general. She told him that it was alright and then said, Let's order some food, I'm starving. After a moment they were able to get the attention of their waiter, and after asking what he wanted, and responding that he didn't care, it was up to her, and while she looked over the menu while the waiter was standing there, she thought of where he would be if he wasn't here. Maybe with his parents. Maybe in the library working on his dissertation. He lived at his parents', though she knew he rarely saw them except on the weekends, ate dinner with them both nights, which he had told her felt like a failure, nearing forty. She would be at home with her husband, probably getting the girls ready for bed. A bath maybe, books before bedtime. Then she thought that this was a weekend night, which in the past meant that her husband might have been out, maybe with the man. He had been friends with her husband first, after all. She knew they had met at a local gallery opening and drank too much. And then after six or seven months of him being friends with her husband, of them playing tennis together, occasionally going for hikes, meeting for pints, becoming friends, then becoming friends with her, she noticed she felt an attraction to him, and then she noticed that he was attracted to her. She tried to suppress that attraction because not only was he friends with her husband, he seemed to like and admire their relationship. After six or seven months, during which time he and her husband drank and talked, and her husband shared paintings in progress, his sketches, his ideas, after she sat in the family room with them, their girls asleep, and her husband asked him about his dissertation and asked to read his work, and after her husband shared his views of existence, which her husband saw as a thinly veiled illusion, and that people were determined, his word, to distract themselves from what was real, and his paintings attempted to address this illusion, after all these months, after flirting with him at school, she'd one day met with him while her husband was out of town. She told him that things with her husband were not going well. She told him they were opening their relationship and that he was the first person she was choosing to tell this to. She felt something like an empty well in her fill with warm water then. And now he was here with her.

She had ordered another beer and an appetizer that would come out quick, crackers with Brie and pepper jelly, and as expected, not two minutes after she ordered, after the waiter had gone away, another server had come out with the platter and two more beers. She picked up a cracker that had Brie and pepper jelly on it and held it up. He grabbed one too and toasted her cracker. She ate her cracker while alternately watching him, his very attractive and kind face, and the skiers and the chair lifts swaying in the wind. There was another pause in the conversation as they ate. The light was gradually dimming on the mountain, as though some patient and attentive being were rotating the dimmer switch of the sun. Most of the mountain was now in shadow, and in the shadow the people still skiing or snowboarding appeared to be simulacrums of real people, slightly fuzzy and pixelated, like she was watching a video game. They both looked to the slopes and distant peaks, where the sun was relatively easier to look at, a bigger, softer orb of orange moving towards the peaks. She glanced at him looking, wondering what he was seeing. He gave her this warm, bright feeling in her stomach that she hadn't experienced in a long time, that was a complete contrast to the cold distance she felt her husband communicated to her. She disliked that the man who was not her husband made her think of her husband, that when she thought of the warm feeling, she thought of the cold feeling. Why was that? She liked that the man who was not her husband was interested in her, liked that he found her attractive, both her body and her personality, liked that he was revealing things about himself today, liked that he was interested in her work, the mundane things in her life, liked all of that even during this most difficult time, and most of all liked this feeling he gave to her, even if, she suddenly realised, it reminded her of the feeling her husband had once given to her. Where had that gone? she wondered now, picking up another cracker, barely registering the fact that she was eating it. Why did she feel only coldness from him? Really, she thought, she hadn't been completely honest with the man who was not her husband when she'd told him why she was done with her husband. It hadn't all just shut down. She still felt something from him, and it was this coldness, this distance, this negativity, and while she felt herself to be done with her husband, she also, she thought now, was not. She was still deeply engaged with all the negative stuff. It was all in her, too. It was not her husband's alone. She'd made it with him. For a moment she felt her mouth hanging open, which made her close it, grab another cracker and eat it, just for something to do. She told herself to stop thinking about this, about her husband, and start thinking about what she was doing, think about the person she wanted to be, the person she really was. She told herself to think of the man here, who was new and interested in her and handsome and kind, and who gave her a warm feeling. Returning to this thought, she remembered how it all deeply excited her, while also making her feel a little guilty. It had been a long time since she had felt this way, and she craved it, it made everything more interesting, and it had been some time since her life had been interesting, since she herself felt interesting. Her husband, more than anything, when not inspiring a feeling of distance in her, a feeling of isolation, inspired an almost raging anger – their arguments could get seriously heated – and being here with this man, skiing with him, watching the mountains and making jokes, drinking here on the veranda, not waiting for him to be done painting, not waiting for him to acknowledge her, not waiting for him to tell her about his life rather than asking about hers, was like being introduced back into reality. This was what the world was *supposed* to feel like. Exciting and wild and chaotic. And the guilt she felt, she knew, was just the part of her that was still attached to her husband, though of course, even while thinking this, she understood that she was being unfair to some degree. Her husband did ask about her, did want to know about her life, was interested in her, she could feel it, but it was always on his terms, his time. That was the problem.

She told the man that she knew that talking about her husband and her problems was probably not exactly what he had in mind for today, and she was sorry about that, they could stop talking about it now and start talking about something else. What did he want to talk about? Really, please, anything else would be great. She was honestly tired of thinking about it all so this would be doing her a favour. Not that she needed a favour, she didn't mean it like that. I'm going to stop talking now, she said. She watched him reach his hand over to her arm, her upper arm, and sort of caress her, comfort her, a little like he was petting a sick puppy. It was odd, an odd way of comforting, his body distant from her, his face leaned in and sincere, and his one hand rubbing the back of her upper arm, yet she smiled, not wanting to make him feel that she was feeling awkward.

The skier watched the rabbit while he cleaned his goggles. It still hadn't seen him, and he knew when it did that it would dart off into the woods. After allowing himself some minutes to just observe it, he reached down and checked his boots, then straightened up, and when he did the rabbit was up on its hindlegs, sniffing. It seemed to sniff near the forest line. He felt a breeze come up. Then the rabbit darted away, down the hill, into a copse of spruce trees away from the forest line. As he was inwardly saying goodbye and was about to take off down the backcountry slope, he saw something in the forest. Near him. It was a deer, he thought at first. Very still. He crouched on his skis, using his poles to balance. No, it wasn't a deer, the legs were too thick, but he couldn't see, could only see patches of brown, tan through the underbrush covered with snow. He stayed very still, waiting. Maybe it was a small bear cub. A fox, he thought, possibly. Then it moved and its head swung low and he saw the large cat eyes and then he too smelled it, he didn't know what, maybe a recent kill, and instead of going down the mountain he turned, walked on his skis in large, loping steps and headed back to the resort. He looked back once and the mountain lion was gone. Then, fear mounting through his chest, his stomach tight, he was gone down the other side of the mountain, back to the resort, away from the wild backcountry.

He brought his hand back into his lap and said that she didn't need to apologise at all and that he was completely happy to help her with this situation and that if she wanted to move on and talk about other stuff, that sounded great to him, but if she wanted to keep talking out her problem, they could, he could, though they had talked about it, not in this specificity, but certainly in general, over the past two months, and maybe it'd be a good thing to get some of this out and off her chest and then to talk about something else, how fun some of those back slopes had been, how much his quads burned on the one black run they did. That one was so hard, he said. She was smiling and nodding. It was fun with her on the slopes, to see her smiling, he said. She said that she'd really enjoyed the day too. She took another cracker and bit it in half, and he took another and began eating his, too. This made him stop talking, but only momentarily, and then, swallowing, he asked her how her husband was taking it all. He chewed his cracker and Brie. She tried not to think the question strange. She tried to just think that he was not only concerned for her but also concerned for her husband. Which he was, she thought. He must be. He wasn't only her friend, after all. He didn't want to hurt her husband, of course, and didn't want her husband to be hurting. He felt bad for him. He liked her husband. But it felt off, almost as though he was trying to show her how good of a person he was, which was annoying. But that couldn't be. He was just trying to be fair, just like she had been earlier.

A man came out onto the veranda. The veranda was not yet completely in shadow, and he walked to a table

– towards his friends – and told them that he'd seen a mountain lion near here, near the resort, on the back side of the mountain. His friends scoffed, laughed. One said that there weren't any mountain lions in North Carolina. He saw a bobcat, probably, and the man said, No, no, I saw it, it was a mountain lion, definitely. Another of the men shook his head and said they were extinct in the region, that wasn't possible. There were children around, families, he might scare someone. The man kind of threw up his hands, said, Unbelievable, and then left. She had been watching, and she was sitting forward now in interest. Definitely not real, he said. He must be confused. His friends were right. They're extinct here. She thought that she was glad for this intrusion. She no longer wanted to talk of what they'd been talking about. She wanted to stick with this, talking about their day, about what was occurring right now, but then he asked again. How was her husband doing? Did he seem to be understanding that things were over, or was he in denial? It could be so hard for a person who doesn't feel the same thing to really understand that things are over. My own relationship in the past was like this, he said. Actually, I was the one in denial. And that caused all kinds of problems and made the pain of the situation that much worse. She furrowed her brow and shook her head and sat back and took another sip of beer and looked out at the mountains and skiers.

She didn't answer right away. She watched the remnants of the sun, the dispersed orange light along the mountainous horizon. The skiers on the slopes had thinned out considerably, though there were still some teenagers who were snowboarding aggressively and wildly, trying their best to fill in the entirety of the winter day with play. She observed him watching this group of teenage boys ski down a black, hitting jumps, wiping out, and scrambling to get back to a lift to make one more run. There had been numerous pauses in their conversation, still points, around which both of them seemed to be orbiting, she thought, as though they were rotating around something that neither of them wanted to define. He occasionally ate a cracker with Brie on it. He chewed quietly. Then he pointed to a boy struggling to get his snow skis off, tripping over himself, a ski shooting away. She laughed. She observed that they both shielded their eyes against the setting sun, looked at each other and then away. There was something pulling them together, two people orbiting some unseen force, and yet something also pushing them apart. Her husband, she thought. She picked up her beer and drank and noticed the way their table sat in a cracked sort of light, the tops of pine trees shadowing and dividing the table in half, but not between them. They both sat in the light and in the shadow, which appeared to have a jagged edge.

She finished another cracker and said that her husband wasn't doing well, and then she added that she hadn't actually said any of this to her husband. Really? Really, she said. I haven't told him any of this. Or, not in the way I'm telling you now. She felt him watching her intently. In her pocket, her phone buzzed again. For a moment she ignored it, hoping it was her colleague replying, but then it immediately buzzed again and she guessed it had to be her husband, as though he had heard her say this. She pulled her phone out of her pocket, briefly looked at the texts, questions about their daughters, their days at school, and what her husband wrote was a 'food situation'. She put the phone back in her pocket, drank some more beer and looked at him when he asked her what exactly she had told her husband then. He was gazing at her intently, his blue eyes wide and mysterious, like small alien stones made of water. She swallowed and cleared her throat and looked down, cleaning her hand with a napkin. A little pepper jelly had got on her hand, and now a pink splotch was on her napkin. She licked and sucked at her hand a moment to make the sticky feeling go away. What she had told her husband, she explained to him, was that she loved him but was not *in love* with him anymore, which she knew was a sort of clichéd thing to say, but come on, how could she say what she'd just said to another person? That he inspires in me a distance, a coldness, or just anger. There was just no way. Yeah, you're right, you definitely couldn't say any of this, the man who was not her husband said. The I-love-you-but-I'm-not-in-love-with-you-anymore thing, she said, was at least a way of saying their relationship had really mattered to her, had mattered to both of them, and had a lingering impact on her, which was the case, it really was, and so the phrase, she felt, was a way of being respectful of that. Also, she hated that she'd had to use this cliché, but you know, she wanted to let him down as easily as she could, so that was the best way to do it, even if it wasn't really how she felt. Or, exactly how she felt. Her phone buzzed again, but this time she made no motion to reach for it. The man who was not her husband looked at it. Then he took a sip of beer, a contemplative look on his face, and said that he could share a little of the specifics of his last relationship if she thought it might help.

The resort sent out the snow patrol, they issued a message to resort-goers through text message, something innocuous but cautioning. A mountain lion had been spotted. There was no cause for alarm. Everyone here at Wolf Valley Resort shared the mountain with wildlife, and as with any type of animal, skiers should stay away from wildlife. Thank you, the management. The ski patrol went out because it was their duty, but they didn't see it. It was no longer where it had been reported, and now the animal moved quietly but quickly through the forest, back to her den, really just a small cave in a granite rock formation, where her three cubs were waiting. She went into the cave and sat against the back of it and lay down and the cubs began to nurse, though it was past the time when the cubs should be nursing. They should've been with her, learning the still-wait of the hunt, but there had been so little to hunt. The deer, the elk, the raccoons, all the animals that were typically the source of food for such predators, which such predators helped thin out, to balance, were all gone, had moved away from the sounds and lights of the ever-expanding resort. This lion, long thought extinct in the eastern part of North America, had returned, moving back from the west. She had somehow returned despite being forced out and hunted to near extinction to protect the farms of European settlers, creating, years later, an excess of deer populations. She was here, though officially declared extinct. She sat against the back of the cave, eyes peering out, watchful in her innate concern for her cubs.

She sat there quietly for a moment, trying not to look at him, but because of the sun going down behind the mountains it was hard not to. On the table, the ringlets of amber light faded, faded, then were gone. The beers sat half in shadow. She drank her beer and tried not to look at him again, though she wanted to look at him, she didn't know why she wasn't looking, there was something fun about withholding, maybe, about not looking and then suddenly looking, and the excitement and power she felt. He stood and said that he'd be right back, he had to use the bathroom, and she watched him go. There was something in looking at him that made her excited and feel powerful, and she knew, because he'd told her over text, that he liked seeing her too, that he found her seriously sexy, and could she send him a quick pic, which she did, nothing lurid, just a good-looking picture of her in a sort of shirt dress, a little leg, and then she'd asked him for a reply in pic pls, and he'd sent her one of him with a tight-fitting dress shirt on, taken in the mirror at work, the top button undone, and she'd been confused by it for a minute, a mole on his face was on the other side of his face, and it took a moment for the confusion to be replaced by understanding, the image was flipped, reversed. Anyway, she liked being here with him, knowing that he found her attractive and that he'd probably looked at the pictures she'd sent him many times, just as she had looked many times at the ones he'd sent, and he had probably, at this point, she thought, masturbated to her. She knew she turned him on. She liked his face, and his body, which was a little squat, but strong, quiet, containing a certain intelligence of its own, she thought. He was funny in a calm and cool way, patient and attentive in that same way. He'd once said to her, because she was so bad at remembering faces, that she wasn't born with facial recognition software but she could buy some on Amazon for like fifteen bucks. Her husband, when she'd told him that his friend was funny, had been almost taken aback. How is he funny? he'd said. Then he'd said, Oh, yeah, he's funny around you. But he's not funny. More than anything, she thought, the man who was not her husband was *not* her husband. He looked different, talked differently, his hair was lighter, his teeth a bit whiter, his eyes not dark, his skin not olive, his mannerisms different, he skied differently, and actually, if she was honest, not quite as well, but whatever, she liked that he wasn't as good. Her husband had to be good at everything. Finally a man who didn't have to be like that. Also, he talked about sex a lot around her, which was a thing her husband had noted as a fault of his, but which she liked – he wasn't trying to win her over, it was just that she brought out this feeling in him. Finally, she thought. It had excited her when she first began hearing it. He saw her sexually, as a sexual being. Not that her husband didn't, but she was so used to that from him, and now here was this completely different person whom she was actually interested in, and who seemed genuinely interested in her, her thoughts and her feelings and also, again, in her body. Your legs look good, he had texted her. Strong. Or: I think about what you look like under your clothes. Or: I'd like to run my hands over your entire body. It had been thrilling to text him naughty phrases and images without her husband knowing. Like she was taking power back in her life. A text that said she was thinking of what it'd be like for him to kiss her neck; a picture of her in some very tight jeans that made her butt look good; a text that said she'd like him to take her to dinner and for her to listen while he told her the things he would do to her later that night.

Though, unfortunately, she thought now, waiting for the man who was not her husband to return, that playful period was over. All of this was occurring because in some deluded way her husband wanted her to be happy and really loved and cared for her, as he had said, and wanted to remain a family with her, and he said he trusted her completely in regard to the rules of their open relationship, though she knew that this was only partly sincere: she found him checking her phone several times, trying to discover who she was seeing. That wasn't an open relationship. That wasn't trust. It made her really loathe him, then. And yet, after opening the relationship, talking to the man who was not her husband became easier, but also a little less exhilarating. Maybe because of the rules she and her husband had laid down. Or that he'd laid down. But also because when the man who was not her husband had asked how the opening of the relationship had occurred, she didn't tell him that her husband had suggested it. She thought that the truth of what her husband claimed, that he thought it might be good and allow her to come back to him and see him for what he was, not just the story of him in her head, would make the man who was not her husband wary, and so she'd told him that she'd asked for it. I'm so glad you asked him for that, he'd said to her. That made things less exhilarating because she didn't like that he was being exhilarated by something that wasn't true. Likewise, since she'd told her husband that she had some interest in someone else after the opening of the relationship, she'd also, strangely, not sent as many of the naughty texts. The relationship with the man who was not her husband began to feel a little more proper. A little more like a relationship, she guessed. She also felt less powerful and more guilty. They texted at regular intervals, began asking routine questions, and even their plans to talk on the phone, which had to be managed and were at first very fun, became a little less fun. Still, she felt it was the right movement, because now she could look at him and talk to him and even meet with him and be close to him and not feel guilty. Though she knew that that wasn't completely true, she did feel guilty to some degree, because after all she hadn't told her husband that the other man she was interested in was his friend, actually was her husband's friend before he was her friend. She thought now that that was probably one of the reasons she was talking to this man about her husband, so that she'd feel less guilty, and it did help ease the guilt some. Though when the man who was not her husband had asked, a couple weeks ago, whether her husband knew, if not the person she was interested in, then at least the extent of their situation, she'd told him she had made it very clear to her husband, because now it was an open relationship, but she hadn't, and the man who was not her husband said that at some point they were going to need to tell her husband that it was him. She had agreed with him enthusiastically, though inwardly she had thought that she might never tell. Or not until they separated, when things went there. She hadn't liked that he'd suggested that, really, but she'd let it go because in other ways the man who was not her husband seemed to know exactly what she needed, he was deeply respectful of her, and of her husband, he genuinely did not want to hurt her husband or want to complicate things between them, and this all made her feel more attracted to him. She saw that he was not willing to engage with her sexually until the thing with her husband was completely over, or not over but completely approved of, perhaps, and what else could you want from a new relationship, after all, except a person whose intentions were clear? She saw his figure moving through the restaurant, almost a two-dimensional shadow, and as he approached the veranda or patio she saw him fully. He came and sat and ate another half a cracker. She leaned towards him and finished her beer. She felt completely full and thought tonight she wanted him to herself, and she wanted him to want her in return.

She would wait and rest and then return in the morning to her hunt. She was weak, but so were the other animals on the mountain. Rabbits, deer, elk, all were experiencing the effects of a difficult winter, with only small amounts of food to forage. Her large paws would help her in the morning after a fresh snow had fallen. By early morning, before sunrise, she would be up hunting already. The sky still darkly blue, but now lightening. Even in this dark she would find the track of a deer, a doe, and follow it. It was easier to track another animal when a fresh snow had fallen, and the lioness knew this. She'd see it from hundreds of yards away and make her slow, hunched approach. Her lack of a strong sense of smell was made up for by acute hearing as she tracked the deer not only through sight but through sound: its nibbling of brush, its hooves creaking the snow. She would approach, then find a place still far away to wait in the cover of underbrush. There was nothing cruel here in the relationship of predator and prey. It was a dance.

After returning from the bathroom, he took a drink of his beer and said that look, he was sorry if he had crossed any boundaries or made her feel uncomfortable. She listened to him, thinking that she detected just a hint of drunkenness, a buzzedness, which she was feeling too. He said that he didn't want her to feel uncomfortable and didn't want this to be only a thing where they were merely sexually attracted to each other, she had kids after all, and look, he was putting it all on the table now, when her marriage eventually came to an end he wanted to be the person who had been there for her as a friend so that then she'd know that he was an upstanding and good person and had been there for her. But at the same time, he didn't know if he could do this to her husband. He was feeling guilty. Her husband had been his friend for much longer than he'd really known her, and he was just not sure it was a good idea for them to really go through with this, he just didn't think he could do that to her husband. It was selfish, he said. I know he's hurting, but part of the reason I can't do it is because I think *I'd* feel too bad. He watched her listening as he said this. He said that he was trying hard here, he really did care about her, he cared about them both, her and her husband, and so he knew this shouldn't happen, they shouldn't do this, but he also wanted to know what it might be like if they were given a chance to be together. He hoped that chance would come of its own accord. He was just so attracted to her in every way. She was seriously very attractive. She was watching him. What he also wanted to tell her, he said, was that his life had for some time seemed like it had been dropped in a hole, like he was a tiny pebble that had slipped into a chasm and which had been there for so long, for three years since the woman he had thought he had loved but increasingly seemed like he hadn't loved, or hadn't loved correctly, had left him. Or had given him an ultimatum to leave. He often didn't know if she'd left or if he'd left, things had got so confusing in the end, and he'd been so alone, living in the basement of his parents' house, with little money, no job prospects, while he finished his dissertation, that he thought that despite the fact that he felt a connection with her, despite the fact that you'd come to me and told me you were interested in me, and I told you I was interested in you, despite all this, I don't really feel like I deserve you. Part of him couldn't believe he was saying this, and part of him felt that it needed to be said. He wasn't a father, he explained, he didn't know what that entailed, he had an okay job but could he really provide for her, and yet he hadn't said any of these things before because he felt like himself around her and he hadn't wanted to ruin that feeling, because he did really want to be with her, for them to be given a chance, so he didn't want to disrupt that chance. Then, he explained, there was the competing feeling that he couldn't do this to her husband, that he knew too well what her husband was going through, that many of the things she'd said to him about her husband were things that the woman in his past relationship had said to him, which he had found unfair, and really it was almost too weird, too coincidental. Anyway, he just couldn't do it unless *she* was really committed, you know?

She said, in a voice that was lower, slower, and clearly sad, that she was sorry she was putting him through all this. She'd been selfish, she understood now, by putting her problems first and not thinking of his situation here and how hard it was, and that was selfish and unfair of her. That wasn't what he meant, he interjected. It was, though, she said, it was what he meant, and it was good for her to hear it, and it didn't dampen anything between them, she was still glad to be here with him, but it did depress her a little, especially that he understood so well what her husband was going through. She was not only hurting her husband, she was hurting him, by making him wait. That is not what I meant, he said. Shit, I shouldn't have said anything. They were both quiet. Then she reached out a hand and touched his arm.

The quiet between them became pronounced as they processed what appeared to be some new, pertinent information. Everyone around them was talking animatedly, while they were quiet – there was, apparently, a mountain lion on the loose. The resort had texted. Cautioned people. Nothing to be alarmed about. But people were alarmed, or acting out alarm. There was danger, this predator, and it concerned them. Sitting next to him now, she could tell he was trying not to look at the part of her snowsuit that she'd unzipped some. She tried not to think of the very sexy pictures she'd sent him and the sexy texts, which somehow felt remote now, though she had expected that part of their relationship to become more real on this trip. Why did she feel this way? Why did this feel remote when they were physically closer than they'd ever been?

The ski slopes had been constructed with a specific goal in mind, in the same way the resort had been and in the same way, generally speaking, that the town below had been: a mind, many minds, looked at what was there and reformed it. The minds that had formed the ski resort had taken what was already there in some way – openings through trees that were easy to navigate on skis, the potential for several entry points up the slopes – and made what was in their mind actual, a river valley and surrounding mountains turned into a resort. Yet form pushed back against mind, which were not two separate things: the old lifts had been replaced twice, and the slopes, each summer, had to be tended, cleared of encroaching plants and seedlings, limbs and trees constantly pruned or cut down, and expansion of the resort considered in a further effort to control and to make profit. Wild nature replaced with something resembling wild nature. But it always pushed back. Signs were posted. Be careful of wildlife. Be mindful of other species. Stay away. But beyond the well-maintained slopes, beyond the ageing town, outside the valley, beyond the farmland, there was something wild. Something right in the slopes, the resort, the town, the people, that was wild: mind and matter wildly itself, dreaming itself, balanced as itself, not two things, no such thing as one or the other, just mind, just matter, together. Two sides of the same thing held in the fold that is the one mind of everything, negatively interacting with itself, positively interacting, forgetting itself, creating itself, destroying itself, alive. A circle of cloud appeared around the moon. The lioness left her cubs to try again to hunt that night. She could see well even in this dim light.

Since their conversation had become more halting, she had begun to feel more reserved and noticed other people going into the restaurant rather than staying on the patio. She said that she guessed she'd like to hear about his past relationship, maybe that would be helpful, though in actuality she wasn't sure she wanted to hear about it. After all, it made her a little jealous. Which was odd. She was jealous of some woman she had only heard about in the abstract, and not only that, a person who was no longer in this man's life. But she told herself that while she didn't really want to hear about this person, she was tired of talking and so she said she'd love to hear what had happened with him and his ex, because after all maybe it could shed some light on the situation with her husband. It made her think about her husband as an ex, and her immediate reaction to that thought was that it was not one she liked, and for a moment she felt a terrible resistance to the entire situation, a terrible resistance both to being with her husband and to being here, as though two parts of herself were finally looking at each other, her mind and body, each causing resistance in each.

He said that he and his girlfriend had been dating for like, ten years when she broke it off. It was seriously hard because even though I was the one who was heart-broken about it all, she was still being so nice to me all the time. She nodded and finished the last of her beer. He said he could tell that she didn't want to hurt him even though she was hurting him, and there had been a very hard period, after separating and moving out, when they still spoke often, even met a few times and got drunk and had sex, which had thrown everything out of balance, had made them both doubt what they were doing, but you know in the end he had got over it, and really it was for the best. You get over it, he said. Even though he had wanted to stay with his ex and wanted things to work out, now he saw that they didn't fit and that their relationship had never really worked, and frankly he was grateful to her.

She was watching him talk, the way his eyes looked down and briefly back up at her, which she understood was a sign of attraction, and, despite his misgivings, she briefly thought about what they were going to do after these drinks, were they going to go somewhere else together, would they get into his car, would he say he wanted them to shower up and then go to dinner, or just go to his room at the resort? Would he remove her ski bib from behind her? Would he run his hands over her breasts and hips? Would she reach back, grab his erection? Would they fuck? Make love? She would have to talk to her husband first, briefly, and tell him how the conference was going, which was not going to be a lie she wanted to say, but she was going to have to do it anyway, and she could possibly tell her husband that she was just so tired from the conference and had actually got trapped in this ridiculously boring conversation, and there was not a minute of downtime at the conference and the panels (she knew which ones there were, she'd looked them all up) were just monotonous and draining and she was going to bed early and could he please kiss the girls goodnight.

So I know what your husband is going through, he said, as though he was approaching some final statement, some culminating insight that would allow them to end this. And while it's incredibly hard, trust me, he will get over it. He said that he could see she was obviously trying to be really considerate of her husband here, he did understand that, and he thought that that was an extremely admirable thing, to be kind to her husband through this, and that really her husband would eventually get over it and would one day be grateful to her. She quickly said that she wasn't sure if her husband would be grateful to her, but she understood what he was saying, maybe he'd eventually see it as a good thing. And that's the thing, she said. I do want him to be happy, and I think he'll probably find a woman who's more like him, you know, some more intellectual girl or something, and maybe that person could make him happy, but she certainly wasn't making him happy, and he definitely was not making her happy, especially because she felt no real romantic connection to him anymore. Saying this made her feel, suddenly, slightly jealous of this imaginary woman, this person whom she had just conjured, and she didn't like it, didn't want to think about it, and then, in what she felt was a wild leap, she was thinking of her husband with another woman in bed, an idea that she'd always been jealous of but which he had never really given her reason to be jealous of, and she wondered why it was that she no longer felt sexual feelings for her husband, since after all he was very attentive in bed, told her how much he enjoyed sex with her, was giving, and often rubbed her feet at night, gave her back rubs. She thought of a couple years ago when they'd had sex doggy-style and he'd begun massaging her, massaging her back and neck while he slowly moved behind her, he'd slowly rubbed up her spine while he thrusted, and that this was really something she very much enjoyed, and that, with the proper guidance – her hand in his hair – he was good at going down on her, and at the same time she was thinking this thought, she told herself that none of that took into account their arguments or disagreements, which had just got to be too much, and he was just what he was: her husband, a man she had been with countless times, who was selfish, who often didn't have enough time for her, and sure he was funny and intelligent, etc., but those were things that were overshadowed by all the things she was tired of – his over-explanation of everything, his need for artistic approval, his need for her to do stupid things for him like take his car in to get the brake pads changed. All of it was part of a man who was maybe kind, maybe decent, maybe a moderate lover, and maybe had a unique way of seeing and thinking about things, but he was not a man she could be with any longer.

The shadow had proceeded up their bodies and now they were sitting in shade. The sun was gone. The mountain was grey. The veranda, the bar, was lighted with soft yellow blubs. Little candles were being lit on the tables and changed the way the people looked. And the people were getting louder, more drunk, and she was now getting cold. She wanted out of her ski suit. Another beer arrived, and she quickly took a big drink and said that, now that she was on her third beer and hadn't eaten anything except crackers, she had something to say, and that something was that for some time she'd been thinking about wanting a man who was a man, who wanted to treat her like a woman, who wanted to put her first, put her on a pedestal, make her the reason for his existence, and who deeply needed her sexually, which she knew was not the healthiest way to be, she didn't want to be just a woman who needed to have a man, who needed a man's validation and approval, and yet at the same time she couldn't help it. She wanted to feel good about herself not through a man, and she said now that she thought it was a little fucked up that she was attempting to get away from this man who had made her feel so shitty about herself, only to be fantasising about another man who'd make her feel good about herself. I mean, isn't that problematic? That's part of why you and I need to take things slow, she said. I need to know that I'm okay with myself. I think the resistance I'm feeling has to do with that, and I'm really sorry you're having to experience this, I hope I'm not stringing you along. I don't know, does that make sense? The man who was not her husband said it absolutely did make sense. She said that one of things she thought was happening was that her thoughts about her situation were just so heavy and negative that it was just infecting everything, like she couldn't escape, and she felt like that's what had happened here, today, and she was sorry. He said, No, that's okay. He said that she really couldn't escape because she was in this particularly bad place and situation and she needed to get out to see herself more clearly, and he really wanted to be the person to help her do that, but she didn't need to be sorry.

She crossed her arms across her chest and gazed into the distance, but they'd pulled the shutters on the veranda and you could no longer see the mountain. Or, you could see the mountain through the slats in the shutters, but really she was just staring at nothing. She suddenly felt closed off, annoyed. He must have registered this because he said that they should stop thinking about it, talking about it. Let's stop spinning the wheels, so to speak, he said. She was putting herself through too much, this situation was so hard. He told her that her husband would seriously be okay, and he was really sorry that he wasn't letting go. The waiter brought the check, and he said that he wasn't going to tell her this, but her husband asked him for a beer this weekend. He'd had to make up a lie, he told him that he might be able to but he kind of doubted it, he had a lot of work to do on the dissertation, but also to definitely check in and he'd see where he was at. Anyway, it just doesn't feel like good timing, he said. It just feels a little off or something.

She said she thought she agreed, the timing wasn't exactly right. It might be right later, and she was so glad they were doing this, right now, spending this day together, but she also thought that they should take things slowly, because, for herself, she really needed to focus on what was going on between her and her husband. She also wanted to be as careful as she could be in this for the sake of her girls. It was so great being here with him, and she wanted to maybe even stay with him tonight, but she also thought she wanted him to know that, in time, after things had settled down, after she was out on her own, she thought they could really try for real then, because, you know, part of me needs to know I'm not just doing this because it feels good to do this, or because I have to have a man in my life supporting and validating me, that I can be okay alone, you know, just as I am. Or I'm not just doing this because I feel shitty at home and so I'm distracting myself with feeling good around you. Or, not that I'm just doing it because it feels good, but that I'm doing it because it's real. I'm sorry, I know that's not the best thing to say to you, but I don't want to be using you, I want to be fair to you, too.

He took a sip of his beer while nodding and said that he completely understood. He glanced at her briefly. Her phone buzzed in her pocket. She took it out, looked at it, and then put it away. Do you remember when I house-sat for you? When your husband asked me to do that? She said that she did. That was nearly a year ago. He explained that not long after he'd housesat for them, while they were all out getting a beer after, her husband had said to him that if he didn't stop flirting with his wife and constantly bringing up sex when he was around her, he wasn't going to ask him to hang out with them anymore. He said that while at the time he'd thought it had just been a joke, he now understood that her husband had understood that he had been flirting with her. He saw me flirting with you, he said. Then he saw me flirting with you, too, she said. He smiled and said that if her husband ever understood that the person she had an interest in and had been texting was him, he would know that it had begun even before the relationship was opened up. He would know that he had been flirting with her for some time and would sort of put the pieces together, so to speak, which was not a thing he wanted. When your husband had said the thing about bringing up sex around you, I hadn't even noticed I'd been doing that. Of course, I knew I was attracted to you. But it was your husband who indicated to me that I'd been flirting with you. Okay, she said. I think that's flattering. What's your point?

He said that he took this as a sign to mean he felt a real, true connection to her. She was a cool person who he'd really been looking forward to this weekend with. He knew they were staying at separate hotels, since she was supposed to be at this conference and had told him she really did need to attend some of it, but now that he was feeling a little drunk he felt it was okay to say that he'd been thinking that maybe she'd stay with him on the mountain, maybe she'd want to free herself to do what she really wanted, he'd got an amazing room on the fifth floor that looked out over the valley, and he wanted to show it to her. We could have another drink at the bar, eat a little dinner, and I have Prosecco back in the room. That's what I'm thinking now, he said.

She watched him finish his beer. People were leaving the veranda and going inside. The shutters were drawn. The mountain was gone, the view, which they had had only moments before, was gone. There were no slopes, there was no town in the valley, no wild backcountry beyond. It was just them in this small, enclosed space, and behind them, through glass, the restaurant-goers getting louder and louder. The heat lamps on the veranda were not keeping her warm. They were the only ones still outside, still finishing their beers. Her phone buzzed again, again with a photo of their youngest girl; her husband had sent a photo, a selfie, of bath-time, in which his face was foregrounded, smiling, and their youngest girl was climbing out of the tub, also smiling, reaching for the camera with a small, outstretched hand, and behind her, in the tub, was a turd. A present for you! her husband wrote. And then, Hope the conference is going well. We all miss you. What are you smiling at? the man next to her said.

Above the mountains, the moon rose white and clear. It rose over the resort, the manicured slopes, the skiers now eating or drinking in the resort restaurants, the restaurants in town, the houses in the small mill town, all the lives inside the houses, the river valley. And beyond, it rose over the wild backcountry, a mountain lion with two cubs, hunting, an elk, pronghorn sheep down in the prairie searching for food. It rose above everything, the body of the world, and in the lake to the south its image was reflected on the water. Its light moved over all things and was reflected on windowpanes as streaked light, in ponds and lakes as in a mirror, in the river as broken white shards, in myriad dewdrops on myriad blades of grass in the valley as small pearls, in the snow on the slopes as fine, crystal light.

*

When she leaves the table minutes from now, he will sit alone on the patio and again be returned to a certain loneliness. All the other couples and families will have gone inside, too cold on the patio after the sun has set to remain there, and he will see that same moon through the slatted blinds and will finish his beer. The patio will darken momentarily, someone turning off the lights. Um, he'll say. I'm out here. He'll sit there, with the light of the moon sort of illuminating the patio, though it's not moonlight, really, it's reflected sunlight. Then, waiting for her to return, on the patio, a light will come back on, and their waiter will put his head out the sliding glass door and say, I thought you guys bailed on me, and after a moment in which he can't speak, the waiter will ask him if he's okay, and he will only be able to say that he's had too much to drink, he's sorry, don't pay any attention to him, he's okay. Where'd your lady friend go? Bathroom, he'll say. Pretty moon tonight, the waiter will say.

The moon will allow the mountain lion to see well into the night, but the temperatures will continue to drop and the first flakes of snow will begin to fall, and she'll have to retreat, to wait until morning. And before the sun even rises, the mountain lion will have tracked the doe feeding in the dawn and lain in wait, and when the moment arises, when the doe wanders too close, she will leap out, clench her jaws around its neck, break its neck and then tear it open. She will eat for her cubs, tearing flesh away. She will eat twenty pounds of meat and cartilage and fat quite quickly, and she will then bury the carcass, cover it in snow so that scavengers don't find it, and after a miles-long journey back to the cave, but fortified now, she will retrieve her cubs, take them to the carcass, and rest while they feed. It will be enough to help them begin their own hunting in the following days. They will follow her out. Once the Smoky Mountains and Blue Ridge were populated by mountain lions, but they were deemed extinct for nearly a decade and were thought gone for nearly fifty years before that. Now a few have found their way back. In the caves and underbrush where they live, their eyes stare out, wide and deep and lighted from within. The prints they leave in the snow are here and gone. In the wild places they roam, all things are still and balanced and boundless in the mystery of their coming and going.

When she leaves the veranda to call her husband minutes from now, before her choice has been made, she will see that same moon, ringed by cloud, making the night sky appear almost blue, and she will also see its reflection in an almost still fountain, a small trickling making the moon appear wavy in the rippled water. She will think for a moment, before calling her husband, how striking the reflection is, almost better than the real thing, the way the water ripples gently and still reflects the moon fully, allowing it to break apart and come back together, and in that moment in which this illusion comes apart and together, she will feel something rise up in her, not unlike the moon itself rising behind the slopes. Was I smiling? Where did that come from? She will try hard to understand it. She will know that she has already understood the two choices to be made: to get in her car and go back to her hotel and back to everything negative in her life, or to stay with the man who is not her husband and be with what feels good. But there is something else. In that moment in the parking lot, she will want to understand this other thing, which she can't define. She will think that it isn't her alone who will make one of these two things real. It is her husband's mind, it is the mind of the man who is not her husband as well. It is everything else also. How is that possible? She will see that the entire night has been leading her to this understanding, that her entire relationship with her husband has been leading to this moment, that her entire life has been moving to now, this: here is her mind, a mind suffused with other minds, and here is how a life is made real. All that is false and unreal in her life did not just happen, was not made by her husband alone, was not made by her alone. She can't quite touch it though. She knows this thing, has always known it, but has never felt it like this, the moon reflecting in the gently rippling pond: herself. It will possibly be then that the real question, not of whether to get in her car and go to her hotel or to go back into the restaurant with the man who is not her husband, will occur to her. What will occur to her is a different question. What if the simple fact that she has come to this place of clarity is indication that what is bad is not bad but only something she is avoiding, and what is good is not good but simply something she's choosing to move towards? That both are necessary. Not created by herself alone. But not created by someone else alone either. Everything in her vision will fall away: the fine cars in the parking lot, the distant lights of the town in the valley, the slopes lighted prettily with floodlights, the moon in the sky and in the gently moving water of the fountain, herself too. She is not one person at home, one person here, one person at work, one person alone. She will be crying, she will be nodding, she will not know what to do, finally, and she will be saying, I'm listening, I hear you, I'm sorry, not knowing whom she is speaking to, and telling herself to hold on to this, crying in the parking lot. A woman who is walking to her car will come up behind her, gently touch her back, and ask, Honey, are you okay? No, she will say, as if for the first time, as though a clenched muscle in her being has finally released. I'm not okay.

But not yet, and only if they each make some other choice first, and then only if the disorder in each mind is great enough, and then only if each can look at that disorder, and then only if each wants to investigate the question that is not theirs in the first place, but which has really always been the only question from the beginning, which is the only question for anyone, just arising now in this particular form, for each of them distinctly, from these particular conditions.

Because back on the veranda as they finished their beers, the man who was not her husband was asking what she was thinking, what was she smiling about, and she said that she didn't realise she was smiling. She put her phone face down. He said, Uh, yeah, you just looked at your phone and had this smile, and she said oh, she had just been thinking about when he wiped out early on one of the black runs, he really landed awkwardly, she'd thought he'd been hurt. He laughed and said that she'd also wiped out pretty good a couple times, and he said that he was glad they were talking about something else, he was really glad to be here with her, while she was wondering if she really had been smiling, she hadn't felt herself smiling, how could she have not known that, though she had felt a warmth in her chest, and she hoped he wasn't suspicious or anything, she didn't want him to think that she was smiling about anything her husband had done, it was all her daughters, though that was too hard to explain to him, and then she thought, it was too hard to explain to herself. All of it, all of it was too hard to explain to herself, too. She felt like crying and didn't know why and found herself inwardly suddenly asking for help, why were things like this, help her make it not like this, so that she wouldn't cry in front of this man. Who or what she was asking this help from was nameless, formless, everything and nothing. What if she were really asking herself? she thought, feeling as though she really couldn't hold it in any longer and trying to. And what if the question she posed to herself was nothing she could understand or explain or answer to herself? What if all things were like this, what if everything was asking a question of itself, presenting itself with myriad choices, to grow or not, to thrive or decay, to be safe or wild, to run or hide or look squarely in the face what was wholly unknowable, unfath-omable, and speak to it and let it speak to you directly, openly? Like a moon seeing its reflection on the face of the earth as though for the first time. She closed her eyes hard to it. Really, she said, feeling her chin quiver. Smiling? She tried to laugh. I didn't feel like I was, really. There was nothing to be smiling about. Really, she just really didn't think she'd been smiling at all.

Spring

Joshu asked Nansen, 'What is the Way?'
'Ordinary mind is the Way', Nansen replied.
'Shall I try to seek after it?' Joshu asked.
'If you try for it, you will become separated from it',
 responded Nansen.
    The Gateless Gate, case 19

He picked her up from her job at the high school during her lunch break and watched her walk out the front doors of the large, brick building, her body small and closed into itself and moving quickly in a brown winter coat, jeans, brown boots. As she walked through the parking lot, he saw her pause and check her phone, type something on it, then put it back in her pocket. Inwardly he noted that she had looked at it before she got in the car with him, probably so that he wouldn't be able to see the screen, probably because she was texting the man she had said she was no longer seeing, though he knew, despite the fact that she had told him she was no longer seeing or texting him, that she was in fact still texting him. He had caught her late one night, then again a few days later, which had led to an argument in the middle of the night, waking both their daughters despite the argument happening in whispers, both their daughters crying, making it impossible for anyone, after that, to go back to sleep, which now made him believe that she was in fact not just texting him but also still seeing him, though she had claimed, when caught, that *she* wasn't texting *him*, it was *him* texting *her*, and he was only texting to see how she was doing. He was only, she had said, checking in on her because he was concerned and wished the best for her, for them both, she had said, he really did hope the best for them both during this very difficult time. He watched her walking, head down to avoid the cold and wind, and felt a disturbing and deeply unpleasant anxiety, more potent than any form of anxiety he had ever experienced, almost like an actual sickness, like a constant flu. This sick feeling was a reaction in his body to what he had come to understand was something wrong with the very nature of things, with the very nature of his existence, with the fact that he was losing her, had lost her, actually, had already lost her in some way he couldn't yet fully define, and he thought that the reason had to do with the fact that she had told him she no longer loved him, she had years and years of accrued resentment towards him, and it was likely they weren't going to be together in the near future, all of which contributed to the anxiety. Not only had he lost her, he thought, he had lost some vital part of himself in losing her. What made his anxiety worse was the additional fact that now that the relationship was closed again, now that he had admitted he had made a mistake in opening the relationship in the first place and had asked for it to be closed again so that they could try to reconnect, to try to correct what he felt was the deeply incorrect way reality was moving, she was still seeing and texting this other person, and this not only increased his anxiety but made him unable to sleep and made him suspicious in a way that he hated – all of which seemed to increase the bodily illness, which had caused him to lose weight, almost physical evidence of losing himself – which she also hated. He knew she hated his suspiciousness because she had increasingly talked about her freedom. She told him that he was smothering her, that when he asked who she was texting, or when she caught him going through her phone – which he knew was not helping their situation, was actually making it worse – she felt violated, which he understood, he really did, but also, what the fuck? There was another problem here that got pushed aside, he thought. Another issue that got ignored simply because she was the one who had a problem in the first place. Because she was the one who was initially dissatisfied, because her feelings were so central here, which he acknowledged they should be, they should be, but because she was the main complainant, as it were, it was as though his thoughts and feelings about things didn't matter, were secondary, were beside the point, which felt completely fucked, almost maddening, and yet each time he brought up his concerns, he came up against what felt like a wall. The problem she didn't want to acknowledge was that she was lying on a weekly if not daily basis and had been lying for some time, had in fact been lying by omission – he had come to know this through searching through her phone, which in itself was shameful and anxiety-inducing and which caused his hands to shake while he held her phone, searching through it, hiding in the bathroom, feeling an awful aversion to what he was doing – even before he had stupidly opened the relationship, and he had tried to explain that he understood that she didn't want to be smothered, but, see, it was *her* lying that led to *his* smothering. Her response to that was that *his* smothering led to more of *her* lying in order for her to feel free and un-smothered.

Now, watching her weave through the cars of teachers and high school students, he didn't know what to trust, and it felt as though everything he had known to be true was no longer true. What this meant, he thought, was that every small gesture or word seemed to carry some banal yet significant information encoded in it. Simple gestures like texting were charged with insidious meaning, coming home slightly later from work could mean she was hiding an encounter, her clothes already changed when he arrived home from work could mean something he didn't even want to think about, but which he thought about: that she was having sex with someone else. The thought was banal and crushing as a cheap movie or after-school special, and all the attendant thoughts, spiralling and pointless – what positions, how good, how often, how long – were equally banal and equally painful and also equally shameful. He regarded her as his, not someone else's, and that possession, that feeling of ownership, was such an ugly feeling that when it hit him in the chest one night in the form of a panic attack, the next day he had felt wiped clean, illuminated, and he had suddenly seen the simplicity of it all: just care for her. First and foremost, just care for her, and all would fall into place, like an apple falling of its own accord, and by design of the universe itself, into his hungry, waiting hand. Despite the clarifying of this simple intention to care for her, which had been covered up, despite this, there was still all the rest of what had occurred between them over the last few months lingering there in the recesses of his mind, occasionally arising like toxic gases from the bottom of a lake, poisoning the clear waters, and all these things that made him suspect that she was doing something behind his back now that they had agreed to close the relationship – at the exact same time that he once again saw how to be kind and attentive, like a child coming out of time-out and giving a hug to a mistreated friend – made him feel insane with anxiety and suspicion. These were things he hated feeling and hated about himself and which complicated and made difficult the intent to be kind and present with her. And the anxiety and suspicion were things that he would normally address, ask her about, to make himself feel better or assured, but now he couldn't because it could make her feel smothered, and where was the kindness there? There seemed nowhere to go, nowhere in all the universe to really be himself, and today he told himself not to say anything, not to ask who she was just texting, not today, despite his anxiety, today was too important. They were beginning counselling.

She opened the car door and sat down in the passenger seat. It was the first time they'd been in a car alone, without one or both of their daughters, in a long time, more than weeks, probably months. He wondered if she was noting this as well, since he thought he could sense from her that she felt the same anticipation he was feeling: what was going to happen here, what was going to be revealed? He said hello and asked how her day was going and she said that it was fine, hold on a second, she needed to reply to a student email. She put on her seatbelt and then pulled her phone from her coat pocket, the screen lighting her face, and began typing with her thumbs. He nodded and said okay, understanding that she didn't want to talk, that was understandable. He tried to believe that what she was doing was replying to a student email, though her phone was tilted away from him, though she had just been texting someone in the parking lot, and he thought now that that person had most likely replied and now she was replying back, explaining that she couldn't talk because she was in the car with him, though at the same time he actively tried not to think this, he actively tried to question this thought, not to assume. He attempted a deep breath – he had again taken up meditation with a renewed seriousness, and simple breathing helped with his anxiety – but it was like there was something keeping his lungs from filling, and he couldn't get a deep breath and he felt his heart getting faster. He tried to ignore it. He backed the car out of the parking space, drove out of the parking lot and began down the road, wondering if she really wanted to do this, because it certainly seemed like she didn't. When he had asked her during the winter if she wanted to do this counselling together, she had said that she really wasn't sure it would help at this point. He hadn't argued with her because she simply wasn't letting him argue with her anymore. It was only after asking a few times on separate days that she eventually said that she was willing to go, to check someone out, she had said, and while he had felt relieved, he had also wondered if she was just doing it so that she could say that she had tried everything, just as she had agreed not to see this other person anymore because, she had told him, she didn't want him to think that this other person was the reason for her wanting out, and now, in the car, her attention directed elsewhere, into the reality inside her phone, he felt that maybe this was all pointless.

In the passenger seat, she looked at her phone while he drove them towards the affluent side of town, without speaking. She was glad for it. She needed to respond to a student who needed an extension on a paper, and she did so, explaining that there was no way he was getting an extension, she had already given him an extension. The gall of asking for another extension was beyond belief here, and she thought it'd be good if he considered that before he wrote her back. She was grateful for having something to do, and as she typed she hesitated more than necessary, performing that she was considering what to write. She typed the email slowly because she wanted to be quiet. She wanted him to be quiet. She didn't want him to ask her how she felt about what they were about to do. She didn't want him to check to see if this was okay with her. She didn't want him to ask her if she was okay. She didn't want him to be the way he had been for the last few weeks, which was kind, understanding, attentive. She didn't want him to be this way because it infuriated her. It wasn't so much the things he was doing. The things he was doing were the same, though he was no longer working every weekend, no longer leaving her with the girls when it was convenient for him and when he thought he could get some work in, something he had been awful about in the past and something she had, over time, come to hate and resent him for. Now he was staying home on the weekends. He was mowing the lawn regularly. He was painting parts of the house, window trim outside, crown moulding inside. He was not the same person. Though she had hated him when he had left her every weekend – pure assumption, no thought to ask – she equally hated that he was making this change now. Why now? Well, that was stupid, she knew why. But still, why now, why not before? What the fuck? Still, those were relatively few changes: he still made lunches and dinners, still kept the house clean and tidy, still did his share of the housework and had added more, and really, still told her he cared about her. What was really different, or most different, what made him feel like an alien implanted into the man she had once known, and what was most infuriating, was the attitude with which he did these things. There was no longer the sighing annoyance when he was doing the dishes or cleaning the house, indicating, she had learned, that he was doing it all again, and she wasn't. And there were no longer the passive-aggressive comments about how many pairs of shoes she had left out. How she left a mess of dishes in the kitchen. How she'd begun a project like sanding and staining the old coffee table, finished it, and left all the materials for him, the maid, to clean up, like he was her employee. That was the language he liked to use. That was all gone. Where had it gone? she wondered.

What the fuck? Mostly, though, there wasn't the same empty stare when she came into his studio with a question. There wasn't the same frustration about being interrupted. He was attentive to her. He put down what he was doing, turned away from a canvas or whatever he was working on, and was suddenly present in a way he hadn't been in the past, or had only been when it was convenient for him. How could he do it so easily *now*? she thought. It was bullshit is what it was. It was unbelievable. Fucking *now*. Now, when everything was broken and out in the open finally, or maybe now that he was seeing the consequences of his actions, or perhaps now that he felt he was losing ownership of her to some other man, whatever it was, *now* he was going to be his best self? No, that's not how it worked. Not only was that not how it worked, it was unfair, and on top of the unfairness, the cruelty of his sudden kindness and attentiveness, there was no way for her to know if it was real. Was the way he was being real or not? She couldn't know, and that put her in this position where she had to figure out what was real or not. It made her suspicious. It made her examine his actions to see if he was being sincere or not, or if he was only playing the role he thought she wanted him to play. What was he doing this for? she wondered. Was his attention to her when she told a story about how a student's mother had been diagnosed with lupus, was that born out of actual interest, or was he only interested because he knew he should be? Was his sudden lack of frustration at home actual, was he really not frustrated, or was he only hiding his frustration, for it to explode later? She tried to read him but couldn't, and therefore couldn't tell what was real. Had he made a change or not, was he doing it for her or not? Was this another version of selfishness, was he just

my questions about Oliver & the
148 *changes he has... barely... made.*

afraid of losing what he knew well? It made her angry to even think about it, that there had been all these years when he hadn't been paying attention and now he was or performing that he was. She shook her head gently as if to shake away the thought and finished typing the email, then put her phone back in her coat pocket and glanced at him. She was mad again. Just looking at him made part of her hate him a little. He seemed to be sitting in the driver's seat a bit too rigidly, as though he were bracing for cold weather or something, but the car was warm, which made her think that he must be feeling nervous or awkward, which meant, she thought, that he was feeling the same awkward tension she was feeling. Then she felt bad for feeling angry a moment ago, that she allowed him to make her angry. Then it occurred to her that this anger at him was also hers. It was her anger at herself for all the years things had been wrong, and she was tired of it. She was tired of being angry at him and tired of being angry at herself for allowing it. At the least, she thought, she didn't need to be feeling that anymore. It wasn't who she wanted to be. Yet at the same time she didn't want to convey to him that going to see this therapist was going to be some cure or that his changed attitude somehow fixed everything. It didn't. And really, all of this, his sudden kindness, though he hadn't always been unkind in the past, but his kindness coupled with his attention, his asking to close the relationship and his explanation that he had only offered to open the relationship so that she might want to come back to him, his wanting to do therapy, and also his constant surveillance of her phone and who she was texting, all of it made her uncomfortable. Like she was walking through the world where the tilt of reality was just off and she couldn't regain her balance.

Anger, suspicion, sadness, these were the things of this world, the readymade emotions, and she wanted away from it. She wanted to turn on her phone again to get away from thinking all of it, but she didn't want him to be thinking that she was texting this other man or something – he was driving her crazy asking who she was texting all the time – she wanted him to know that this was between them. That this other person was not the reason she didn't want to be with him anymore, that had been a mistake. She could admit that. This other person had been an escape into something pleasant and kind and fun, and yes, sexy, pleasurable, but the problems between them remained whether this other person was involved or not. So best that he wasn't involved, she thought. Maybe, later, once all of this was done, she could contact this other person, but right now she wanted to be sure of her reasons, which were reasons that had to do squarely with him, with her.

The trees along the roadside were leafless and grey against the cloudy sky, and from the car the trees were a part of their vision, a part of their world, but they remained unseen, somehow outside the reality that was inside the car. That morning it had been sleeting, but now it was only raining. It was unclear whether it was spring yet or still winter. Temperatures had climbed in early February into the sixties and suddenly rue anemone, those early bluish-purple flowers of spring, were blooming along the road-sides, until temperatures dropped again, killing the new flowers, ice on windshields in the morning. Then there was wet snow that came down from the mountains and dropped big, heavy flakes and closed the city for a day, but not twenty-four hours later the air was warm and the day was sunny and bright and the snow was gone, as though the seasons themselves were confused, uncertain where in time they were. People wanted to know what was going on, they were laughing, what's going on, is it spring or not, global warming is lovely this time of year, they said laughing, and others chastised them for it, and others didn't notice at all. Despite the too-early rise in temperatures, most of the deciduous trees remained dormant. These trees had growth inhibitors that would cease their function and end the dormancy of the tree only when the tree had experienced enough chill hours, regardless of occasional warm temperatures. Additionally, trees sensed light. Their branches, the tips of roots sensed light in a way not completely dissimilar from the way insects, animals, mammals sensed light with their eyes. Except for some early flowering plants, the deciduous trees in the region physiologically experienced several things: that they had not been dormant long enough, that there had not been enough warm weather, and most importantly, that the days weren't long enough though temperatures were warm. There was not enough light. Thus they knew to stay resting in order to avoid injury, frost or freezing, which could harm or kill small trees and new growth. And though some trees opened their buds too early, most waited through the false springs until they had remained in dormancy long enough. The trees waited for the signals from the rest of the trees, emitted in chemicals in their root systems and passed along, though pass wasn't correct, it was more that the root system of a single tree interacted with the root system of another tree of the same species, chemical signals firing between them, almost so that the trees were connected. The forest or copse was actually one thing, not two. Any two trees might pass information in the form of chemicals between themselves and then to the other trees, perhaps waiting to hear from the tallest, the biggest trees in the forest. Was there enough warmth and light? All forms of communication, of an intelligence that no one in the buildings, in the cars on the roads, at home in their houses, was even considering, not even as though it was of no importance but as though it didn't exist at all, wasn't real.

He pulled into a neighbourhood with large, old two-storey houses, big trees and yards with elaborate landscaping. She peered out the window, already feeling both envious of the privileged lifestyles, judgemental of those same lifestyles, and a little intimidated – some wealthy, privileged white woman was going to try to fix her marriage – but then she heard him say, Whoa, I like this therapy already, I think it's working. He heard himself say this, the first thing he'd said since hello, completely spontaneously, and he wondered if he shouldn't have said it, shouldn't have made a joke, but then he heard her laughing. She felt herself smile and then laugh and then heard herself say that they'd have to quit their jobs as teachers and start working as bankers to ever be able to afford someplace like this. Or just become therapists, he said. My god, the people here are so happy, he said, motioning to the houses around them. These houses make them happy, she said. And all the therapy they're doing on each other makes them happy, she said. He turned off the car and they both got out, going up the brick paved walkway to the very fine ranch-style house, and as they walked up to the house where this therapist would decide if she would take them on, and where they would equally decide if they wanted to do this, they both inwardly noted certain details of the previous moment: he noted that she still thought he was amusing, and also that she had said they would have to quit their jobs as teachers *we?* breaks the dream

if they were ever going to be able to afford a place like this, noting that she used the word *they*, that this joke, however improbable, included him in it, and him as part of their family in some imagined future, and in this imagined future that was a joke, they were still *they*, and he told himself to try to hold this very lightly, because maybe it was nothing. But maybe it was something, he couldn't help thinking. He was aware he was looking for something, he couldn't help looking for it. While he was thinking and feel- *how it felt* ing all this, she was walking beside him noting that she *around* still enjoyed being amused by him, that there was still, at *again* times anyway, a basic, almost elemental ease between them. Despite the awkwardness in the car, something effortless occurred, and maybe what this meant, she thought, was that they were meant to be friends. If he could get over them having to be together, maybe they could still be friends, which would be difficult, she knew. Certainly difficult for him since he was having such a hard time letting go, but it would also be difficult for her, because her life would have to change as well. Still, that was her hope. She did want them to be friends. She thought maybe he was beginning to see this, and maybe, after they did what felt to her like this almost unnecessary step of trying out a counsellor, maybe then he'd really see this for himself. Then, right after having these thoughts as they approached the front door of the house, she almost put her hand to her mouth because she realised she'd made a joke about both of them becoming bankers and living in this neighbour-hood, implying, of course, that they were and would be, in the future, together. She needed to be more careful about that, she thought. She didn't want to lead him on.

this is all so relateable

He knocked and she watched him knock. She thought he knocked maybe too eagerly, and he watched as she crossed her arms across her chest, either to keep warm or to separate herself from him. Neither of them could tell what the other's gestures indicated. Neither could read the other's body or understand the codes of their own language anymore, and as they waited on the porch, standing apart, for this other person who was going to force them to see in ways they hadn't for a long time, neither knew what was going to happen next. Neither liked it, and as soon as the counsellor opened the door, introduced herself – thin, mid-sixties, with a creased, hawkish face and alert, dark eyes, and dark hair with streaks of grey – they felt even more uncomfortable because here was someone who, they could both sense, was going to really look at them, who already was.

She took them into the sunroom at the back where she conducted the sessions. She instructed them to sit on the small sofa in front of her. She asked them to tell her a little about themselves first. She said she'd heard a little bit of the trouble from him on the phone, but she liked to start with just a little bit about the two of them. Neither said anything for a moment, the woman sort of looking at the man. He took this as a signal to begin. He explained that he was a teacher, they had two daughters, he was an artist on the side, though he didn't know why he said on the side, and things were not going well and that was why they were here. He looked over at her sitting away from him on the small sofa, her eyebrows slightly raised. She explained similar things: she was also a teacher of literature, AP literature, two daughters, yep, and yes, she agreed, things weren't going well. The counsellor said, Okay, how long have you two been together, how did you get together? Let's start with you, she said to the woman. The woman explained that they'd met in a graduate seminar nearly fifteen years ago, they'd begun dating then, and she'd followed him as he'd got his degrees in art history, while he was also painting, and she'd become a teacher in that time, teaching at several high schools. They were together seven years before they married, and then another three or so before they had their first child. Why so long before you asked her to marry you? the counsellor wanted to know from the man. He thought it was an unfair question somehow, though he didn't know how and didn't have time to think about it because she was watching him. It was simple, he said. It was that he, that they, didn't have any money, weren't really settled, and that after living apart for a year – she had a job in South Carolina, he had one in East Tennessee – he realised it didn't matter if they had money or not, so he'd asked her. And how would you characterise the relationship? she asked the woman. Well, she told the therapist, they were really young at first, passionate, and you know, ups and downs. Drinking too much, I think, in those first years, which led to fighting. The counsellor looked at the man without asking him anything. I agree, he said. We drank too much. The counsellor wanted to know if that was a problem now, and they both laughed. No, they each said, almost simultaneously. We rarely drink now, he explained. The counsellor wanted to know if one or both of them was in AA, and they laughed again, and he said, We just don't really enjoy it all that much, which is sometimes problem-atic with friends. The counsellor wanted to know how so, not asking either one, necessarily, and he paused a moment and then said that people took it the wrong way, like as a judgement of a lifestyle or something when it's much less calculated than that. We just don't like being hungover. The woman was nodding. Okay, so ups and downs and fighting when you're younger, partly due to drinking? Yes, they both said. Bad fights, the woman said. Nothing physically violent, but really ugly, mean things. She looked at the man and he agreed. And now? the counsellor wanted to know. Yes, the woman said. Those ugly fights still occur, not as frequently, but there's something else now. The counsellor wanted to know what the something else was, and the woman explained that all the fights had accrued or something over time, and not only that, but he was always doing his own work, leaving her to deal with the kids, and when he was home it was like the entire family had to be careful around him, he was always frustrated. His frustration about his own work, this thing he did alone and in complete isolation, it infected the household. The girls felt it, they asked what was wrong with him. To be completely honest, I'm just done with it. Not only that, she said, he's failed me in so many ways, and after this one fight last summer, I was just done. The counsellor wanted to know how he had failed her. He wasn't there for me when my grandparents died, the woman said. He didn't take me to the airport, for instance. He actually threw a party one time when I was out of town with my sick grandmother. A party. He wasn't really there for me when I needed him. That's not completely accurate, the man said. There's a lot more to that story, a lot more subtlety. The version that she's presenting is too black and white, too neat. I didn't, for instance, know how sick her grandmother was. The counsellor looked at him. You'll get to say your piece in a minute, she said. She's talking now. Go ahead, the counsellor said to the woman. The woman continued by saying that that was really it. These were things, along with the fighting, along with his selfishness, that she now resented him for. There were other small things, of course, but these were the big things, and she was just done, she didn't love him anymore, and she didn't know how to love him again.

The counsellor turned to the man and said that it was his turn, and he said okay, that was all fairly accurate, he had made mistakes, he was selfish and inattentive, and he conceded that he had let her down when her grandparents were ill. Not ill, the woman said. Dying. Okay, but *he* didn't know they were dying, as he was explaining a moment ago, and additionally, it hadn't been *his* idea to have a party, one of his friends essentially insisted on it, and yes, he knew he had let her down when her grandparents were sick, but there were other factors to consider. Say dying, the counsellor said. He looked at her for a moment. If you want to know her reality, the counsellor said, you have to say it. He took a breath and said, Okay, dying. Now say the whole thing, the counsellor said, if it's true. Think about it, the counsellor said. I don't want you to say anything that isn't true, that isn't honest, and I don't want you to say it if you don't genuinely believe it. He thought a moment, then said he wanted to explain it, yes, that was true, on some level it was true, but the thing is, he said, pausing, thinking again. No, stop, the counsellor said. You don't get to think or explain yourself out of responsibility here. She's hurt, you hurt her, the counsellor said. Do you see why or not? He looked at the ceiling, considering. From a certain point of view, I see that, he said. But there's another point of view to consider. I'm not asking about other points of view, the counsellor said. I'm asking if you see her reality. He hesitated, and she said, Don't think of the correct answer. Just answer it. Do you see that? Yes, okay, he said. I see that. Okay, the counsellor said. You have to work on that over-thinking stuff. The perfect answer stuff. That's your job for the week. Now go on, explain how your answer is a yes.

He said that okay, yes, it was true, he didn't drive her to the airport and he wasn't attentive when her grandparents, each of them, were dying. He admitted that he hadn't really cared for her in the ways he maybe should have sometimes. He was, had been, selfish with his time. He was, *had been*, inattentive, at times. Okay, the counsellor said. That sounds fair to me. Now, what's your side of it? He said that part of the problem then was that her grandparents were essentially her parents, and so she sort of thought of them differently, thinks of them differently. For instance, when his grandparents died, he only went to one of their funerals, and he in fact didn't even really know one set of grandparents very well. For her, it was different, her relationship with her grandparents was different, they had raised her for a good part of her life, and he didn't really understand that at the time they were sick and dying. But at the same time, he should've known that, too. I mean, I knew it, he said. But I didn't really know it, if that makes sense. I didn't feel it to be true, I suppose. I should've known better though. I acknowledge that.

The counsellor looked at the woman – her body still, her eyes wide and blank – and she said okay, what about his view of her? What problems did he see here? He thought a moment and explained that he hadn't known things were as bad as she claimed, and then suddenly, out of nowhere, at least to him it was out of nowhere, she was one day explaining to him that she didn't love him anymore, or, actually, he was having to figure out that that was what she was saying, and on top of that, she was seeing another person, and yes, he had opened the relationship up because it seemed, or was implied, that that was what she wanted, that that would somehow release some pressure, and that was admittedly stupid. Pretty stupid, the counsellor interjected. But once I told her I wasn't happy about that arrangement, she continued seeing this person, a friend of mine by the way, behind my back, and so I felt betrayed in several different ways. Why wait until the point you no longer love me to tell me you have a problem? he said. I told you I was depressed, the woman said. Is this my turn? the man said. I thought this was my turn. The woman shook her head a little and the counsellor said, Yes, it's your turn, go ahead. The man adjusted his shirt and crossed his legs and said he guessed he was done, but he thought it was important to note another thing. What he meant was that she edited the past and his past self to fit a version of events that lined up with her state of mind, she was always doing that, editing out the good parts of him and only seeing the bad parts, and that was one of his complaints, that she didn't really see him fully, and he acknowledged it was true that he often didn't see her fully either, but he also didn't sort of look back at their past and only select the memories that fit a narrative of bitterness or resentment. He tried to be a little more even about how he saw her, and he wished, at the very least, that she'd attempt that as well.

The counsellor asked the woman if the things he had said were true and she said that, yes, generally speaking they were, but one of the things she wanted to point out was that this wasn't about another person, this was between them. That's fine, the counsellor said. I don't care about that. Is this person important to you? the counsellor asked her. No, the woman said. Not really. Has there been anything like this in the past? Yes, the woman said. Other infidelities? Not exactly infidelities, but yes, flirting with other men. That was hurtful? the counsellor asked the man. Of course, he said. I felt betrayed. Were there sexual ways in which he betrayed you? the counsellor wanted to know. Oh, definitely, the woman said. I mean, maybe I'm prudish here, but it always hurt me when he looked at porn. The counsellor looked at the man and he said yeah, of course he looked at pornography. Can you stop doing that if you know it hurts her? Yes, I can, the man said, and then he said he had a question. Go ahead, the counsellor said. He said that he didn't understand, he had to quit looking at porn, but you don't care that she's been seeing someone behind my back? That makes no sense to me. The counsellor looked at him steadily and said, Look, she just said this other person is of no importance to her. Yeah, but, he said, his wife was going behind his back and seeing one of his friends, and it was causing him anxiety and paranoia, which was, if she wanted to know, nearly debilitating. The counsellor looked at him while he said these things, waited for him to finish, and when he did, she said, There's nothing I can do about this. She said this person wasn't important to her. Do you want me to tell her not to see this other person? You know I can't do that. And that can't be what you expect from this, right? It has to be her choice. She's going to do what she wants to do, the counsellor said. Can you deal with that? she asked the man. Can you be okay with that? He said he could try.

The counsellor sat back and observed them both. Look at yourselves, she said. Rigid bodies, sitting away from each other at opposite ends of the sofa. It was common, a form of communication she had seen many times, she said: they were indicating to each other how much they disliked each other, and yet, they looked to one another when answering questions. That's worth noting, she said. Then, after writing something down, she said to them that what she was hearing here was something she had heard many times before, and what they probably wanted to know, for different reasons, is what the outcome of therapy would be, and what she could honestly answer here was that she had seen hundreds of couples at this point in her career, and many individual patients with a relationship crisis, and the only thing she could say with certainty was that any crisis in a relationship led to change. What form that change took was thoroughly uncertain. Also, that change might be painful, it might not be exactly what each party wants, but it will be necessary, and she said what she saw right here between the two of them was that the way they had been in their relationship was now over, something had ended it, *they* had, actually, they had ended it, not thoughtfully or skilfully, but they had, though it probably didn't seem that way. What she liked here from both of them was that there were acknowledged mistakes – that was good. Now they had a decision to make. For her part, she'd like to see them again. The rest was up to them. There could be healing here whether they remained together or apart. Remember, you have children, you'll still have to have a relationship even if you divorce, okay. That's not just me wanting money. That is a reality most people don't want to consider, that sometimes therapy is important for a healthy, non-traumatic separation. But to do that, you have to see what I see, and this is subordination. You, she pointed at the woman, have been subordinated by him. I feel that's true, the woman said. And here's the other part of that, the counsellor said. You subordinated yourself to him, too. You did it, too. It wasn't just him. You allowed it. I'm willing to bet there's a reason for that. Is there? What are your past relationships with men like? The woman took a breath and then said that she had abuse in her past. Her stepfather had done things, massages, when she was twelve. Can you talk about that? the counsellor wanted to know. If this isn't something you want to discuss with him here, you don't have to. But at some point I'd like to hear about this. I can talk about it, the woman said. He knows about it, she said, indicating the man. What happened was, my stepfather, he would tell me to lie down after soccer practice and tell me my muscles needed to be rested and massaged, and he'd massage my legs, but then also touch me. The counsellor nodded and said she was sorry. How long did that go on for? A few months, the woman said. My mother eventually found out and they separated and then she divorced him. Okay, is there anything else from your past that was like this? the counsellor said. Same deal. If you can't or don't want to share here or now, you don't have to. The woman said she was fine. When I was fourteen, an older boy, twenty-two, manipulated me and made me do really ugly things. Okay, were you in therapy for that? Yes. How long did the abuse go on for? Can you tell me whether this was sexual abuse or physical violence? He used me for sex, the woman said. He made me steal things from my mother. My parents were divorced and I didn't get along well with my mother when I was a teenager, and he'd make me steal money, once a television. He sort of used sex as a way to control me. If I didn't give him what he wanted, I was a bad girlfriend or a piece-of-shit person and a prude. He was verbally abusive, too. Again, do you mind if I ask how long this lasted? Probably a year, a little less. How long were you in therapy for it? Two years. What kind of therapy? Cognitive behavioural. Dissociative techniques, too. Was it helpful? Extremely, the woman said. It literally saved me. It allowed me to see from a very young age I was conditioned, programmed, sort of, to believe that relationships were a certain way. I had better ones later, but even those had problems, and for some time, it was like men who weren't good gravitated towards me. So would it be fair to say that in some way, unconsciously, you gravitated towards them? Yes I think that's very likely, the woman said. Is it fair to say that this is a cycle then, to some degree? I'm not saying this man sitting next to you is anything like that, but there's some subtle cycle of subordination here. What do you think? I think so, the woman said. Okay, so we're going to break that cycle, the counsellor said. Whether you two stay together or not, we're breaking that cycle now. How does that sound? the counsellor asked. That sounds good, the woman said. The man nodded and said he agreed. Okay, you two go home, decide if you want to do this or not, the counsellor said. It's a decision you come to together, okay? You, she pointed at the man, don't get to decide. You decide together. Okay, let me know.

The week passed, nearing the end of February. There were days of rain, days of sun, days of frost. Winter was harsher in February despite the added minutes of daylight, almost an hour since the winter solstice. Though the days were longer and the sun was higher in the sky – though higher in the sky was a complete misnomer, suggesting that the sun was sitting somehow differently in the sky, but this was not the case, the sun was no different, the planet itself

was different, tilting on its axis as it moved at nearly eight
miles per second around the sun, and thus it was the sky
itself that was different – the effects of the shortened days
were still at work: over several months, heat had slowly
escaped the surface of the planet, and though the days
were now longer, it would take time to reheat this particular
part of the earth, and during the week, as February moved
to March, heat from the more direct sunlight accumulated
on the planet's surface. Viewed from some distant place in
space, from where the observer could see both sun and
earth, it would appear that a dangerous amount of light and
radiation was hitting a new part of the planet, but what was
actually occurring was a vital kind of interaction, one that
could only happen because of the particular atmosphere
of the planet, which filtered ultraviolet rays, the magnetic
field around it that deflected highly charged particles, the
speed with which the planet rotated on its axis and the
speed with which it moved around the sun, all things just
so, so that a harmonic interaction began to occur once
again: the planet and the beings on it could better use the
energy of the sun. The week also passed for the man and
the woman, though they took little note of the warming
temperatures, the few extra minutes of sunlight at the end
of the day, and instead performed their tasks mechanically,
with a tacit anxiety informing their actions: for him, taking
the girls to school had to be done right, and he tried to do
this without complaint or worry, noting internally when
he felt annoyed and, rather than expressing it, attempting
to see it as just what he had to do, not necessarily for her,
though that was also the case, but also just for the girls, and
going to work, he tried to feel, meant performing one's job,
not feeling as though it was taking away from creating art,

and he also made sure to make her feel that things were taken care of at home, that dinner would be ready, laundry done, the house clean without either bringing attention to the fact that he had done these tasks or getting annoyed that he was doing them, and additionally, when she arrived home in the evening, he was not in the studio but drawing with the girls or playing with them in the yard, both a performance, he thought, and a kind of sincere relief. He was glad to be out of the studio and away from himself. For her part, she tried to allow herself to be okay in the home, to not feel as though it was someplace that she wanted to escape from, because the truth was that for some time it had been a place she'd wanted to escape from, both from him and the role he had put her in, and from the girls, whom she loved unconditionally, but who also turned her into a narrowed version of herself, just a mother. So she was aware that she was faking it sometimes, but she did feel better in the home. She noticed that he wasn't as annoyed and was also more present, both in actual time spent with all of them and in body and energy. He listened to her, wanted to know what was going on with her and her day, and she liked that, though she wondered how much he was performing it, this supposed interest. Additionally, she made a pact with herself. Not with her husband and not the other man but with herself: not to contact the other man until this was all done, to be as present for this process as she could. They ate dinner with the girls, they read them books, got them ready for bed, and then slept in separate rooms, just as they had been. Neither of them had noticed, but their lives had narrowed down even more than before: this moment, this one, now this one. Then one night, after the girls went to sleep, they had a discussion about whether or not they were going to go to the counsellor again, whether they thought they had got something out of that first session or not, whether it was worth the cost. It was expensive, the woman said, and she didn't know if it was worth burning through that amount of money, a statement which she felt to be a manipulation, as she didn't want to go, while also being true, which he countered by saying that he thought it'd be good to spend the money if it kept things healthy and balanced for the girls, a statement which he felt was a sort of manipulation, since he wanted to go again, while also being true. They eventually agreed to go again, the woman saying that there was some merit to it, she knew that better than anyone. They called and made another appointment.

Now they were sitting in the counsellor's sunroom again. The sunroom was small. The counsellor sat maybe three feet away, in a chair in front of where they sat on a small sofa. They each had coffees, though the counsellor's was in a mug on an end table, steaming, and theirs were in to-go cups. The room was cold, and the counsellor had brought in a space heater and placed it in a corner of the room near a window. Its coils occasionally glowed orange. The counsellor began by asking a question about their decision, and the man began to reply by saying that he was all for it, but he was quickly cut off and told to wait his turn, this wasn't a question for *him*, not yet, and really this was something he needed to learn, that it wasn't always his turn, and his thinking in this way, that it was always his turn and had always been, was indicative of something that he needed to consider deeply and that was connected to the subordination thing she had explained last week. But not right now, the counsellor, who was sitting opposite them, said. Then the counsellor nodded towards the woman and said she wanted to hear from *her* first. It's just a very easy flipping of the script, the counsellor said. It probably feels insignificant. But you beginning things is a way to disrupt that cycle we talked about last time. The woman looked briefly at the man, and she said okay, if she had to answer she'd have to say that she hadn't really known most of the week. If you'd asked her last week if she thought she would do more than one session, she probably would've said no. She probably would've said that she didn't really see the point, but now she was ready to say that she'd at least give it a try. She thought it was at least worth giving it a try, because she wanted things to go well for the girls no matter what happened. There was quiet in the sunroom for a moment, light and shadow seeming almost to undulate in the glassed-in space as a result of clouds moving across the face of the sun, and then the woman continued by saying that since he was willing to give it a try, she felt she had to give it a try, too. Or it wasn't that she *had* to, but she felt it was important to do this, to know for sure. She knew that was maybe impossible, knowing for sure, but as close to that as possible she thought was worthwhile. It was worth seeing. She paused, momentarily looking down at the floor as if searching for a lost earring or contact there on the rug. Then she looked up and said it was worth seeing if things were too irrevocably fucked or not. She suspected it was all too irrevocably fucked. They had made too much of a mess, they had fought in front of their daughters, they had said unspeakable things, she had done this thing and now he couldn't trust her, and not only that, she didn't trust him. He had let her down too often. On top of all that there were just years and years of, sure, yes, good things, but also all this bad stuff between them, it really did seem impossible to her. But okay, she said, she was willing to try if he was willing to try. There was something fair in that and she wanted to be fair. She wanted this whole thing to be in some way decent, and though she felt like it was impossible, she acknowledged that this was just a feeling and part of her really didn't know, she couldn't know until some effort was made, so this was it, she guessed. She was making the effort. The man looked at the counsellor and she nodded to him, indicating it was his turn, and he said he was obviously willing to try, he was the one who had made the phone call in the first place, and also, he said to the counsellor, he knew he could do better, he was *certain* he could do better. Yes, he acknowledged and understood all that she had said, that things had got bad and unpleasant, but that was just how things were sometimes, sometimes things were difficult, but there was something important here that he didn't want to lose, that he didn't think *they* should lose or just give up on, which he understood was corny, but to him it was still worth trying.

They could see out the windows, if they wanted, that there was snow on the ground, which had melted a little, revealing brown, almost tan grass. They could hear, if they listened, a dripping sound accompanied by birdsong. They could feel, if they were inclined, that the air in the room was warm and that the air outside coming through the windows was cooler, despite the fact that it was sunny. But their awareness was not directed to these things, they were only paying attention to the words in the room, the words in the room seeming to be the only reality, and they engaged with them as though these words were in fact the only reality, and they did not perceive that outside it still appeared to be winter and that, though the crepe myrtle, dogwood and elm trees were all leafless, there was a beech that had kept its brown leaves, and whenever there was a breeze, the brittle leaves rattled. They didn't see that there were buds on the branches of the dogwood, and soon there would be buds on other trees and plants as well, as though spring were ready to bloom, though that was not what was occurring, spring was not blooming into life. What was occurring was that the axis of the earth was again tilting the northern hemisphere towards the sun, and the energy of the sun's more direct rays was again warming the surface of the northern hemisphere, lengthening the days, which caused the ground to unfreeze, which in turn allowed seeds, deposited in the ground the previous summer or fall, to begin to germinate in the softening soil, and the warmer air and longer days finally signalling to trees, whose buds had formed in summer and fall, to come out of dormancy, to begin chemical reactions, though there had been several false springs and it was unclear whether it was really here, whether the time was right. Nonetheless, the warmer air was creating the right circumstances, the right conditions, for insects to emerge from hiding and animals to return from warmer climates or hibernation, the sun's energy on the surface of the northern hemisphere of the tilting planet creating the optimal conditions for myriad forms of reproduction. The people in the room did not see this, did not even feel it, their feelings connected only to the words in the room, words that spoke only to a certain part of reality, excising everything else, which was, of course, what all beings did, partly in order to survive and partly in order to avoid the terrible reality of what they were.

The counsellor listened to their answers to the questions with which she had begun the session: what was their mutual decision, and were they really sincere in what they were doing here or were they just going to go through the so-called motions? Because, she had explained, she didn't have time for insincerity and neither did they, and she really wanted them to think about it because she had no intention of wasting her time or theirs. As she had told them in their first session, whether they stayed together or not wasn't what she was interested in. She wanted to know if they were really doing this to learn something or not. Staying together or not wasn't the issue, they could still learn a great deal and grow even if they didn't stay together. She wasn't here to magically put them back together. So what would it be? What had they decided together? had been her question. Were they invested in this process? Now, hearing their responses, she shook her head at what appeared to be empty space and said, Okay, this is our second meeting, so you're still learning, and I like what you've said, it feels pretty honest to me, but here's the thing: don't say it to me. Say it to her. He turned his head towards the woman sitting next to him on the small sofa, and the counsellor said, No, turn your entire body, and she reached over and said, May I? He nodded, and she moved his shoulders like he was a puppet, and he turned his entire body and looked at the counsellor. Try it again, she said to him. To her. He nodded at the counsellor and momentarily looked at the woman sitting next to him on the small sofa and said he could try, he could do better, and the counsellor interrupted and said, Okay, that's a good try, but you're looking down. Can you look up, at her? He looked up and into the woman's eyes and said again what he had to say, thinking it was difficult to be sincere when it felt like someone was forcing him to be sincere, like he was performing sincerity, and not only that, it was difficult to be sincere when he felt like he was trying to impress both the counsellor and his wife, though he was trying to impress them each in different ways, but he told himself to ignore this thought, this type of thinking, partly because that was one of the things the counsellor had told him to do in their first meeting, and partly because he knew, he already *knew*, that it was this type of thinking that always got him in trouble, he needed to stop considering every possible outcome of his actions and words, and thus not try to manipulate outcomes with his words and actions, but just be sincerely himself. He said again that he knew that he could do better. He was certain of it.

The woman listened to what he said and said she'd heard him, and she said in response that she didn't know if he even knew *what* he was supposed to do better at, though. That was the problem. The counsellor leaned over again, and said, May I? The woman nodded, and the counsellor gently moved the woman's head and moved her shoulders and said, Now, I'm moving you because I want you to feel that, feel that posture of attention and facing him. So, now, don't say it to me. Say it to him. The woman thought that the counsellor was intimidating, an intimidating woman, but she also liked her, and at the same time that she liked her she felt free with her to say what she really wanted to say, and she now turned to him and said it. Do you even know what you're supposed to do better at? He said, Yes, I have to, you know, be more attentive, not be, not be so self-involved, and then, after a moment of hesitation in which he felt himself thinking of the correct and most appropriate and most impressive response, the counsellor said, Just answer with what you feel. Don't overthink it, don't try to come up with the perfect answer. He didn't say anything for a moment, thinking of the appropriate response to that, and she said, I know that hesitation is your way of thinking, but it's also a way that you kind of control the narrative. Would you agree with that? That's what I saw in that first meeting. Do you feel that way? The man said he did. Okay, the counsellor said. That's good sometimes, but here I'd like you just to speak first thoughts, first emotions, unless you really are confused or something. I can tell you like to have it all pre-thought out, but now I'd like something I call first response, best response – there's honesty there, okay? That other thing is not going to work here. You just have to say it. No filters. No figuring it out. You *can't* figure it out. There's nothing to figure out here, okay. Both of you. Nothing to figure out. Nothing to fix, even. You just have to be direct. That's going to be hard, but that, *that's* why you're hesitating. Does that make sense? She was looking at him intensely, with these wide eyes that were not scolding or mean but were alarmingly direct, and though he felt that there was a kind of affectation he disliked about her, that there were ideas here he had heard before that were clichés, he equally couldn't deny the force of the way she was. It was as though she saw past his body into his mind, or maybe saw him as a body and a mind, seeing all of him, and in that moment it felt as though her eyes were pulling all of existence into them and sending it back out to him. And she said, Okay, so why'd you hesitate before? When she asked if you knew what you had to change, why did you hesitate? He nodded and then he shook his head and said he didn't know, and the counsellor said, That's good. That you don't know. I'm glad you don't know. Because here's the thing, *you don't know*. She paused. So what *do* you know? she said. He said, I know I can do better, but I don't know in what way, and the counsellor said, Her, not me, and the man said it again to the woman. The woman looked at him and then at the counsellor, and the counsellor nodded towards the man. The woman looked at the man. The counsellor said, Tell him what you want. The woman said that she wanted him to listen, she wanted him to hear her when she said she didn't felt like a whole person, it was like he dismissed that feeling. You dismissed that I felt like I was playing this role. She stopped, wanting to say more, more about the other man, but she thought that she shouldn't or that the counsellor would tell her to stop or that such information wasn't pertinent here, but the counsellor leaned towards her and said, What else do you need to say? What else does he need to hear right now? The woman felt an awkward tension in her chest, like a faulty electrical wire inside her attempting to send the pro-grammed signals, which were signals that were meant to hide something, she understood, but she was now being told this wiring was wrong, and, removing her arms from across her chest, she rubbed a spot above her breasts like she was having a hard time breathing in fully and needed to loosen and warm some cold pathways of communication.

The counsellor leaned towards her and said, He's not here right now. What would you say to me? Just me. Just us girls. What do you think you might say if it was us? The woman felt it to be such an abrupt move she couldn't de-cide what to do, and then she thought that the phrase 'just us girls' was so trite she could barely get past it, like what was this, were they suddenly inside a Hallmark card? But then the counsellor smiled at her and said, Here's something to consider. He hesitates because he likes to have it all figured out and sounding perfect when it comes out of his mouth so that he can control things. Just in a small way, a subtle way. It's based in a kind of fear and anxiety. *You* hesitate not because you want to control but because you're afraid of saying what's really on your mind. Because you're afraid of hurting people or exposing yourself. So it's fear either way. So, knowing that, seeing that, try now to say what's on your mind to me. There is no right or wrong, I promise you. The woman took a breath, feeling that maybe she had been a bit too callous a moment ago, and said that well, what she'd want to tell him, what she thought he needed to hear, though she didn't like it and it was obviously really hurtful to him, but what she needed him to hear was that doing this thing – the counsellor stopped her and said, What thing? The woman paused and then said, Seeing this other man, and the counsellor said, Good, go on. The woman continued by saying that what she'd want him to know was that being around this other man, it made her feel like she was no longer playing a role. The woman paused, her hands smoothing her pants, her eyes momentarily down, and then she added that it gave her some relief from her life, being around this other man, and not only that, but this other man listened to her completely, he was in a similar situation to some degree, in that he was alone, and she had felt alone for a long time, and they were able to be alone together and that had brought them closer in some way. It just felt like there was someone who understood what it felt like to feel alone, stuck in a role. No one else, none of her friends, not him, seemed to understand that, or they wouldn't admit it. Everyone she knew, so many people, had these deep anxieties and worries, but they couldn't communicate them. It was like people hid themselves and put on this pleasant face all the time, when they were really feeling pain, and this other person, he could share this with her. He *had*. He had allowed her to feel that she wasn't just performing her life but that she was actually living it. He had offered himself as a person who could really hear and understand her, understand that she was tired of performing her life, and just that understanding made her feel like she was not just performing her life anymore but was living it again.

The counsellor sat back and looked at him and said, Okay, you're here now. He took a breath, thinking that what she was really saying was that it was he who had made her stuck in this role, it was he who had made her feel alone, it was his fault, and it was infuriating to hear that, but at the same time he thought that he shouldn't say any of that, it wouldn't do any good, he *was* the one to blame here, and some part of him acknowledged that, some part of him knew what she said was true, despite how infuriating it was, and yet he was still angry about it and he said, Okay, so I'm addressing that or what? You are, she said. If you want. Okay, he said. So I hear that, and first I just want to say that I kind of think it's a little unrealistic that she was around this other person because he wanted to *listen* to her, but okay, okay, fine. I mean, this person was my friend, so I know him, and I remember very clearly that he told me one night that he found her very attractive and I was lucky, so I think there's some bullshit there, but whatever. I didn't say that that wasn't part of it, the woman interjected. The man looked at the woman and then at the counsellor, his eyes wide, like, see? The counsellor said, It's his turn.

He allowed you space to speak, and now you grant him
that same space, okay. Go ahead. So, he said, angrier now,
my response would be that I didn't put you in that role,
you did that to yourself. Okay, the counsellor said. See, that
was defensive. That's an answer born out of defensiveness.
Can you consider the ways in which you contributed to
her feeling that way? Maybe not consciously, and obviously
it wasn't all you, but didn't you have a hand in it? I know
you're angry, but I'd like you to try again. The man looked at
the woman, tried, thought, thought okay, fine, yes, and then
said, Okay, I can see how I sometimes made my time more
important, which caused you to sort of be stuck in the role
of mother. The role of mother, wife, the subservient role,
the counsellor said to him. Is that right? the counsellor
asked the woman, looking at her. He made me small, she
said to the counsellor. Him, not me, the counsellor said.
You made me small, she said to the man. Not all the time,
not when we fell in love, not for many years, but there were
times you made me feel small, and lately, the last year, it
was all you did. Or it felt like it. You did it over and over
without paying me any attention, and I was done. I am done.
You aren't doing that anymore. There was another muted,
language-less moment in the room, and the woman felt
so good getting to say this, she almost didn't care that it
hurt him, and then she was a little glad it did, and then she
felt bad that she was glad about it, but equally glad that he
was struggling to come up with a response. The man said
slowly that he hadn't realised it at the time, but he saw it
now. Didn't realise what? the counsellor said. She said that
she wanted him to say it, that it was important that there
was no vague language here, and she could see that this
was what they were both good at, speaking in code, like so

many others. I didn't realise I'd made her feel small, he said. And the counsellor said emphatically, Do you see that you didn't see it because it benefited you? That makes sense, the man said. But now you have got to do better than that, you've got to do better than you didn't *realise*. Give it another shot. He was quiet for a moment and the counsellor said, Look, I know this is hard, I know this probably hurts, but this is what she experienced and it is real. Suddenly something released in him, like the anger he had been feeling was a clenched fist in his chest that suddenly opened, like it was tired of holding on to whatever it was holding, which was in reality nothing, and he was shaking his head and saying that he was so sorry, he couldn't believe he'd done this, been this selfish, and the counsellor said, Okay, that's okay. She looked at the woman. I'm sure this is not his first apology, the counsellor said. No, the woman said. Has he apologised enough? Yes, the woman said. You know he's sorry? the counsellor said. Yes, the woman said. Good, so we're done with that then, okay. Both of you, done with it, you've said it and you've heard it. Now, she said to the man. Do something, say something that matters. He collected himself and wiped his face and looked out the windows of the sunroom. He wasn't seeing anything out the window, he was seeing his own reflection there, ghostly and transparent, superimposed on the wooded lot behind the house.

The snow that had made its way down from the mountain that weekend had now almost completely melted away. As they sat in the room, sunlight warmed the air, which in turn melted the snow into water, which seeped into the frozen ground, softening it. Small blue and purple flowers grew in the corners of the yard where the most direct sunlight hit. The flowers were there because seeds moved by the wind or a bird last year had sunk into the ground, waiting all winter to germinate. The tiny brown seeds of these particular plants, round and dry and mature, found their way somehow into the ground and stayed there, not really waiting, though people like to say that a seed waits to grow, that a tree waits to open, but it is not waiting exactly, it is resting in its proper place, as a seed, until the arrival in the ground, softened by water, of water itself. Water which the dry seed is nourished by, the exact right amount of water and oxygenated soil: too much water and the seed is oxygen-starved; not enough and the seed will not be nourished. Though that is actually incorrect as well, the seed is not nourished by water, the water only allows enzymes to begin working again, allows the metabolism inside the seed to increase so that the proteins and starches in the seed itself, already there, can be broken down into the necessary chemicals. The seed breaks its coat, establishes roots in the softening ground and begins to grow, and in a few days a seedling pushes through the wet mud and soil towards the surface of the earth, seeking oxygen. The seedling comes up and begins aerobic respiration. Leaves emerge off the stem, rosettes growing towards the sun, and photosynthesis begins converting the sun's energy into carbon dioxide and expelling the waste as oxygen, and eventually, as in the corner of the counsellor's sunlit yard, the small blue or purple flower opens, welcoming insects, ladybugs, bees, the wind, to live out its life just as it is, and just as it is means all that it has come from: water, soil, oxygen, sun, insects, birds, and all that those things come from – the sun, the stars, the collision of molecules in space that formed the planet, the universe itself – are the flower, too, this flower that came from everything and now gives itself back to everything just as it is.

Looking out the window, though really looking at a reflected image of himself, barely there, he felt himself longing for something, though he didn't know what exactly. So often it was her, but now it was also something else. He didn't like what he was seeing: that he had been so selfish, that it did nothing when he apologised. All of it was new to him still, and what was worse, it was not new to her, and it was nothing new at all to the counsellor, he was just one of many men, many males, who was still a boy, still childishly selfish, and what was worse, he was just as bad as any of the males in society that he claimed to dislike, to be different from. Then he thought he needed to give a response, and just that notion, that he had to respond to this, made him recognise just how self-pitying he was being, which was just another form of selfishness, he thought. So he shook his head a little, shaking the thought away with force, and he said, Okay, you're done with it, with this way of being, so am I. I'm done with it, too.

There was a pause in the room, language again muted momentarily. The dry leaves of the beech rattled in the wind. Okay, the counsellor said. In the space between the okay and the counsellor's next words, the woman thought that the counsellor was going to address that, was going to address the man's I'm done too, and she thought that she would call him out, as she had been calling him out, but when she didn't, when the counsellor said what she said next – Now let's take a little break, that's a good stopping point anyway – the woman suddenly felt the need to reconsider this, this I'm done too, and momentarily she heard these words, words she'd used to describe her love for him, echo inside herself, and for a moment she felt like crying, but she didn't know why exactly, and she composed herself, began listening to the counsellor, not wanting to think of the idea that all of this was pointless because she didn't love him anymore.

I like that as a stopping point, the counsellor said. Now I want to emphasise some stuff. This is how you communicate. Open and direct. There's too much coding, too much not meeting or seeing the other point of view. That also means you have to stop bullshitting yourselves. This is just the beginning of whatever happens next for both of you, so you're going to have to look at each other, really look at each other, and really look at yourselves. For the first session last week, we got to know each other. You told me the problems. You both agreed there were problems, you both acknowledged mistakes had been made. You, she pointed at the man, explained something about your selfishness, acknowledged it. That's a good start. You're beginning to see just how hurtful you've been. And you, she said to the woman, you told me that you held grudges, became resentful, bitter, and that you don't love him anymore. Another good start. For you, she looked and pointed at the man, I can't change you, and for you, she looked and pointed at the woman, I can't make you love him. That's what we know. Now we're here, and the old life is over. Okay, I said that last week. That is the end. Whether or not you keep going together or apart, and I don't know that and I can't direct you, but either way, that old life is over. It ended when you stepped in here with your decision that you'd keep going with me. Make sense? They both nodded. In some way, this is starting over. Beginning again. There's no way of knowing where it'll lead. Okay, so today we did this exercise in which I think you were both pretty direct. Now, I've got the complaints from you both, the complaints are duly noted, and frankly, it's all either of you can see right now. You, she turned to the man, you're probably beginning to see just how selfish you really are, and that's good, but if that's all you're seeing, nothing's going to change. It's too narrow. Do you understand what that means? Neither of them said anything. That question wasn't rhetorical, the counsellor said. Do you understand what that means? The woman and the man looked at each other. Okay, the counsellor said. One thing you both need to do is look at what you have, because you're failing to do that in any real way, and what I mean by that is that you're failing to see what is real, right in front of you. So here's what you do. Go home, write a list describing your ideal partner. Not describing each other. Your ideal partner. I realise that sounds simple, clichéd, but this is how big of idiots you both are, she said, laughing lightly. Everyone is an idiot in their life sometimes, and this is your moment. Here's the other thing. You're not married anymore, okay? You're not partners. You aren't even to-gether, really, except as parents for your children, and you have to bring the attention and awareness that you're learn-ing here there, too. For as long as this goes, you're not really together. Do you know what's going to happen to you two? They didn't answer. Nod yes or shake your heads no, she said, smiling. They both shook their heads. Right. Exactly. Thank you. You have no idea. Live with that. That's how things really are all the time. You don't know. Stop pretend-ing like you do. You think everything is nice and pleasant and you want things to be nice and pleasant all the time, but guess what, you've been living in the mud, in shit, and you didn't even want to pay attention to it until it got really ugly and you were nearly drowning in it. So okay, here it is, the shit you made, she smiled and laughed, her hands both palm up, as though presenting a huge pile of shit to them. And now you have no idea what'll happen next, and it's uncomfortable and unpleasant, but you made this, so deal with it. Okay? They both said okay. You, she said to the man. Your homework is to listen to her. To not dominate. That's it. Give her space. Let her pick what's for dinner. You're not getting Thai food tonight, she's wants Chinese. Okay? Nice to see you both again, she said. Next week? She didn't wait for them to respond. Yes, okay, next week. I'm putting you in.

On the drive home they were talking animatedly in the car, and she was saying, She scares me a little. Oh, definitely, the man said. She doesn't put up with bullshit. She sees right through things, the woman said. I'm kind of amazed. She's also funny, the man said. I mean, she really likes that she doesn't put up with bullshit. It's like the one part that's bullshit, he said. The woman laughed and said that that was true, but Jesus, she's a little scary. I sweat when I'm in there. Me too, he said. Me too. And it's because I don't want to let her down. Oh, same, he said. They drove through the downtown where he would drop her off at work and then head back to his school. The trees were bare, but they could see little buds on the branches, getting larger. A warm wind was blowing. Spring soon, she said. He turned onto Academy Street. What do you want for dinner tonight? he said. I'll pick it up. Oh, so you've been paying attention, the woman said. Asking me what I want now? He felt himself blush a little and said that it wasn't as though he hadn't asked what she wanted for dinner before, it's not like that was a stretch. The woman said she was only messing with him. She just thought it was funny that their therapist used the dinner metaphor as the main descriptor of the problem in their relationship. Like you always choose dinner and it's my turn. She keeps saying that. You, and then she points at you, let her pick Chinese food tonight. You're not getting Thai. He smiled and said that he hadn't noticed that, but he could see it now. Do you feel like that's somehow reductive, like it reduces your, you know, complaints? There was a pause in the conversation. My complaints? she said. You know, he said, your issues. My issues? she said. Jesus. I'm not trying to be a dick, I just, I'm saying the wrong words. I'm trying to be on your side here. I'm trying to say that I acknowledge that what you experienced with me this last year was shitty, and I'm sorry, and that, you know, if her using this dinner thing, fuck, I don't know. The car was quiet as they drove down the city street, buildings around them like walls, a blue sky above like a ceiling. That was my bad, she said after a moment. I get that you didn't mean anything by that. I think just the way you said it felt reductive, but I get what you're saying. Okay, he said, quietly. Hey, she said. I apologise. He glanced at her. Thanks, he said. Okay, she said. To answer your question though, no, I don't think she's reducing anything. I think she's making us both aware that there's something serious about this and also something playful. That it doesn't have to be so fucking heavy. That's a good way of thinking about it, he said. Yeah, I know, she said, pointing to a red light. Pay attention. He stopped and then made the turn onto the street where her school was and the separate lives they would live until the evening, each thinking of what had just transpired, their latest session, which would inform their week, until the next session and whatever the counsellor gave to them then to look at.

In this way they proceeded. The counsellor told them she was their coach, their guide if they didn't like the sports metaphor, sorry, she was a runner. Over the next two weeks, as the temperatures warmed, they met with her. They each thought of how this crisis had happened to them as individuals rather than just as a pair. It had been slowly becoming apparent, like a Magic Eye painting that is just coming into focus and then fades again, and now they could see things more clearly. The counsellor reviewed information with them that should've been apparent but that somehow wasn't, that should've been considered, she said, but hadn't been. The woman, she reminded them, had grown up in a family that split up before she was five, she was constantly swung between parents, and then, because both her parents were so young when they had her and subsequently divorced, she was raised by her grandparents while her mother worked. According to her own recounted history, she had a father who manipulated her as she was growing up, whom she had to take care of when he was sick. Even as a child she did this, was asked to do this. This is correct, right? the counsellor asked. Yes it is, the woman said. Okay, so later on, when she was a teenager, her father had disowned her twice, then allowed her back into his life while at the same time hanging the threat of disownment over the relationship, through the precedent, and also demanding not only attention but an ongoing and exaggerated demonstration of her concern for him. That's right, the woman said. The woman said that he had promised to pay her way through college in Texas if she forewent a soccer scholarship in San Diego and stayed in Texas, near him. When she did that, he didn't pay her tuition. He kept saying he would, that he would get her the money, he'd take care of tuition, now the loans, and he did give her some cash here and there, but he didn't really pay, and she had tens of thousands of dollars in student loan debt to this day. It had all been a way to get her to stay near him, she said. That was it. And so she was home with him many weekends: she cooked for him, she cleaned his house, when he got very sick and had to have polyps removed from his colon, she took a semester off and became his nurse, and when, after that period in which she sacrificed a semester of school, she explained, he claimed she had stolen a photograph from when she was a child, and then had claimed that he had been so out of it on pain medication for his ulcerative colitis that he couldn't know what else she'd taken, money or valuables – which she had vehemently denied was true, had argued that that wasn't even close to true (this well before she knew of the anxiety and paranoia long-term opioid use caused) – when she didn't admit that this false claim was true, he disowned her. Didn't speak to me for nearly two years, she explained. It crushed her. She went into a depression, and then, in hindsight, to cope with that depression, drank too much, partied too much, nearly failed two classes, got into relationships with shitty men. This is important for each of you to know, the counsellor said to them. It's important for you each to know that the world for her was one filled with dangers, one in which she couldn't act without feeling some threat.

Moving from demanding attention to complete dis-ownment was not only dysfunctional for her but resulted in trauma, she said. I don't think it's some epic trauma, but it is traumatic. But more than that, this is a continual trauma, it's ongoing, it's still occurring. I definitely agree, the

185

woman said. So there were learned behaviours here, links in a chain of causation, the counsellor said. The man thought of all this as though re-seeing information for the first time, as a lived life. He scolded himself for missing it before. How had he not seen? How selfish had he really been? So many things that had begun deep in the woman's past, when she had felt abandoned by her parents' divorce, leaving her to be raised by her grandparents. Then another abandonment, moving on her own with her mother, feeling that she herself abandoned her grandparents. He had known these things. He had known that when she lived with her mother, she was abused some years later by a stepfather as well as by an older boy, both of whom demanded things of her and then made her feel as though she was unworthy and threatened dropping her. He recalled now – as though this was information that he had put in a vault, never to consider when thinking of her, she was just who she was – that her stepfather had told her what an amazing soccer player she was while at the same time telling her that if she told anyone what they did together, her mother would leave her. He'd known this was already a complicated relationship, since her mother had had her so young and often wasn't even really involved in her life. How had he not paid more attention? The sessions bled together, days of cloud, of sun, of warming weather in which he learned new information about himself but also, most importantly, new information, or newly registered information, about the woman next to him on the sofa, a woman he thought he knew so well but who he had come to understand he didn't know as well as he thought. He was both angry with himself and somehow relieved. She was more than he had imagined, and he had taken her for granted.

In the sunroom, the counsellor said that the way the woman's life had unfolded had programmed her to feel that there was something always being demanded of her, that she had some role to play that was not a central role, that was secondary to the most important role, and that if she did not fulfil this role successfully she could be abandoned at any time despite the demand, or she could choose to do the abandoning, and so she had learned to want to seek escape, namely through other men, who happened to be like her father simply because that was her model, who only reinforced the demand–abandonment dysfunction, thus leading her to seek escape again, namely through another man. It was her solution to the ongoing dysfunction, it was what she taught herself, what she cultivated, a way to keep herself safe. You are playing it out in your life to this day, the counsellor told her. And you've done a noble job of handling this. You're successful, a talented teacher, a good mother, even a good partner, if you don't mind me saying that right now, but there is this pattern. So now it's time to see the pattern very clearly and then change the pattern. Right, the woman said. The man, next to her, felt moved for her, saw his own wants in the situation as small, insignificant, almost beside the point. Then he felt happy for her.

In one session, on a day in which temperatures plummeted, seeming to revert again to winter, the counsellor asked the man and woman what was going on, how were things going. The woman said that things were going pretty well, he was giving her room, and she liked this, it was pleasant. The house was, for the first time in a long time, a place she wanted to be in. She glanced at the man briefly, then looked back at the counsellor, who was writing something in her notebook. She did have to admit she was enjoying being around him, in the house with him. That didn't mean she loved him, she was quick to add, but she was enjoying being around him. I'm glad to hear that, the counsellor said. But there's something else. There *is* something else, the woman said. Her father was sick. It was such strange timing, she said. After what they'd discussed in the previous session. Her father, who lives in Texas, had called late one night, nearly incoherent, and had said that he was really sick, very sick, he hadn't left his house in four days, he couldn't eat, he was going to the bathroom all the time, all the time, one day he hadn't made it all the way and had shit on the floor and slipped on it and hit his head on the toilet and woke up in his own faeces. He had a cut over his right eye and he thought he maybe needed stitches. He wanted her to fly down. What he didn't say initially, what she had eventually got out of him, the woman had explained, was that the reason he had slipped was that he was mixing hydrocodone with beer. He took hydrocodone because he claimed that it helped his ulcerative colitis, it both helped with pain and helped him to be regular. That's what he claims, she said. And so she had eventually found out that the reason he was calling was because his doctor, whom her father had been seeing for nearly fifteen years because he prescribed him hydrocodone without any questions, an enormous band-aid on a very serious illness and which was in fact destroying his kidneys, the woman said, well, his doctor was retiring, moving to Florida. Her father was out of hydrocodone and needed more, she said. He called her to help him get another doctor who would do this. She said that this was nothing new, he did this kind of thing several times a year, and it was once again time to do it all again, but it was so much worse this time. He thought she could call up a doctor and be like, hey, my dad needs some hydrocodone, and it was all extremely stressful, and if she didn't do things in the time he wanted or didn't set up a doctor he liked – as if she could figure this out from six states away – then he was disappointed and angry and short with her, wouldn't speak to her for several days, and just generally made her feel like shit, like she was a bad daughter, though then he was calling her again because he was genuinely sick this time and needed help, he couldn't do it on his own.

What do you need here? the counsellor asked. I don't know, the woman said. I think I just needed to say it. To see, like you said, the cycle. To put it into words. To really know it. I think I do now. This is difficult, the counsellor said, but you do have the ability to create boundaries. You need to come up with what those are for your father, but you are not his servant, you're his daughter. Right, the woman said. Now, I think this is very clear. This cycle is playing out in your relationship. That isn't meant to absolve him, the counsellor said about the man. He played into it too. And of course there are other factors at work here. His general selfishness, need to be viewed as impressive and intelligent, and inability to communicate important things clearly. But this goes deeper than just this relationship, and I want you to see that right now, she said to the woman. While he may have neglected you and left you alone in the relation- ship, he also is not going to abandon you. Despite the fact that you *felt* abandoned in the relationship, that you have been abandoned in relationships before. He won't do that, the counsellor said. Will you? the counsellor asked the man. Of course not, the man said. No. The counsellor asked how the woman felt he'd been doing through all this, the situation with her father, and the woman said that he had been good, actually, but she didn't know, it was still hard to know, he was listening, being supportive, he was, just, *there* in a way he hadn't been. What does that tell you? the counsellor wanted to know. The woman hesitated and then said that she was doing better with it, but she still couldn't trust if the way he was being now was real or not. He was doing better about not smothering her, he was there for her in a way he hadn't been in a long time, and though she did feel better, she still had the question of whether this was all a show or a performance of some kind in order to maintain the status quo. The counsellor said that that was a reasonable position to take. She suggested exploring what the woman felt, rather than what the woman thought. Pay attention to whatever it is you're feeling, rather than figuring it out. Now, as for the stuff with your father, she told the woman. Your father is a grown man. He can figure his own stuff out. Don't let him put it all on you. You're allowing yourself to be subordinated. You're playing into it. Don't do it.

Another set of sessions were devoted, they both noticed, to the man, as though things were out of balance and the counsellor was evening things out. She asked him to tell her about his past. He said that his was very simple, he was part of a family unit, upper-middle class, his parents still together, vaguely religious, but they were also deeply controlling people, obsessive in their cleanliness and concern for material possessions, and that maybe this led him to need to control his life and other people in unhealthy ways. He explained that he thought that, based in a basic religious upbringing, he had separated the world into the sacred and the profane, and, accompanied with a privileged position, he was always trying to make things the way he wanted them to be, and when that didn't work he got frustrated or depressed, or any other negative reaction. He felt he had to be perfect, unflawed in all his thoughts and actions, and when he wasn't he was distant or annoyed, both at himself and the world. And yet he was aware that there was some other way to be, and he felt that he was in a vague, active, low-level struggle with himself at all times. Struggling to be intelligent and impressive while at the same time actively trying not to be that, actively trying not to be so controlling and self-concerned, and he'd come to think that maybe art was a way for him to continue this struggle against himself. Years before it had been a way to end the struggle, but now it was as though he was wrestling against it as well. It was as though he was wrestling with his entire life. You've found out that the world does not exist for you alone, the counsellor said. That might seem like banal information, information that you should already know. And you should. But most people never really get it. They truly believe that the world is for them, and in my experience males, white males, struggle with this. Not everything is there for you. And guess what, she's finally awakened to that fact, and I think you didn't understand this at first, and now, little by little, you're getting it. Here's the other thing she saw: it was obvious that he overthought things, a thing, she suspected, that was related to his confused notion that he could control everything, and so he rehearsed his responses both in order to control and in order to appear a certain way, which was just another form of control, controlling how people saw him. He wanted to be viewed in a particular way, she told him, she told them both. At the same time, she could see that he could listen, and he could also answer beyond his rehearsed answers, and really, finally, he seemed to be hearing the woman again, to some degree, rather than only hearing himself. So that's very well done, she said. She's even said that things are more pleasant in the house, and that's no small thing. Additionally, she said, maybe neither of you have seen it, but while you've been meeting with me, your relationship has been tested. Her father getting sick was testing them, she told them. It was asking him if he could pay attention to her when she needed him, and he was responding, and it was asking of her, could she trust him for support, and she was, she was going to him, talking to him, asking for his help. When she had asked the man specifically what he'd been doing to help the woman out, he'd sort of shrugged and said, I'm just trying to take in what's going on with her dad, and just letting her know that I think she should be able to help her dad and be there for him without feeling threatened by him and without having to do so much, or without having to do *all* of it for him. That's really it, the man said. She asked him if he thought that his way of being with her had changed in some way, and he had said yes, definitely, he'd thought for a while that he'd been doing certain things a little differently, maybe for the last month or so, but it was true that things were different in the past. For instance, her stress with her dad would probably have caused him personal stress, he'd explained, which would've made him frustrated. In the past, maybe, he said, I would've viewed it all as just a difficult thing that I'd maybe try to be supportive about but which, because it was interrupting my teaching or painting, I'd be annoyed about. That isn't to say that he wouldn't have recognised it was difficult for her too, he would have, and he would've made some gesture towards understanding that, but he also would've tried to help her get over it, or he would've tried to fix it, and so he would've been trying to control things, trying to control her, which amounted, he said he realised now, to the fact that he wouldn't have been fully there for her. In some basic way, he would've made her father's sickness – clearly things that were not about him – somehow about him, how it was inconvenient to him, and if he wasn't able to fix the thing, he would've let her know he was frustrated with her in a passive-aggressive way, maybe moping because he needed to do things with their daughters in the evening rather than painting because she was calling various doctors, her father's insurance company and her father himself. Maybe he would've just been annoyed and would've ignored her. But he felt different now, he said. He felt that that had been so stupid. He couldn't believe it. He couldn't believe how stupid he'd been. Now he felt that his first priority was to be there for her. He wasn't sure what that meant, exactly, but it definitely did not mean his frustrated distance. And really, it made all the other stuff, all the other concerns about his job or his art or his need to be alone, it made all that seem a bit less consequential, like it was almost a relief to be outside his own concerns and be there for someone else and really mean it. He didn't know why it felt like a relief, but it did. He couldn't explain it really. The session ended, and they went out into the cold, clear day. It was mid-March.

Then, in yet another session, the man said that he had found out that the woman had again been texting the other man she'd been seeing. He found this out, he explained, because their phones were synced, and a phone call came in from the other man, and then he'd, yes, he admitted, located her phone and found the text messages. He didn't even read them, he said. He just verified that this was in fact occurring. The thing was, he said, he'd spent the entirety of the winter losing weight, losing sleep, literally becoming physically ill because of this, anxiety coming to dominate his life, and he knew these things were true for her too, and he wasn't going to do it again, he couldn't abide it, and he didn't want her to have to abide it, abide him, and he wanted to address it here, he wanted to talk about it. And he knew, he explained, that some of this anxiety was because they hadn't had sex in some time, some of his anxiety surrounding the other man had to with the idea that he suspected she didn't find him attractive anymore, that she in fact found another person attractive. He knew that was part of his anxiety here, that he in some unpleasant way viewed her as a sexual object that was his, that no one else should have. He didn't like that about himself, but it was true, but also part of his anxiety wasn't sexual, or wasn't purely sexual, it was emotional, there was a connection, or so he felt, between them, and he felt he had been trying his best during this process, and so seeing those texts had caused him paranoia. It made him believe that she might just be going through the motions, that really she had this other person she was waiting for, so that when they were done with all this she could feel good about it and say, well, I tried, and then go to him. The counsellor said, Okay, good, sex, finally. There's a lot to unpack there, but let's start with the sex. I've asked you not to consider each other married or together, but I'm sure there must be some forms of affection. Let's start there. Are there? she asked the woman. The woman said yes, there were. She let him rub her head at night as they lay together on the sofa, watching TV or reading. And what about him, do you find him attractive?

Note that my question is not are you attracted to him right now, but just, in your estimation, is he attractive? Of course, the woman said. He's good-looking, handsome. I've always thought so. She looked at the man and said, There, so now you know. And what about this other person? she asked the woman. Are you attracted to him? Well, yes, she said. Have you had sex with him? No, she said. Do you want to? The woman thought for a moment and then said, No, it's not about sex. I mean, I'm glad he paid attention to me, I was longing for that, to be seen, but no, he could've been anyone. I've said that before, and it's true. I'm not going around pining for this particular person. Do you love him? the counsellor had asked. The woman laughed, Of course not, Jesus. That's all you need to know right now, she said to the man. As for your anxiety about it, she said, you don't meditate for nothing, right? Now, as to this other stuff with texting, tell me again, what's going on? Well, the man said, the problem was she was saying one thing – that she thought he was doing better and was somehow coming to trust him again – and doing another, texting this other person. Just like she was doing right now. She was saying all this stuff, she didn't love him, hadn't had sex with him, but then she was secretly texting him, so all that felt like bullshit to him. And he was supposed to just deal with this? To not have suspicions? I mean, it makes me feel like they're constantly going behind my back and having secret meetings and fantastic sex. She's supposed to trust me, right? So I'm trying to do things that are trustworthy. When I confronted her with this information, she got all upset and told me that I was smothering her. And I'm supposed to trust her? Okay okay okay, the counsellor said. We got it. She then asked the woman why she had got upset

at him, was that true, and the woman said, Well, yeah, he
had a bag packed and said something dramatic like it looks
like you've made your choice, so I'll go to a hotel tonight.
The counsellor looked at him. Why would you do that? she
said. It just seemed like, I don't know, he said. Okay, look,
she said. You don't pack a bag and threaten to leave, you say
something like you feel like leaving. Do you see that? Can
you get at what you were feeling in that moment? Rather
than acting impulsively. Keep in mind we just talked about
the fact that you wouldn't abandon her, like, last week, did
we not? The man said they had, but that it was his understanding that he and she had come to an understanding
that this other person would not be involved while they
worked out whatever they had to work out. So I felt violated
by that, like it was breaking a pact or something, like she
had made a choice, and not only that, I don't think it's abandoning her when these lies are occurring. I see all of that,
the counsellor said. But look at it this way: you need to
understand the difference between emotion and action.
It's fine if you're angry, you can say this makes me so mad
I want to leave, but you don't act on it, because guess what,
I bet that feeling passed, didn't it? The man didn't speak
right away, like he was trying to think himself out of the
corner she had put him in, but then he said that that was
accurate, yes, it did pass. She said to him, Do you want to
leave her, now, in the past, or in the future? He immediately
responded that no, he didn't. He had overreacted. Look
at how deep these grooves are, she said to both of them.
These grooves, the pattern of your relationship is so deep,
you can't see what's actual. We're going to play a game, she
said to the man. It's called What is Real? And I'm playing
you, the counsellor said. Here's what you say: Hey, I've got

to ask you a couple questions because I'm feeling insecure. I saw a text come in on your phone. It was a shitty move of me to look at your phone, but I did. I want to ask you this, and if you feel willing to answer, I'd really like to listen. Who texted whom? she then asked the woman. He texted me, the woman said. Who called whom? He called me, the woman said. Why? The woman said that he had called to check in on her, and frankly, the woman said, I then contacted him because I decided it was time to tell him that I was no longer waiting to maybe contact him, that I thought it was time to tell him that I was deleting his contact information from my phone, that I was sorry to have dragged him into this but that it was time. And then what happened? Well, the woman said, he wanted to talk to me about why. He said he thought he had been respectful of me and of what we were going through, and he wanted to know why he was going to be cut out completely. He said he had a right to know. And why did you want to do this? The woman said it was because she was feeling more committed to this process, actually to him, she motioned to the man sitting next to her. The counsellor looked at the man, who was sitting there looking like a sad little boy, and she said, Do you see why it's best not to just run with your emotions? Yes, he said. And you almost screwed all this up. Yes, he said. Did he screw it all up? she then asked the woman. No, the woman said. Actually, the whole thing ended pretty quickly, it didn't go on and on like it normally does. He acknowledged the mistake. Well that's something good, the counsellor said. Do you see, though, that if you can actually say what's happening, what's really on your mind, what you're really feeling, that there might be something revealed that doesn't warrant you packing a suitcase. The man said yes, of course, he saw that now. Okay, the counsellor said. We're getting there.

*

Dogwoods were the first trees to open their buds, and it seemed as if they did so across the region in unison, as though they were planning it, which of course they weren't, at least not in the way people think of it. The trees grew in clusters at the edge of forests, and the opening of all their flowers at approximately the same time, within hours and minutes, even, was evidence of a vital communication: chemical signals passed between tree roots bearing the information that day-length was appropriate, that there was enough light, that the temperatures were warm enough. Rosettes of leaves formed near the flowering petals, the sun's energy being photosynthesised again, the forest re-spiring again, as though, upon waking from sleep, it was taking one enormous inbreath, a yawn, and then an out-breath. Viewed from above, the grey-brown edge of the forest was dotted with white. Closer to the ground, the flowers on the trees were myriad as the trees themselves, delicate white petals holding and protecting the pistil and anther and stamen. One thing holding another thing holding another thing. Though the petals on the dogwood weren't actual petals, they were bracts, white leaves that photosynthesised as well, and which expanded as the tiny yellow flowers in the centre of the bract matured and became ready for pollinators, now a bee, now a butterfly, the first step in the production of the fruit, which wouldn't occur for many months but which was already occurring now, all time future contained in time present. In plants, the process took the entire spring and summer, until fruit was produced in the fall, which was then distributed by birds, insects, chipmunks and was seeded in the ground, where it would rest. In spring, there was summer, fall, winter. All present already and all equally existing in their own states. A bee hovered at the bracts of the dogwood and the forest began to buzz.

In the sunroom, the counsellor asked – as she did at the beginning of every session – how they'd been doing, it was their eighth session. Two months. They said fine, pretty okay, good, really. She asked them what had been going on. After a few minutes of talking about their jobs, the schools they taught at, it was revealed that he'd backed the car into a pole while they were getting lunch with their daughters one afternoon, an outing that was supposed to be a joyful activity, which was the counsellor's phrase, another homework assignment. But it hadn't been joyful. They'd had an argument, the man said. What'd happened was, they both explained, seeming to trade sentences, was their daughters had argued during lunch, the younger one claiming the older one had stolen her chocolate chip pancake, which the older one had done a good job of ignoring or remaining calm about, until their younger daughter attempted to take their older daughter's bowl of fruit, which had led to them both momentarily pulling on the bowl, and before either of them could get the bowl away, it spun from their grasp, dropped onto the floor, shattered, and splattered a man's shoes with fruit and juice, causing, at the same time, their younger daughter to cry, their older daughter to pout. And I was on my knees, the man was saying, wiping this guy's shoes off, apologising. While I'm trying to get our little one to calm down, the woman said. Okay, so what about the pole or whatever, the counsellor said. The man didn't say anything for a moment, understanding that it was his job to let her speak, to let her go first, though he had the urge to speak first. After a moment, the woman said that this was a perfect example of what she didn't want to do anymore. The restaurant thing wasn't fun, but that wasn't the problem. The problem was him backing the car into the pole and then how they'd argued for like an hour after that in front of their children. On the one hand, the woman said, the argument was about him not paying enough attention while he was driving. I was trying to entertain our kids, he said. She ignored him. But on the other hand, the woman said, what I was trying to get him to see was that he wasn't letting me feel frustrated. He'd done this stupid thing, and yes, it was true, I got angry, but what he did was he turned into a child and wouldn't talk to me or hear my frustration, and after all it was his fault, and I'm not going to do this thing where if I have a feeling that he doesn't like, he just gets to ignore me.

The woman paused, and the counsellor asked, So he was ignoring you while you fought for an hour? No, the woman said. No, not like that. She said that he ignored her *at first*, but then he was all mad that she was upset about him cracking our bumper, and it's like, that costs money, money they did not have, and not only that, that was her car he was driving, he wasn't paying attention to something that mattered to her, and then he ignored her, so what's the message there, that she's not allowed to be frustrated for a moment? She shouldn't have to feel like there's another child who can't deal with the fact that she's upset when he does something that's going to be costly for them, something they really can't afford, and something that could've been easily avoided if he wasn't doing whatever he was doing, clowning around with the girls. The counsellor was nodding her head, looking at the woman, taking notes, then turned to the man and said, Your thoughts on this? He shook his head and said that it was an accident, he'd accidentally hit a pole that was behind him, he hadn't seen it, and yeah, he had been joking around with the girls, but that was partly in an attempt to keep them entertained because they'd gone bonkers in the restaurant. It was true, it happened, he hadn't meant to do it, he'd apologised. Okay, the counsellor said, what about what you just heard her say? He inhaled and said that it was really hard not to want to just shut up and be quiet when her initial response was to yell in front of the girls and make it seem like he'd just strangled a squirrel or something. That's exactly what I'm talking about, the woman said. Censoring my emotions by ignoring me and then making some ridiculous analogy. The counsellor turned to the woman and said that that wasn't what was happening here, in this case she didn't think this was one of those times he was subordinating her. The woman, sitting forward on her side of the sofa, remained there momentarily, then sat back in her seat. The counsellor said that what she was hearing here was that he perceived that she was more concerned about the car than him. The counsellor looked at him. Is that accurate? That's exactly what I was trying to say for the hour we fought. How did you try to tell her that, the counsellor wanted to know. He said he had no idea, she was so mad even after he apologised that he just stopped talking, and then when he finally said, again, that he was sorry but he didn't think she should do that, yell like that, that it seemed like she was way too angry given the situation, she got super angry again, and then I was angry and yelling about her getting angry, so I was basically really angry too by that point and saying awful things now, I acknowledge that, but only after she'd not let me just be quiet. He loves doing the you-started-it thing so that he can then be angry and blame me for his anger, the woman said. You never take any responsibility, he said to her. You always think you're justi-fied, any feeling you have is justified. And you make sure to tell me what feelings of mine are real and justified and which ones aren't, the woman said. Thank you oh wise one for showing me the error of my ways, that meditation is really making you insightful.

The counsellor sat back in her seat and was seemingly watching them go. The man felt that this was embarrassing, to be defensively attacking each other in the meeting, and the woman felt the same thing, that she couldn't believe this argument was still going. If there wasn't something painful at the centre of it, it would almost be amusing. The real thing that she's not willing to say, he said, is that she doesn't like that the girls actually like me, and so because I was messing around with them, something I also acknow-ledge, definitely a mistake, but because this happened when I was clowning around with them, she just loves it because it justifies her notion that I'm somehow irrespon-sible, that I can be the fun dad figure but I can't do the hard stuff, which she perceives she does alone, which isn't true at all, I just don't bitch about it. The woman now broke off from their argument and looked at the counsellor and said, This is who he really is. That is so unfair, he was saying, and she was saying at the same time, Oh that's unfair, really, and the counsellor was saying quietly, Stop, stop, lowering her voice, making it lower and lower, saying, Stop, stop,

stop, neither of you are talking now, let's be done with this now, and after a moment they both agitatedly sat back on the sofa, away from each other, and the counsellor said, Thank you for that. That was helpful.

For a moment she didn't say anything and let the tension in the room, which had been catalysed in language, hang there. Let's take a moment here, she said. To pay attention to what's going on. The room is no different, I am no different. There's a pattern of sunlight flickering on the floor there. It was on the wall when you first arrived, but beyond that, the room is no different. Maybe it's a little warmer because we've been sitting in here, but otherwise it's no different. But I'm guessing it feels pretty different to you both now. That's something I want you to think about, to just pay attention to. They both agreed. Right, so let's pay attention to that. What's creating the difference? Your bodies, for one, please pay attention to the way you're sitting. The energy of your bodies. So let's loosen our bodies a little. Both of you, take a deep breath, breathe deeply. Just settle in here with me in this room in this moment. You don't have to return to the argument in the car. Do you see that that's what you did? I asked about the argument, and rather than simply observing it and relating it, you returned to it. Why? the counsellor said. She didn't speak for a few moments, just sat watching them, and they sat there, not knowing where to look. Sunlight flickered on the floor of the sunroom, fading in and out. Dogwoods in the backyard were white and moving gently in the breeze; they smelled as dogwoods do, almost fungus-like in their odour, the unmistakable scent of spring. The woman felt herself calming down, the anger she felt a moment ago dissipating, but also feeling that there was really no hope here, they couldn't even behave in front of a therapist, and not only that, he wasn't changing, not really – he was claiming to have changed, but the incident in the car and now this revealed to her that he couldn't change, that he was still just a man looking to win an argument. While watching the sunlight on the floor, he thought that he needed to be more gentle, he shouldn't have allowed himself to get so angry, and then he thought he should apologise, feeling anxious that he was doing the wrong thing, and then didn't apologise because he'd been told not to, which left him wondering what to do, so often he felt he had no idea what to do anymore, he hadn't encountered such a feeling so frequently in a long, long time, and it was unnerving, so he sat there quietly, waiting, feeling depressed that the process was really hopeless and that he'd been stupid to believe that something like this could fix something so broken. She didn't love him anymore, she loved someone else, that was that, this was just what the counsellor had warned them about, it was the motions, it was what they were supposed to do, no amount of honesty or sincerity would change the fact that they had, that he had, fucked things up irrevocably.

Okay, now back with me, the counsellor said. In this room, this moment. When you returned to the argument in the car, you took this moment and refashioned it, you re-created it, you took what was simple and plain, this moment, and turned it into something else, in this case, whatever was in your mind about the car. You created a new reality. First of all, you don't have to do that. More importantly, here's the thing, the thing we've been going over since day one. Neither of you are hearing each other because you're both afraid to listen and be open. You, she pointed at the man, you don't ever need to say what she shouldn't do.

If she gets angry and you tell her she shouldn't be angry, all she's going to feel is that you're trying to control her, and it's going to piss her off more. Instead, you say that her getting angry at you in the way she does makes you feel shitty. Say something like that. Isn't that the actual truth here? He nodded. Okay, and you, she said to the woman, you have to cut him some slack, as the saying goes. Is your car more important to you than him? The woman didn't immediately respond, and the counsellor said, If there's some question about whether the car is more important than him then I don't know what we're doing here. So I'll ask again, is the car more important than him, this person, sitting here on this sofa, this actual human being? The woman looked down into her lap and shook her head and said no. My god, the counsellor said. Right. What a revelation. So, what the hell? He messed up. So he can be an idiot sometimes. We're all like that. He did the same thing, or almost the same thing, like three days earlier, the woman said. Well, the counsellor said to the man, drive better. Take a class. But listen, she said to the woman, does that really matter? What is more important? The woman looked down again and said, Okay, yeah, I hear you. Not good enough, the counsellor said. The woman looked briefly at the man, then back down at her lap, and apologised for getting angry. The counsellor sat back and said, Yes, he may subordinate you, he may be selfish, he may not hear you, but you also don't hear him, you weren't hearing him when you fought in the car and you weren't hearing him now, you need to listen to him when he says that he feels attacked, you do attack him. I'm not excusing his behaviour in the argument in the car or here, but you both take things too far. Way too far. There is no need to go that far. The reason you both go that far is because you're not really communicating. So, he has to do better at expressing what's on his mind, but you don't get a free pass to attack him just because he's an idiot sometimes or because he's been a selfish jerk in the past. Has he been a selfish jerk lately? The woman said, Well, besides the car. Yes, the counsellor said, besides the car, which you had a solid part in, definitely a mutual part, besides the car, how have you been feeling about how he's been treating you? Yes, pretty good, the woman said, now feeling a kind of blossoming in the area of her chest, like something there was letting go, and she didn't have to feel so despondent, that it was okay to acknowledge he was trying, that it felt nice, more than nice. Are you feeling that the car episode somehow makes the way he's treating you unreal? Is there still that same question about whether his change is real? There is, sometimes, the woman said. But now it feels more like I'm scared that he hasn't changed. It does seem like he's seen something, she said. Okay, the counsellor said. She quickly shifted her attention to the man and said, And you're not hearing her. You need to listen to her when she's saying she feels you're being passive aggressive, purposely neglectful, which was what you were trying to do by not responding to her in the car. See that there's a reason for the way both of you are acting, that it's a dysfunction, she said. You both need to learn that you've been speaking in code to each other for a long time, and it's time to end that childishness. As she was speaking, he felt his body seem almost to emerge into the room, like he had been holding it back somehow, and suddenly it was there, and it wasn't so bad, there was nothing to win or lose here, there was just an opportunity to be here, where he was, he didn't have to be afraid of it, he was glad to be there. Look, here's the thing, she told them. She thought for a moment and then said it because they had been here over two months. She said, You wouldn't be fighting like you are if you weren't connected in some way, but what you're doing is you're both stuck in these grooves of passive-aggressive communication, subordinating behaviour, defensiveness, and you're living a life that is the inverse of the life you want because you've accepted that this is how things are. But it's not. You've just made it like this. The car example and your argument in this room is a perfect example. You both seemed to be doing pretty well, but when you went back to that moment in the car, you brought all of it here. Why? Why not just say, we had an argument, it's over. You get that choice. You get to create your life as you see fit. It's like the negative you got back when people still used film for pictures. That is your life. It is the exact negative of the life you both want, but you've made it that way, and now you have to try some of the stuff I'm telling you to do here, and from what I just heard, from the little argument that just occurred here, you've done a good job with daily life, with everyday occurrences, but when things got hard neither of you took to heart what I've been trying to teach you, neither of you was direct or open about what you were feeling when it was difficult, you just looked for ways to attack and blame the other person.

She paused for a moment to observe them. The counsellor looked at the woman and said that a few minutes ago she'd asked them to pay attention to their bodies, and she wanted them both to do that right now, starting with her. Do you feel your body right now? The woman wriggled in her seat a little. How's it changed in the last few minutes? The woman looked at the counsellor and then at the man and said, I don't really know. You didn't notice that for most of this session you were really closed, facing away from him? The woman said yes, maybe she'd felt that way. It was evident in your body, the counsellor said. Why was it like that at first? Just because, I don't know, the woman said. The argument we were discussing, I suppose. And you didn't like that? the counsellor said. The woman waited a moment and then said, Well, yeah, that was awful. What exactly was awful about it? the counsellor wanted to know. The woman shook her head a little and said she didn't know, just all of it, it wasn't fun, it was boring and stupid, it made her feel bad, and the counsellor said she'd have to do better than that, and the woman said just her anger, she didn't like it, didn't like being that way. And that made you closed to him? she said to the woman. The woman thought for a moment and said yes, that was true, she felt this way around him sometimes, he was the cause of it. The counsellor said, Do you feel like you're often closed to him? The woman again hesitated and said that she was sometimes. Okay, the counsellor said. That's fine. Just know that he's not causing it. He can't cause anything in you unless you let him. Think about it. When he hit the phone pole, did he *cause* you to be angry? Again, I'm not excusing his anger, and I'm not condoning his you-started-it thing, but you need to really think about this, did he *cause* your anger? And you, she said to the man, do you think that you can care for her anger, rather than rejecting it? Try to care for it? You didn't cause it, but the way you're addressing her when she's angry is not getting you anywhere. Both of you think about this on your own this week. But first, look at the way you're sitting now, she said to the woman. Describe it. The woman thought for a moment and observed that it was true:

a few minutes ago she had been sitting there with her arms across her chest, as she often did, her legs crossed at the knee, and though her head had been facing straight ahead, her body had been turned slightly away from his, towards the door. Now her arms were down, hands in her lap, and she'd turned her body slightly towards him. The man observed that his hands were resting on his legs, one sort of cupping and uncupping a knee. The ankle of his right leg was resting on the knee of his left leg. It was his right knee that he kept messing with, as though he didn't know what his hands should be doing. And while he'd been facing straight ahead not a moment ago, he also observed that he was now angled more towards the centre of the room and towards the woman. Well, I suppose I'm more open, the woman said. I'm facing him more. And why is that? I just felt that it, it wasn't so daunting for a moment. It felt good to be here, like something got communicated. And you? the counsellor said to the man. Your body language changed too. The man said he'd felt something similar, that it was clear to him that there was some kind of connection here. He looked at the woman and the woman looked at him and they both looked at the counsellor. Me too, the woman said to the man, looking back at him, drawing his gaze away from the counsellor. I felt that way too. That's about all we have time for now, the counsellor said. No homework this week, just go keep practising this stuff. Do something together. Good luck. It was nice seeing you both. Bye-bye.

Petals dropped from the trees, and the first green leaves were apparent. The days were longer, there was more daylight in the afternoons and evenings. Spring was early, but not irrevocably so. If viewed in a particular way – as though the animals were separate from the plants and the plants were separate from the ground and the ground was separate from the sky, which was separate from waters and mountains, which were separate from humans and human endeavour – then there was really nothing to do, nothing could be done. There was no reason to do anything, there was no reason not to mine the land for whatever it would give, there was no reason to worry whether this species went extinct or if that insect no longer existed, this was all here only to be used, for its usefulness to be exhausted. But if viewed in a different way, if instead of viewing separate bodies as evidence of separate existences, with another kind of awareness it could be seen that in the plant was the animal, that in the sky was the sea, that in the winter was the summer, that there was only one hard and fast body of reality, and in this way, the beings on the planet who were aware and who were watching, acted not as individuals but as the body of the planet itself, the part of the planet that was intelligent attempting to communicate with the rest of itself the importance of the balance and harmony that maintained this body, like a tree that speaks to other trees of its own uprightness and stable awareness and this the same in relationship to the myriad things of existence. The briefest glimpse of another way to be, with the world and one another.

They walked their daughters home from school one afternoon, holding hands, something they hadn't done in half a year or more. She told him she liked doing this again. She'd forgotten. The neighbourhood was old, a historic district, and the spring was a palpable thing, it could be felt in the air. Pollen dusted cars and the windows of houses and then became caked onto windshields when it rained. The trees were light green – pin oak and beech and poplar and sugar maple – and the perennials were out, flashes of pink and yellow and purple. An almost cloying scent of sweet honeysuckle in the air. Bees, butterflies, insects of all kinds moved through the streets, giving the world depth. They were talking about something. It didn't seem to matter what, was what they both thought for a moment. For so long, every word had mattered, and for a moment, now, they no longer did. The girls were running in front of them, the older one pulling the younger one along. They were clapping at bees in the air. Then he said he didn't want to ruin this moment, and she quickly said, But you're going to, so go ahead. Okay, he said. He told her that whatever the outcome of this, whether they would be separating or not by the end of it, he had decided on a small experiment. Oh god, she said. No, no, hear me out, he said. He had this plan. They'd talked about it in the past but never made any effort, had never begun. He wanted to now. If she was interested, he'd like to do this with her. He had bought the books and done the research and it didn't seem that difficult, and since this had been a year of certain kinds of change, why not go all the way and bring in a little weirdness. What are you talking about? she said. He told her he was planning on growing psilocybin mushrooms. Did she want to do this project with him? She looked at him in disbelief for a moment. Then she smiled. I'm listening, she said, twiddling her fingers together like a mad scientist. It was a project, a kind of science experiment, and something that he had been wanting to do for long time – he had done hallucinogens in college, but with his background in meditation, he wanted to do this substance with a clearer intention – and she said yes, that sounded good. He thought that if they were still together, they could do them together, and if they weren't, they could be a kind of amicable parting gift. She grabbed his hand and pulled him a little towards her and said that he shouldn't tell anyone, but she was committed to this and to him. He stopped walking and said that they were supposed to be in this uncertain place. Hmm, she said, I know. She walked away from him to catch up to their daughters, and he followed.

He made the cakes: brown rice flour and vermiculite and water. He put the mixture in glass jars with tight lids, then sterilised them in a pressure cooker. Afterwards, he inoculated the jars with spores sold online for microscopy purposes, and then placed the jars in a closet, at around seventy degrees, and waited for the mycelium to begin colonising the cakes. They checked on the cakes occasionally, and the brown mixture inside the jars soon had spots of white, in a rhizomatic pattern, forming on the wall. It was like a little spring he was creating, as the real spring arrived, he said to her one evening after the girls were down, and she said, it's like a little spring *we're* creating. Right, he said. He woke earlier, made the girls' lunches, made her breakfast. He didn't go into the studio as much, but when he did, painting came easier, he didn't care if it was right or wrong, it was just what he was doing again, like he had forgotten he was doing it because he enjoyed it. When she came into the studio, he put his brushes down, turned from the canvas, went to her. Hello, he said. Hello, she said. He didn't want to look at her phone, in part because he knew what he'd find might make him feel anxious and shitty, but also because he just didn't want to. It was her business, her choice, it had nothing to do with him. He slowly stopped worrying about it, stopped worrying what it meant that she'd changed her clothes when she got home. She had just changed her clothes. He'd stopped worrying if she got a text in the evening. She was just texting. The hidden meanings and hidden codes in their life were being vacuumed out, and in their place was a kind of plainness. It was like stepping into his body for the first time and taking a breath. He checked on her, asked if he could do anything, grade some of her papers, some tests, while she figured out insurance stuff for her now chronically ill father. Most importantly, something had switched tracks in his thinking: the things he was doing were things he enjoyed, making a lunch, playing with the girls, grading some papers for her, putting on a record, asking her what she wanted to do that weekend, listening to her as she explained that she just wanted to be friends with her dad, that's all she wanted, but instead she was his secretary, and it was stressful. He could hear her again. When she was gone, he lived out his days like there were a series of doors that had once been locked and that someone had opened, then one day he realised he'd opened them, he'd done it himself, then he further realised, no, the counsellor had helped, and then he further realised, his wife had helped, too, they all had. She watched him do these things. He stopped by her work, brought her lunch. She watched him paying attention to her and began to feel that it wasn't a performance, that he was genuinely interested, genuinely wanted to be there. Or it was a performance and genuine at once. She left work early and went on walks, enjoying time to herself when he was with the girls. She did small things for herself again: she decided they needed a new dining room table, she didn't like the old one they'd made all those years ago, so she bought the wood and a saw. When he asked her what she was doing, she figured he'd get annoyed, he'd have to clean up the sawdust and mess or something, he'd say something like that, but instead he said, That's cool, can I help? They made it together, a simple rustic thing with a pine top and oak legs. They stained it dark walnut. It took three days. She looked at it very literally as a thing they'd built, that had been her idea, that he'd joined in on with her, replacing their old one. She felt like she was emerging from a dark, cold pool where the world had been barely recognisable, murky and distant and distorted, and now she was out and everything came to her with clarity. They still argued, but the arguments were over quickly. They hadn't had sex in nearly a year and then one day he gave her a massage. She'd just graded nearly eighty papers, the quarter was over, and she needed a massage, her neck and shoulders were tight and ached, and he'd massaged her back, her neck, her head, then lower, her legs, hamstrings and then calves, the taut Achilles, the balls of her feet and the arches, his hands strong and kneading, then smoothing, then kneading again, his hands following the curves of her body, and she felt again that warmth in her chest, like someone had blown on a coal that she'd believed was out. He turned her over. He massaged her temples, her forehead, then her arms and pectorals, he didn't touch her breasts, though his hands followed, slowly, the curve of her body down to her thighs and quads, which he kneaded, then smoothed out, then her lower legs, the tops of her feet. Her eyes were closed and he seemed to be pulling her to some dark but safe room in her mind, and the coal burned and when his hands slowed even more, tracing the outlines of her body, the massage over, she heard him say, just breathe in deeply, just let yourself rest there, focus on the inbreath down into your diaphragm, then the out-breath, and let yourself dissolve with the outbreath.

Inbreath, then dissolve, inbreath, then dissolve. Dissolve into the world. Dissolve into that still point inside you. As his hands slowly moved up her thighs and then along her sides and past her breasts, he brushed a nipple and said, Oh, sorry. She opened her eyes and told him he didn't need to be sorry, she wanted him to touch her everywhere now. Take your clothes off, she said. She pulled him into her and told him that she was as surprised as he was that this had turned back on. She told him that she had missed this, and he said that he had too. It was slow, slow, then fast. It was like the first time, which was a cliché, they discussed afterwards, but it was true, it felt that way: they were different. They talked about how the codes they'd been using for so long had dropped away, the passive aggression, the buried annoyances, the accruing resentment. It was easier to communicate now, so why had they been so stupid? I'll take responsibility for that, the man said. The stupidity part. She laughed. You're the dumbest smart person I've ever met, she said to him. But think about me, I hold on to everything and then soak up everything everyone else feels – why was I doing that to myself? He shook his head.

They continued going to their sessions. They sat closer to each other on the sofa and then they sat together. The counsellor asked what had been going on, and the woman said that one of the things she'd recently noticed was that the girls had stopped bickering so much, and in fact she'd only noticed that they'd been arguing so much when they stopped, and the woman had begun to feel that they'd modelled some terrible behaviour for them and the girls had copied it, and she was really glad that was over. She hadn't realised they were having such an impact on the girls. The counsellor listened now more often than she spoke, and the woman said that she felt, actually they felt, she'd talked to him about it – was it okay if she said it, and the man nodded – and the woman continued and said she felt released somehow from an old life. She said that they'd had some disagreements, but she was beginning to feel that this was possible. She was committed to doing this with him. Committed to him. The counsellor looked at the man and he said he felt the same way, and that they'd talked and felt that things had got misplaced, what was important had been misplaced, and this was a process of recognising what was important again, and part of that was the relationship between them, part of that was individual. He, personally, he said, had been paying attention to the wrong things, and it felt good to be paying attention in this new way.

The counsellor said she wanted them to try an exercise. Now, look, turn to him, look him in the eyes. This isn't punishment. Look him in the eyes. I want you both to look at each other for a moment. Just look in each other's eyes. Because if what we're trying to do here is really look at each other again, we have to actually look. We're going to do this for four minutes. I'll keep time. The woman felt a hesitation, a fear, things had been going better but she was afraid of what she'd see, if she might find evidence that what she was feeling wasn't completely accurate. She looked at him. Brown eyes with flecks of green in them. Big eyelashes. A sadness there. She could see that. Though whether it was for himself or for her, she couldn't tell. Probably both of them. She knew she had hurt him, she had caused some of that sadness. While that was there, what was missing was the look of judgement, the look of annoyance that he could give her at home in the past. She hated that it had gone away, almost like some part of her actually wanted evidence of it here, and at the same time, she was glad it was gone and didn't like the part of herself that wanted the evidence of it. She kept looking, and then she saw both sadness and something smiling through it. It made her smile despite herself. She felt herself going into it, allowing herself to go. The man saw her blue-grey eyes, which looked hurt, which had for so long looked as though they were peering at the distant mountains in longing, and he knew he was the one who had done the hurting. He felt this sadness for what he'd done, for her, for the many bad things that had happened to her in her life, and a regret that he'd contributed to these things, sadness that she'd lived through it.

He couldn't believe he'd done it, and then he told himself to stop focusing on himself, to focus on her, like he was unmaking his mind, and in doing this he saw her sadness and wanted to hold it, to take it from her, and in seeing this he saw something in her eyes smiling, and it made him smile. For a moment, which was only an instant but contained every moment past, present and future, they were ever so slightly smiling at one another.

Time, the counsellor said. They looked back at the counsellor. That didn't feel like four minutes, the woman said. Not at all, the man said. I enjoyed it. Good, the counsellor said. Now, she said to the woman. What happened there? Can you explain a bit about your experience? It was hard to do it at first, the woman said. Even with how things have been going, it was hard to do. But once I sort of let go, it was nice. It was really nice, she said. Or, it was sad at first, there's a lot of sadness between us, I felt that, but then it felt like we were both smiling at each other. Our eyes were. She began to cry a little and wiped her eyes. What did you feel then? the counsellor said. Grounded, the woman said.

I allowed myself to feel grounded. Oh, the counsellor said. You *allowed* yourself. *You* allowed yourself? *He* had nothing to do with it? She was pointing at the man. The woman smiled, looked at him and said, Yes, he helped me feel grounded. The counsellor turned to the man and said to him, But I want you to know, centre-of-all-existence-guy, that she did allow herself. It wasn't just you. Okay? Okay, he said. She surveyed them, and she said that when they had arrived four or five months ago, they had sat apart on the sofa, though he had been sort of leaning towards her, and now they sat together, their knees occasionally touching, and they were more turned towards each other, though the woman liked to protect herself with her arms. Would it be fair to say, the counsellor said to the woman, that when he's not being selfish, he grounds you somehow? I think so, the woman said. Look at you two, she told them. Smiling at each other. Who knew? You can smile and look at each other without any words or codes or the mess of language between you. You don't have to, but you can. Keep in mind there are other ways to communicate. You don't have to do things the way you were doing them. You've already seen this, but there are different ways of communicating. Find those ways. You know there is nothing I can really do but show you that, right? Some people are incompatible, that's true, and some people are in destructive cycles. But most of us are just living out our stories, and you brought your story here. Once you see that, you get to do the fun part, which is create some other story the way you see fit. All I can do is point that out. I can't say, okay, here's your deal, now be this way, and I can't say but here's your deal, now be that way. That's not a relationship. You have to learn to see your own minds, and you have to do it separately and with each other, and then make the story the way you see fit. This is it, okay? She looked at her book, her calendar, and said, It's almost June. You've been coming here for nearly six months. I thought it was less, but you guys started in January, and it's almost June. I'm going on sabbatical for the summer, and I was going to say let's continue this online, but in the last month I've changed my mind. I think it's time for you guys to do this on your own.

They thanked her, they shook her hand, and she walked them out of the sunroom and towards their car, parked along the kerb. She told them to email if they needed anything, and if they needed an online session they could do that while she was abroad. She said goodbye and good luck and turned and went back to her house. They got into the car and drove away, passing under the new green of the trees. There was a dusting of pollen on the windshield. They turned out of the neighbourhood onto the urban streets, past restaurants and bars and gas stations. They were taking a different route because they had the day off. They weren't going back to work, they were going home, and in the distance, beyond the city, the sky was brimming with bluish clouds. The woman suddenly said, This has been so hard, and began crying. He asked if she was okay, and she shook her head and wiped her face. He waited to see if she was going to say anything else. After a moment, she said there was a part of her that was still scared, and he felt some part of himself almost want to say why would you feel that way, after all this, but another part of him understood, or wanted to understand, and he opened himself to it just as she'd been open with him, too. He agreed. Yeah, I'm a little worried too. What if we can't do this on our own? she said. What if I go back to the way I was? the man said. What if I'm just selfish by nature? What if I allow you to do that? she said. What if I contribute to you being the way you were, and also make myself subordinate to you just because that's the way I know? I don't know, he said. It's like we've had some practice, but I don't exactly know the way forward. Neither do I, the woman said. Then she wiped her face and said, We just try. I want to. It's been working, I think. Do you trust it? she wanted to know. He looked at her and widened his eyes and shook his head, and then nodded his head and said, Yes, I think so, I don't know. What about you?

Summer

Once a monk asked Changsha, Zen Master Jingcen, 'How do you turn mountains, rivers, and the great earth into the self?'
Changsa replied, 'How do you turn the self into mountains, rivers, and the great earth?'

Dōgen, *Treasury of the True Dharma Eye*, Case 16

Their youngest daughter was helping with the packing, while their older daughter was having her first overnight at a friend's house. He was pulling clothes from drawers, stacking underwear, socks, shorts, which his daughter was putting into a bag. His wife was looking at something on her phone and he wanted to tell her that he was vaguely nervous about their oldest girl spending the night away, but he didn't because he had already expressed his concern earlier that week when their oldest asked if she could stay with her friend, Casey, on Friday night, this night. He had asked her whether she really thought she was ready or not, and their oldest girl had said yes, she was the big sister, and he said that he knew that, but staying at a friend's house was different from staying at Grandma and Grandpa's, and then his wife entered the room and asked what they were talking about, and he told her his misgivings and she'd said, Don't put that in her head, that she can't do it. I'm not putting that in her head, he said. I'm only trying to be realistic. No, you're being defeatist, she said. And you're probably thinking about the fact you don't want to have to pick her up at night if she ends up not going through with it. That is so not what I'm doing, he said. I'm only trying to talk to her about her choice so that she realises there are, you know, I don't know, things to consider. He had looked down to see the confused, slightly scared, wide-eyed face of their oldest daughter. Of course you can go if you want to, his wife had said to their daughter, which had made her smile and that was the end of it, though he'd felt shitty for the rest of the night, partly because he couldn't tell if he shouldn't have said the things he'd said because it had implanted negativity in their daughter's mind or if he was actually right and should've explained in more detail that their daughter needed to know there were repercussions to her choices. Now, though their daughter was already at her friend's house with her pillow, sleeping bag and several books, he said to his wife, I still think it seems too early. I feel like six is the right age, not five. She's going to be fine, his wife said. She's done it with Grandma and Grandpa plenty. There's no difference. I still think we're going to get a phone call, he said. His wife didn't look at him. She was searching for a match to a sock in the pile of clothes on the bed, and said, And if we do, we'll deal with it.

They were together in their bedroom, folding clothes for their trip to Ohio. Their youngest was neatly putting the clothes they'd folded into a large duffel bag. He allowed himself to stop thinking about whether their oldest daughter was going to do okay on this sleepover and watched their youngest, feeling that, like with their oldest, he couldn't believe how much she was changing on an almost constant basis. Here she was, quietly folding clothes. There were no lamps on, though evening had just begun to darken the room. Outside, the high drone of cicadas increased as the sun went down. He listened to this, observed the darkening light, and watched the little girl while she folded one of her shirts. He enjoyed this: her small hands picking up a folded shirt, placing it gently in the bag, then patting the top of the shirt. She asked, again, where they were going. He told her Ohio. Then she asked why, to which her mother replied, To see your grandparents, who are his parents. The girl asked why again, and he replied, Because it's summertime. When their daughter asked why because summer, her mother said to her, Because, I don't know. Because it's the best time to see what we can see. Their daughter asked them, with that uptilt in her voice that indicates a question,

See what we see? Her mother said to her, Yes, summer is the best time to see things. Like butterflies and bees that bite, go chomp chomp, their daughter said. He said, That's right, we're going to Ohio to see bees that go chomp chomp in the summer. That's right, their daughter said. Yes. She asked about her sister, was she coming too? Yes of course, he said. But she's not here right now, she said, her face looking concerned, her small brow furrowed. Well, like we told you, she's at a friend's house for a sleepover. We're picking her up in the morning. Their youngest seemed to consider this while stretching a sock in her hands. Then she said, I miss her a lot.

He put a shirt he'd folded onto a stack in the duffel bag, watching both of them, his youngest daughter and the woman who was his wife, both framed by one of the bedroom windows. Out the window, in their backyard, it was cool evening, the hot, humid day nearly over. Cicadas were again crescendoing. Waves of electric noise. He went to the window and opened it to hear better – the sound of the cicadas, thousands of them, was like a bell being struck and slowly fading. He could see the moon above a streetlight, which was flickering on. Trees in the backyard, a chestnut and a swamp oak, were black against the dark blue sky. When he turned back to the room, he told himself to hold on to this. It could all go away. It already was going away. He watched his daughter put a pair of socks in the duffel bag, standing on her tiptoes to put them into the bag, which was on the bed. After doing this, she walked out of the room, saying, I go watch *Dora* now. It felt as though something were about to fall into place. Like this was the way things should be, and if he could do something, something – he didn't know what – he could keep it all. And yet he also knew it could all be lost. He knew that now. He wondered if his wife felt this way too. That while things were good now, or better, they could always return to how they were. He wondered if he could be vigilant enough, watchful enough. Maybe that was what it took. At the same time that he thought that, he thought, who wanted to live like that? Shouldn't he be trying to be easy-going and careful, not vigilant and watchful? He was as confused as he'd ever been – he thought that the months of counselling would have revealed with an obvious clarity the way he should be in the world, but instead it had just served to scramble his intentions. It was true that the counselling had been helpful in some basic ways, but it was also true that he felt more confused than he ever had before. Or maybe, he thought, he was just aware of his confusion now. Then it was there again: the crescendo of the cicadas from the backyard and the trees all around their house. He opened the window wider.

His wife picked up her phone, the screen glowing. He watched her walk over to a bedside table and turn on a lamp. Its yellow light brightened the room. He watched as she was texting whatever it was she was texting, feeling a brief burst of anxiety clenching in his chest, which he actively released, breathed through. He told himself that it didn't matter who she was texting – she was here in this room with him. The pulsating buzz again swept through the trees and he allowed it to fill his mind in the same way it filled the room, and the tightening in his chest loosened. Sitting on the bed, she said that she'd just got a text from Casey's mom – their oldest was doing well, apparently, and was still excited for her first sleepover. They were getting ready to watch a TV show. What time is it? he asked. She told him it was nearly eight-thirty, and he said that when nine rolled around they'd know whether this was really going to happen or not. She'll be fine, his wife said. Then she asked him wasn't it weird that she'd just said what she said? What's that? he said. The thing about seeing, she said.

Three summers prior, when it was hot enough, the female had laid eggs the size of a piece of rice in the bark of a tree, or she had made a crevice in the trunk with an incisor-like claw, her ovipositor, and laid the eggs there. For six weeks the eggs rested, safe in the crevice, where water running down the tree seeped into the eggs and allowed hydration. Then, after those six weeks, the nymphs emerged from the eggs, looking like small white ants. They crawled down the tree and fell to the ground, where they immediately burrowed into the dirt in order not to be eaten by birds or bats or other predators and to drink the fluids inside tree roots near the surface of the ground, the water and sugars there. For years the nymphs grew underground, moulting several times in the dirt. As the nymphs grew and moulted, they developed powerful forelegs for burrowing. They dug deeper, to the thicker roots, where they grew into whitish, almost marbled insects each the size of an adult human thumb. They had red eyes. *Neotibicen canicularis* stayed underground anywhere from two to five years, maturing and feeding, through summer, fall, winter, until one hot, humid day in early June – the heat signalling that the time was right – in South Carolina, outside in their backyard, a cicada burrowed up through the ground, past tree roots, and emerged at the base of the tree where it was first spawned. This night, it crawled to the top of the tree, wet and whitely opaque, where it waited to moult for the final time.

She said wasn't it strange what she just said about seeing? He put three pairs of shorts into the duffel bag and shook his head, not understanding. She said that at first she'd thought it was just a nonsensical phrase – see what we could see – something to end the 'why' questions their daughter was asking, but as soon as she'd said it, she realised it wasn't nonsensical at all. She'd thought it was strange, but then immediately understood that it wasn't. It was what they'd been doing now for several months. They'd been seeing what they could see about themselves. We're still doing it, she said. It had become programmed into her thinking, and it had come out, and it surprised her, almost scared her a little, how programmed it'd become, she told him. He asked if she thought this was a bad thing. She watched him adjusting some of the clothes already in the bag, making room for other clothes he was still folding. She thought of course he would ask that. It was one of those things he could easily twist, she thought. She felt she could see the way his mind was working. He probably believed that she was bringing up this phrase because she was still in an uncertain place regarding their relationship. Like she hadn't fully seen something about them, or about him, and that she needed to see something else from him. He was asking for reassurance. Reassurance she didn't want to give. At least not in this way, through this coded question. She knew it came from his insecurity, but still, she could feel this train of thought already in his question. It made her wish she hadn't said what she'd said. And yet she couldn't help herself. Part of her was unsure: was this really what he was asking? She felt like so much of their relationship was peering around the corners of themselves to see if the other person was there. To see whether the other person was really there and was who they said they were. She saw him doing it. She was doing it too. She hated it a little, but she couldn't help herself.

What do you mean a bad thing? she said. He looked at her, then briefly at the ceiling in thought. The light from the bedside lamp extended up the wall in a widening V and then became diffuse on the ceiling. She heard the cicadas beyond the window and saw the twilit backyard. Here in their bedroom, a room in which they were both sleeping again, together again, was their dresser, two end tables, the bed, which on the weekends both their daughters crawled into to wake them and then play under the covers. She briefly thought of her daughter waking in another house – she wouldn't be in their bed tomorrow morning to wake them. He said what he guessed he was wondering was whether it was okay with her that things still weren't certain. She watched him folding a pair of pants, looking down, folding carefully but also quickly, putting the pants in a spot he'd cleared in the bag. She didn't know if she should be surprised or not. Was he being open to this uncertainty or was he seeking reassurance? But she was surprised that he didn't take the opportunity to explain what he was feeling or thinking. She'd been so used to his feelings and thoughts taking precedence. It was almost unsettling, uncomfortable, that he wasn't always explaining things anymore. There was more room, more space for her. It was good, but also strange. Now, he seemed to want to hear from her. This had been happening for some time, but it still felt new and strange, and it made her feel a little bad that she'd thought he was only attempting to learn how she felt about their situation. It's not at all a bad thing, she said. She said it was a good programming, a reprogramming that she liked, that she thought was a better way to be. Actively seeing rather than just being swept along by her own thoughts or emotions. Which of course still happens, she said, but I like the intent, I guess. He said that he'd liked the phrase but she'd seemed taken aback by his question. Should I not have asked that? She shook her head and said that she was sorry, some of this was still new. She knew he'd heard this before, but some of this was still confusing to her. But she said it was a good confusing, because he was surprising her. He told her not to be too surprised, after all he had to admit he wanted to be done with this phase where everything was uncertain, but he was really trying to do things differently. It's not as though everything was uncertain, she said. He tilted his head like a dog and said well, sure it is, and she said no it wasn't, they'd done a lot of hard work, they were together, and then she paused, picked up a pair of shorts and folded them and tossed them in the bag, feeling anger rising quickly in her chest, and then she said, See, I was all surprised there because I thought you wanted to hear what I was thinking. Now I just think that was all a manipulative way for you to get some firmer answer from me about where we stand. And I don't like that. I'm not going to do that. I've told you I'm committed. He said that he knew that and that he wasn't trying to be manipulative at all, he genuinely wanted to hear if she thought this was a good or bad thing, but he was also attempting to be as honest as possible here. Of course part of him was concerned, how could he not be after all they'd been through? It did sound like she might still be wondering about certain things, but this need for certainty wasn't as big a part of him anymore, or it wasn't as though it was all he wanted. It was hard to describe, hard to articulate, he both wanted to hear from her and wanted things to be certain, yes, that was accurate if that was what she was asking. He threw his hands up in an annoyed, frustrated gesture. Right, she said. He looked at her. Look, he wasn't trying to manipulate anything, he explained, he was just having a hard time navigating things here too. This new place they were at was unfamiliar, and he was trying. She picked up another pair of shorts, shaking her head, and said that this was what happened: a thing she wanted to talk about turned into some other thing about him, about what he was feeling. This was exactly what she was tired of. He went quiet for a moment and shook his head, doing another hand toss. I'm sorry this is so annoying for you, she said. He sarcastically nodded and continued folding. Right, he said, looking up, looking at her eyes. He seemed to take a deep breath, and then he said, Okay, yeah, I hear that, that's my bad. She felt herself soften and said, Okay. No worries. You're fine. He said he heard her, please go ahead, he really did want to hear what she was thinking. She almost said that it didn't matter now – a thing she would've done in the past, taking his subordination and imposing it on herself, internalising it – but she knew, no, she felt, that was no way to be, and, additionally, she saw him trying, and that was what she'd been wanting to talk about anyway, how they were both trying. Okay then, she said. Even now the phrase see what they could see was apt. We're having this discussion, and in the past it would've just devolved into an argument. Either I would've become defensive, or you would've been dismissive, but right now, she said, we're making an attempt. Seeing if we can be different in some of these moments. She liked that. He said that he liked that too. She said that she shouldn't have been so surprised to have said that particular phrase because that's what they'd been actively practising, and though it was a good thing, parts of this awareness were still a little odd. Again, take this moment, she said. I feel like we can both feel the old tracks in our mind, the old ways of being, and if we're not careful we slip into them, but also, if we're careful, there's another way. That little thing that just happened between us, that could've devolved into an evening where both of us cold-shouldered each other or something. Right, right, he said, smiling down at the clothes, the bag. So it's a good thing, a pleasant thing, she said, but it also makes me a little scared. He asked her what she meant, and she said it made her a little overly aware of this whole trip. You know, she said, like there's a certain pressure, almost. We're going to Ohio, going out into the woods, going to take mushrooms together, after this year where our entire relationship unravelled. I mean, what we're actually doing is sort of testing the relationship on a whole different level. That's a little terrifying. Aren't you afraid? What if what we see is that we really shouldn't be together?

She watched him put a pair of socks together, then drop them in the bag, and then suddenly walk towards the door, saying, You're right, I'm out. That's not what I mean, she said, grabbing the sleeve of his shirt. That's what I mean, he said. I'm out. There's no way. Not after you said that. That's bad, you know, vibes. That's bad mojo, bad juju. That's probably a racist thing to say, he said. I don't know, she said. Either way, if it is, he said, it's bad energy on top of bad energy. This conversation has the potential to really mess up our lives. We definitely can't do this now. She looked at him coolly. No way, I'm done, he said. Can you imagine how classically fucked that would be? What happened to your marriage? Well, after a really bad year, after counselling, after we righted the ship, after reconnecting, I suggested we do a serious dose of psychedelics to *really* connect, and frankly what we found is that we are not even close to soulmates. We are, in fact, not even good buddies. The universe showed us this. I'm going to Nepal to be a lama and she's now a realtor. What the fuck? she said to him. I'm the realtor? No, she said. You'll figure out you want to try out for the local semi-pro soccer team before your 'playing days' end, and I'll start an organic farm-to-table restaurant whose chairs and tables are actually made of sustainable cornmeal. He cocked his head in what she knew was mock thought. That doesn't feel accurate, he said. I'll become a helicopter pilot and you'll become a horse wrangler. How's that? Better, she said. But you're not smart enough to be a helicopter pilot. Either way, he said, it's not a great story. She gave him that cool look again, then she said, I know you're being funny, or you're trying to be funny, but show a little backbone. This is me showing backbone, he said. She thought for a moment while tossing a balled-up pair of socks between her hands and then said that there was no point in backing out now. Not at this moment anyway. We'll go to Ohio, she said, see how things are up there, check out the cabin and see how we're feeling, see how the girls are doing alone with Grandma and Grandpa, and then we can decide to do it or not. We don't need to make the decision right now, but I think if we do it that should be our intention. To see what we can see. I've been reading some of the things you sent me and it seems like having a very clear intention is important. And I want that to be ours. Do you agree? Just see what we can see. Nothing more. To see what we can see about ourselves and the world. She observed him take a deep breath and nod and agree to the plan. Then he said thank you for reading that stuff. She helped him finish packing, then their youngest yelled from the family room, Mommy, come watch *Dora* with me, and she went.

Their daughter was sitting on the sofa, a bag of Goldfish crackers in her lap. She sat down next to the girl and put an arm around her while she also listened to her husband gathering his toiletries in the bathroom. *Dora the Explorer* was on the television and their daughter was entranced by it, her eyes wide, her right hand bringing one goldfish at a time to her mouth, which she crunched with an open mouth. She heard him in the bathroom opening and closing cupboards. It was true that she liked this sound, his body moving through the house. When he had been away she had felt two things, one that she was so glad he was gone, she could breathe again, and two, that she missed him. These two feelings had been irreconcilable. She didn't know how she felt them at the same time. She didn't know how he engendered so much hate from her, a wishing to be away from him, and also, at the same time, a longing for him. She thought now, sitting next to her daughter, maybe it was just attachment. She was attached to him. Or worse, dependent on him. Or they were codependent. They had worked, it was true, to get to this better place, and now that they were in it, it was difficult to tell if she had made the right decision. She was committed to him again, and things were better, but was this right, was it correct, was it the choice she should've made? Had she given anything up in this choice? Another, freer way of life? Had she fallen back on what was familiar and comfortable? She equally wondered if these feelings of doubt existed simply because she was afraid of being wrong, and it was the fear itself that created the doubt. She wondered if the doubt arose from the wish for some fantasy version of life, another life in which she was with another man, whose flaws, she knew, she would have seen eventually, but who now remained some idealised version of a man. Alternatively, when she imagined being alone and free, and that this might be better, having no man in her life at all, she knew that this too was a fantasy, another ideal. This fantasy was one of complete and pure freedom. She had seen through such an ideal already when her husband had left to give her space in the fall: it had been incredibly difficult to go to work, take their daughters to school, pick their daughters up, make her own dinner, make their daughters', keep the house clean, and then find any time at all for herself. But she was able to imagine that he'd have custody on the weekends, giving her her freedom back, at least to a degree. And yet it was all a fantasy. When he was gone, there had initially been a sense of relief and openness, of possibilities and potentials. But this faded quickly. She was still mired in the same routine. Without him, she felt even lonelier. And, she felt, she was almost using the other man to fill that loneliness. She recalled a night when she had managed to get both their daughters to bed early. It was supposed to be a night when she stayed up, read a book or watched a movie, felt that she could do things. But rather than staying up, rather than having a glass of wine or smoking a bowl, she'd turned on the television, felt vaguely annoyed at every show – one mindless entertainment after another – and had gone to bed and cried. In an effort to make herself do something, she'd tried to masturbate. It had been so long since she'd felt anything good, and she was sick of feeling tired and depressed and lonely all the time. Lonely even with her daughters. Even with the other man. With people at school. In bed, under the covers, she'd masturbated with a vibrator and tried to make herself come, but couldn't. She had cried in her bed, feeling as though life had become an ugly, unknowable, superficial thing – work, clean, watch television, look at the internet, eat, all of it the surface of something that seemed to contain infinitely more depth, but which she couldn't access – and there was no escaping it. She had felt in bed that she had no way of managing this world, she didn't know how to be alone, and to cover over the vacuity of modern life she had to have a man help her, which was infuriating and wrong. A man to make her feel good. It'd all got confused. What else was there? she'd thought that night, touching herself, no longer masturbating but just gently touching herself in contemplation. And now, she thought, sitting on the sofa with her daughter wasn't sitting on the sofa with her daughter, it was thinking about how she should be feeling about sitting on the sofa with her daughter. It was maddening. She remembered that she had stopped crying that night. She'd told herself to stop crying, to stop being so self-pitying. This was what she'd wanted: to be alone. To feel something good alone, for herself. She had picked up the vibrator with renewed purpose, determined to feel something good. She'd turned it to its highest setting. Let's do this, she'd thought. Then she had realised she was giving herself a sex pep talk, and then she started imagining she was: come on woman, you can do it, focus, enjoy things, turn that thing down, let's warm up, start on the slow setting like you like, and she'd then been both laughing and crying in bed. It was going nowhere, and she eventually gave up. She didn't want to go back to that past

– alone in her house with the girls – but she didn't know if being here was exactly right either.

From the bathroom, she heard him yell, Hey, check your texts. His words pulled her back into the room. Her daughter was still slowly bringing goldfish to her mouth, munching on them, a slight smile on her face while she watched *Dora*. She picked up her phone and saw a new text message in which her husband had been included and which read, Uh-oh, with a sad face emoji. She clicked on it and read the text, which explained that their oldest daughter wanted to call them, and then yelled back to him. Looks like you're right. Quiet, Mommy, her daughter said. I can't hear. She laughed. Her daughter tugged on her shirt and held up a goldfish. Mommy, you want one? She smiled and took the goldfish and said thank you. The bugs are loud tonight, the girl said. They are, she said. Very loud, but not mean. I don't like mean bugs, just nice ones. But sometimes there are mean ones. It's okay though, the youngest girl concluded, because there are nice ones too. She listened to her daughter and then to the sound of the cicadas outside and tried to hear the cicadas as her daughter would, as a child would. How does she hear them? she thought. It was, of course, like so many things, impossible to know. She texted Casey's mother back, asking if she should call now. A text message quickly appeared that said, Yes, please do. She yelled to her husband, Do you want to call her? He appeared from the bathroom. Yeah, what're we going to say? She said, Not we, you. You're the one that did this. But if he was asking what she thought, what she thought was that if their daughter wanted to come home, that was fine, at least she tried. He stood still a moment and then said that he wasn't so sure that was the right strategy. What do you mean? she said. You're the one who thought she was too young to do this. Yeah, but now that she's doing it, I think she should have to try. He looked at his phone. It's only about nine. She hasn't even tried to go to sleep yet. She needs to try. If this is really what she wanted, she has to try. She looked at him for a second and said that that seemed a little unfair considering he was the one who had put into her head the idea that she wouldn't be able to do it. How? When you told her that she wasn't old enough yet and that this wasn't like Grandma and Grandpa's, she said. That is so not what I said, he said. That is exactly what you said, she said. Or that's how a five-year-old would take it. That you were worried she couldn't do it, which would in turn make her feel like she couldn't do it. It's not like this is new, she said. You used to do this to me all the time. He looked at her in surprise and then said, That's unfair. Is it? she said. Don't be mopey. I know you didn't mean to do it, but you could've approached the thing differently, and now you want her not to give up. She could see that he wanted to say more, his body was rigid, his shoulders sort of pinched in and his eyes not looking at her. It was the way he looked when he got defensive. Then his shoulders fell a little and she heard him take a deep breath and he said, Fair enough. I hear that. So what do we do? She was surprised, that he was putting certain things into practice, and then she said, well, it'd be better to talk to their daughter on the phone first and hear her out before deciding anything. He looked confused for a moment and shook his head and said, If we don't have a plan going in, how are we going to – I mean, she's just going to get what she wants. She needs to try again. Okay, she said to him, see, you're just saying how it is. You realise that, right? I'm not actually a part of this decision. I wasn't a part of the decision to let her go over there, he said. I didn't want that to happen. Yes you were, she said. We talked about it. I listened to your misgivings, which I heard and understood, though I didn't think you should've communicated them to her, and then you eventually said she could try. He stood motionless listening to her, like a kind of mannequin, then he said, Okay, yeah, I guess so. Alright, let's just talk to her on the phone. Thank you, she said.

When ready, the cicada nymph found a place high on a sturdy upper branch. Through a crack on the back of its body, a new body began to emerge. The process took all night: three hours for the new body to fully break free from the old, and several more hours for the new insect to fully become what it was. The white nymph's outer shell split open, from the eyes to the thorax. Gradually, the split grew wider, the teneral cicada beneath the shell now visible. Slowly, the blue bug wiggled its head free from the shell, struggling to pull itself out. All around it were the sounds of a thousand cicadas, which the people inside the house heard almost as one sound. After an hour, the head emerged from the now brown shell casing. The upper half of the cicada body vibrated, so as to loosen itself from the shell, until it was able to pull its forelegs out, looking sickly, weak. The noise of the other cicadas around it shook the tree. Then the upper half of the teneral cicada emerged, its lower abdomen still inside the shell. It hung upside down. It took nearly two more hours, a significant portion of its adult life, just to do this one thing. To change. Its lower body was still attached to the shell, the old body. If a person were to view such a metamorphosis, it would be impossible for them not to consider how difficult it would be to remove oneself from what one once was. How painful the change appeared. After more vibrations of its body, panicked and violent, which seemed to become more and more panicked and more and more violent, the cicada grabbed the exuvium, the cast-off skin, with its forelegs, which now looked to be stronger, and pulled its abdomen out. *N. Canicularis* flexed its wing buds, and over the course of twenty minutes, during which the people in the house could not possibly know that this was occurring outside, the wings appeared to grow, to unfurl. Blood began moving through the wings with each flex. They expanded. The cicada remained hanging on to the exuvium, the shell that was once its body, waiting for blood to flow and for its wings to be ready. It was at its most vulnerable in this moment: fully changed, yet also almost larval. A bird or another insect could eat it at any moment. But blood kept flowing, hardening the body of the adult cicada, turning it from a light blue to darker greens and browns. The wings hardened and acted as a protective layer over its body. Now fully in the world, the cicada turned the colours of the earth.

They went again into the bedroom so that their youngest could continue watching her show while they called their oldest daughter on speakerphone. He watched his wife sitting on the bed and then he joined her, the phone between them. When their daughter answered she immediately said, Mommy, I want to come home. His wife said okay, that was okay, could she please explain why she wanted to come home? Their oldest said that she was scared and missed her room, and Casey's room had a big window and you could see the sky out the big window, and it was just too big and a little scary. His wife looked at him, which he took to mean it was his turn to talk, and he asked their daughter if she had she tried getting into her sleeping bag yet. She said no, she hadn't tried yet. His wife said, Well, sweetie, why don't you give that a shot first? You haven't even tried your sleeping bag, and you've been really wanting to try it out. Their oldest was quiet for a moment and then said maybe she could try it another day, because she really missed her room a lot and also Casey didn't have any goldfish and she liked to eat goldfish before bed. His wife put her hand over the phone and whispered to her husband, What do you think, let's go get her? He shook his head and said, She's manipulating you. I know she's manipulating me, she said, but she doesn't want to be there. She's not going to fall asleep. Thinking that he had stated his case, he said, Okay, if you want to go get her, we can. He watched her hesitate a moment and then say, Shit, I think you're right. She told her daughter that both she and Daddy wanted her to try to go to sleep in her sleeping bag, and if that didn't work, she could call back, okay? Their daughter said okay, and then said goodnight. She looked at him and said she had no idea if that was the right thing to do. There's no such thing as the right thing to do, he said. They went back down the hallway together and then split up: she went back to the family room and he went to the bathroom.

In the bathroom, vaguely wondering when their daughter would decide enough was enough or whether she would stick it out, he looked for the contact lenses he hadn't been able to find earlier. While searching, he thought that he'd been thinking for a while about finding a way to paint all this, though he didn't know how he would paint it. He thought now that maybe he would use text. Maybe the paintings of their dissolution and reconnection would be accompanied by text, maybe writing would feature on the paintings themselves. He didn't know. He also didn't know why he felt any of this was worth portraying, worth telling, and compared to other things that were going on in the world, their suffering in the last year was small. It was true that their relationship had come to a breaking point, a crisis point, had fallen apart, during which time all things were changing and uncertain. It was true that there had been sadness and anxiety all around them and inside them, and now that all their lies and foolishness were exposed, not only was it clear that these things were meaningful, of central importance to them, it was equally clear that they were small in comparison to the pain of the rest of the world. The world spinning at 1,000 miles an hour, depending on where you were on the planet, and during its spinning, the planet speeding through the cosmos around the sun at 67,000 miles an hour, travelling about 1.6 million miles a day, the planet a perfect balance of life, and humans ruining it in every conceivable way, trying not to, trying to correct what's been ruined but failing miserably, ruining not only the planet but their minds through a superficial culture radically distanced from nature. And here he was in his bathroom, looking for his contacts, thinking of making paintings about two people who'd lost themselves and lost each other. It felt a little pointless. What did his pain, her pain, mean to anyone else? What did the pain of two middle-class white people in the middle of the very artificial construct of the United States mean to anyone?

He opened a cabinet and moved bottles around, looking for the blue and white box. He knew he had contacts left but he couldn't find the box. He thought it would be better if he weren't a painter. If he were a writer or a filmmaker, he could write about their last year. But even that would be difficult because there wasn't the drama of most novels or movies. He didn't want to write a novel with characters, he only wanted to write about them, the two of them. He'd written when he was younger, and he thought now that maybe he could again. There wouldn't be the gritty realism of some writing, with drinking and drug-taking, recklessness of all kinds and a chaotic relationship suddenly exploding. There weren't going to be scenes in which they yelled at each other in front of their daughters, blaming each other, and though versions of these things had happened, they were always more sober than what appeared in certain books or films. There wouldn't be a literary location, there would be no New York, no Europe, no Greece, no Paris. Just two people who had been confined by the structures and technologies of their modern life-styles, who had also been confining themselves and each other. He wondered if he could write not the scenes but the minds that experienced these things. Maybe he would ask her if she approved of him writing about them, and maybe he would ask her if she could help him get it right? After his wife had asked for space, he had packed a bag and driven from South Carolina to Ohio to stay with his parents. He stayed there a week, then stayed another three weeks with a friend. He remembered driving home to Ohio, crying while listening to Bonnie Raitt's, then Bon Iver's cover of Bonnie Raitt's, 'I Can't Make You Love Me' on his phone. Could he write the mind, he thought, that experienced being at his parents' house in Columbus, where he cried in the kitchen over breakfast, suddenly, mid-bite, just crying? His mother had got up from her chair and rubbed his back while he cried into his plate of scrambled eggs, as if, once again, he was a child, which he knew he was in that moment. Maybe that was a painting, he thought now, in a series of paintings titled *Divorce*, and the subtitle of this particular painting would be *Crying over Eggs*. Could he write any of the moments in which he thought of his wife at night and masturbated and cried, unable to finish masturbating due to crying, and then just crying holding his penis, but then sort of getting turned on again while thinking of moments when he and his wife had been together, of her body, the particular curve of her thighs, aching for those moments again, to be with her again, and masturbating more, about to finish but unable to because he would remember what he had done: moments when he had neglected her, hadn't really heard her, hadn't been there for her in the ways he could've been. He recalled pathetically crying in a hotel room three blocks from their house, holding himself while crying, trying to just simply cry. In the bathroom, still looking for his contacts and moving bottles around that he had already moved, he recalled being disgusted that it took some effort to actually do that, to simply cry. It made him want to cry now. Could he write that he had cried in a hotel room three blocks from their house where his wife and daughters were living? Could he truthfully recount that he was crying at the clearest loss he'd ever experienced? A loss of a certain way of life. A loss also of a certain way of being. He didn't know if he could write that, let alone paint it, in an honest way. He'd hated the thought of losing something about himself as much as he hated the thought of losing them. He hated that he had thought so selfishly, that he had been concerned with what he was losing, and now, equally, he didn't like thinking about writing it. He also knew that under all that, under all that he disliked about himself and the situation and the overwhelming sense of loss, he had also had the clear feeling that something was happening. There was some excitement mixed in with all the sadness. He couldn't write that, that he had been excited that something was happening to him. That something was happening to her, too. It was terrible, but they were alive, wildly alive. As though he'd been birthed into some new body that finally felt and sensed and experienced in a real way, and he both liked it and hated it.

He collected the other toiletries he needed for the trip – deodorant, aftershave, toothpaste, toothbrush, nose and ear hair trimmer – and went to the cupboard near the shower and began looking for his contacts there. He moved some hair tonic, some lotions, a bottle of perfume, found a travel-size bottle of Listerine and then stopped looking again and sat on the toilet seat and recalled a particularly grim vision: lying supine in a hotel room eating gummy bears and pizza, and drinking Sprite, things he almost never ingested, at midnight because he couldn't sleep, while alternately viewing Netflix and images on Reddit of women who looked like his wife on his phone. He recalled this image of himself as though he were outside his body, the screen of his phone lighting his face and head in white light, as if his mind were imprisoned by the light itself, his face and head the only thing visible in the hotel room, everything else just barely there in darkness. He'd hated himself then. He had thought of their daughters visiting him two weekends a month, then one, then only in the summer, then hardly at all, until they were strangers, so that one day he would be a stranger to his daughters and a stranger to his wife, because that would be what his wife, now not his wife, wanted, and eventually, in this sad, novelistic version of his life, he'd end up a stranger to himself, barely human in a decrepit little apartment eating instant ramen and raising chickens and selling the eggs to locals as his only source of income. That was the time he was in the biggest, most expensive room at the Marriot in Spartanburg, South Carolina, which he didn't ask for, which they simply gave him, because when he'd arrived at the front desk and the woman had asked, with a big, bright smile, What's the reason for your stay? he'd said, after a moment of hesitation and trying to figure out what a person normally says in such a situation, he'd said, I don't know, I'm lost, and began crying. That'd got him a corner suite. Sitting on the toilet, allowing himself to think freely of these things, he heard his daughter yell, Daddy. *Dora*.

It could take three or four days for the hardening process to complete, and when it finally ended, as it just had for a particular cicada near their home, the cicada flew, clumsily, to the higher limbs. There, the male cicada began its song, vibrating the tymbals at the base of its abdomen. The electric noise people heard and associated with cicadas was the tymbals of the male cicada vibrating, which was its mating call. The chorus attracted both males and females, the chorus growing louder. The cicada outside their home did not eat, would not eat; that had all occurred in the nymph stage, and the cicada now focused solely on finding a mate. The male sang, the female responded. The cicadas in the trees now outside their home were dog-day cicadas, *Neotibicen canicularis*. They appeared every year during the dog days of summer: when Sirius, the Dog Star in the Canis Major constellation, appears above the horizon before dawn. Their song was a song of summer, of connection, of reproduction, of mate finding mate, fulfilling a cycle, and then, in not a few weeks' time, the cicada that had just flown to a high limb and was creating its whining, screeching sound would die, having lived through transformation after transformation and having fulfilled this purpose, which would lead to more change. But not yet. Aided by everything around them, the cicadas sang, unable to complete their cycle without the warm weather, the trees, the dirt, the sap and water running into the ground, all these things allowing them to make the one connection that would ensure their ongoingness. Their song was a song of ongoingness, one that was threatened now, that arrived earlier each year, a symptom of the times that was discussed by scientists, who wondered if the insects' earlier arrival was an indication of climate change, and activists discussing it the way activists do but nothing being done, and even those attuned to the change were not able to see what was really there, which was not just the destruction of the natural world or the planet but the other loss, the thing that can't be seen, the mystery of the connection of it all.

She heard him come down the hall and say that he couldn't find his contacts, did she know where they were? She said she had no idea. He sat down on the sofa so that their daughter was between them. His face looked concerned, like there was something on his mind that had to do with more than finding his contacts. She asked what he was thinking about, and he said, Nothing, why? and she said, Your face. My face? he said, and she laughed. Really? she said. He said it was really nothing, and really it was nothing he wanted to bother her with. She knew this meant something was bothering him. In the past she would've pressed him on it, but she decided not to. He could say it or not, she thought. If he didn't want to say it, she didn't need to know it. In the past she would've felt like he was hiding something from her, about her, about something she had done or failed to do, about a thing she'd said or some way she'd failed to be, but she tried to see now that things could be bothering him that didn't have to do with her. Their daughter, who had been eating goldfish, pushed the bag away and then put a hand on each of their legs, as though, she thought, to make sure they weren't going anywhere, while she devoted the rest of her senses to the television. She watched her daughter, who was watching the show, and had the brief thought that she should only watch this one episode, maybe two. She glanced at her husband, who was looking out a window. The noise of the cicadas was quietly fading for the day. The first crickets were beginning their rhythmic chirping. She liked that sound. How the sound of the cicadas in the evening came in sweeping waves of electric noise, waves that if you went outside and stood under the trees and listened to seemed to generate an electric response from her body, a warm feeling in her chest. She knew her husband liked the sound. He said he liked to sit on the porch and let his mind drift while he listened to them. She'd wondered what he meant by this, let his mind drift. Then one summer evening, on a walk with their daughters, it had happened to her, the waves of sound had carried her mind away. It left her with a windblown, clear feeling, like a mirror swept of dust. It had been the first time in months she'd felt peaceful and content. Then it was gone. She looked at him and couldn't help wondering what he was thinking. Their daughter looked up at her and said, Are you ready to sing, Mommy?

The song, which the family called 'We did it', came on. Their daughter jumped from the sofa and said, Sing

Mommy, dance Daddy. She almost said she'd hurt her foot and couldn't, but with not much effort she restrained the impulse and got off the couch. Just dance with your kid, she told herself. She began singing, We did it. Her husband was singing it too. Dance, dance, their daughter said, wiggling her legs and waving her arms. Then they were all dancing in the family room of the bungalow. He was doing his little hop dance that he liked to do, sort of hopping in place like he was in the kindest, most compassionate mosh pit ever, and she was doing a rendition of the twist. Their daughter ran between them, bopping them on the knees. She laughed at this. Good, Mommy, their daughter said. She watched them all reflected in a darkened window. She could see that she was smiling. It made her smile more. For a brief moment, it was the strangest thing, watching them do this in the darkened window. It was also joyful. Then she thought that this was a place that for the last year hadn't seen much dancing, let alone joy, and yet it was present here again, somehow. It felt strange to feel joyful again. When she thought about it, she couldn't tell if she should feel joyful. If she had earned it yet. She didn't fully recognise it. It was equally true that she didn't fully recognise her husband any longer. Or her youngest daughter, for that matter. She also didn't recognise herself. She didn't see herself as someone who could be joyful. Had it really been that long since she'd experienced joyfulness that she couldn't see herself, or anyone else, clearly while experiencing it? Why was she suspicious of the joy inside and outside her? Or was she not actually experiencing joy at all, she thought while dancing, was she only acting it out? Was her husband? She glanced again at their reflection in the window and just saw them, the people they were, the people she sort of recognised and sort of didn't, standing in the family room.

The song was over and she sat back down on the sofa with her husband and daughter, who immediately reached over and patted her leg. The little girl put another hand on her husband's leg. The girl smiled at each of them, then began watching the television again. She had taken note of this, the way their youngest was always touching them, almost as though the little girl was holding them in place. Then the screen of her phone lighted again and she looked at it and said to him, over their youngest's head, Here it is. What're we going to do here? Your call, he said. She answered the phone and listened to her daughter patiently explain that she was too scared to do this, the big window was a bit scary, Casey's room smelled a little funny, and she missed her bed and everyone and she wanted them to come get her please. She listened to their oldest daughter talking and said that was okay, thank you for trying sweetie, and she said they'd be there shortly. She turned off the television and told their youngest that her sister was coming home, to which the little girl said, Yay, I miss her so much, Mommy. She put on her shoes and heard him say, Why don't we all go? We'll walk together. I don't want to walk, their daughter said. Almost simultaneously they told her she could get in the stroller, and she smiled and asked for a blanket.

*

Outside, there was a thin line of light near the tree line. He pushed their youngest daughter, who had pulled the blanket up to her chin. Insects were chirping in the trees and bushes, and overhead there was the occasional high-pitched chirp of a bat. A crescent moon hung above the trees, a star near it. The air smelled of honeysuckle. The streetlights that they passed beneath buzzed like insects. After a block, their daughter was asleep in the stroller. The woman watched him while he pushed her, his face seeming calm. She thought that there had been a point in time when she didn't believe that walks like this one would happen again. She could still feel the possibility of some other life, and, along with that, the ugliness of the way they had been living. On this walk, which was one thing, she felt these other lives. She said to him that she sometimes felt as though it was hard to believe they were here, walking together. He glanced at her and nodded and said me too. She said she was struggling with certain things, struggling with how things had changed. Even on this walk, there was behind it the possibility that it might not have been. She could see both at once. Even though we're actually on this walk, she said. He said he knew what she meant. There were times when he could see the house and them in it, and then there were times when he also saw all the times he'd slept in the other room or they had fought. She said that she looked at the kitchen some mornings and saw him and the girls eating breakfast, but she also saw the time she cried on the kitchen floor. Do you remember that night? I'm so sorry about that night, he said. Don't apologise, she said. I'm just remembering it. But I see the kitchen, just a normal morning, but like, behind it I also see that night. It was a long winter, he said. February, I think, she said. It had all become too much, and I sat down on the kitchen floor and cried. I couldn't even pinpoint exactly why. You were kneeling next to me and both girls came in and they were, like, petting me, trying to get me to feel better. I felt so pathetic then. You weren't pathetic, he said. I felt so bad for that, she said. For letting our daughters see me like that. That's one of the things I hated the most, letting them see me like that. I wanted to be strong for them. I want to still. She watched him. In the past he would've said something like, you are strong, you were strong, but now he just nodded and agreed. I didn't want them to see how I was either, he said. They turned down another street. Maybe it was good they saw you like that, he said. That it's okay to be lost even as an adult. The moon went behind the tree line. She said maybe, but what about all the things they had said? They had said awful things, they had done mean things, to each other. She wondered if it would ever go away. I don't know, he said. I hope so. It'll always be there at least a little. She said she was sorry for bringing this up, and he stopped pushing the stroller, looked at her and said don't be sorry. I'm glad you're telling me. They continued walking. A warm breeze shook the trees. Thank you, she said, feeling like both the words and the breeze had swept something out of her and she was clear again. I feel better. He smiled at her. Ahead she saw the house, the porch light on, and then she saw their oldest daughter standing in the front entrance, holding her sleeping bag, books and a flashlight, waving it in the night like a beacon. She's such a cute dork, she said.

Not a few weeks after they'd begun that high, electric whine, the cicadas mated, male and female often looking like one strange insect, connected at the rear and with two heads. Then, after mating, they began to die. They'd be eaten by birds, by wasps, by just about any small creature looking for food, or their lives simply ran their course and they fell to the ground. They became food for animals in the summer, they became nutrients for the trees when they died off into the soil, and they helped prune the trees by acting as parasites. After mating, females deposited eggs in the dead branches, which caused those limbs to eventually fall off, making it easier for the tree to supply energy to healthy limbs. The dead bodies of cicadas became nutrition for various fungi on the ground. All this, and to the people in their neighbourhood they were just one thing: the sound of summer across the continent of North America. To the people in the house, in the neighbourhood, at the university, downtown, there was an innate understanding that the disruption of any one thing was a disruption to myriad things, and yet that understanding was buried under other things – a microwaved dinner, a child's toy, a television show, an artwork on a wall, an argument, a glass of wine, an emotion, a six-pack of beer, a bratwurst, homework, a ball game, the news, an article on vegetarianism on the internet that contains a link to another article on how eating soy is a danger to the environment or an article on sustainable farming or on climate change, all viewed at the end of a day in summer when the cicadas had arrived too early – so that what was heard that night throughout the South was merely the vibration of the bodies, the hum that can reach 100 decibels, encompassing an area in a kind of magnetic energy, that then went still and quiet as the humans waited for night to begin again.

*

The West Virginia Turnpike cut through the Appalachian Mountains, switchbacking as it climbed. It was early afternoon, and their daughters were asleep in the back seat. The mountains were green with trees in full bloom. Summer, under deeply blue skies and big white cumulus clouds, rang like a bell. He liked this, driving through places he had never been to some place he had once lived. He liked looking at his daughters' sleeping faces in the back seat, mouths slightly open. Their oldest had her head tilted back and their youngest's head was tilted forwards, as though the two were balancing some unknowable equation. Both positions looked uncomfortable, but he felt good, empty. All of it, the day, the drive, sleeping daughters, would soon be a memory, he thought. He touched his wife's thigh. She was asleep too. He said they were coming to a rest stop, did she need to pee? She woke and said she did.

On the exit ramp to the rest stop, they passed a lump by the road. She was tired and couldn't tell what it was. When they'd parked, she got out, stretched and then told him she was going to see what was on the ramp. He told her he'd stay with the girls. She walked in the grass along the side of the road, back towards the on-ramp. Being outside was like stepping directly into an unending embrace: warmth, humidity, the scent of honeysuckle, insects, birds, deer, and then also the stink of a dead animal. The lump they had passed was the carcass of a dog. She walked to it and thought of all the cars that had passed the dead thing. Not one had stopped, no one got out, no one moved the dead dog off the road. When she got close to it, she saw flies were buzzing around its face and bloated stomach. Its eyes were oozing. There were maggots in its mouth and nose. She could see a trail of blood. It had probably tried to move after it had been hit. She pulled the animal and for a moment found it stuck against the hot pavement, then it came loose. Fur was left stuck to the road, in blood that had dried. It smelled worse after she moved it. She dragged the stiff thing to the grass. She looked at it a moment, sad for what it had once been. It was alive, it had suffered, and no one had comforted it, and now it was nothing. The person who hit it drove on, and the person after that didn't stop. She walked back to the rest stop bathrooms, washed her hands, peed, and washed her hands again, and then, her mind feeling vacant, she got back in the car and they went.

They watched summer out the window. The girls had been talking and singing and arguing and playing, colouring and snacking, and now they were both still napping. He said he was glad they were asleep, and she nodded in agreement. He said he was glad they hadn't seen the dog. Normally she would've said it would've been okay for them to see it, that they needed to see, they needed to know that things didn't last, and they needed to understand that now, but today she agreed. She said she was glad to be on the road and to be out of the house. To be away from their life. Me too, he said. We needed it. She said being out made everything feel a little easier, like there was no longer the weight of the last year on them. There was no longer the weight of either failing or succeeding. It was almost as if she could look back at the last year and see it like it was a novel or a film. He asked how so. She said it had almost felt like she was playing a character. He asked what he saw as her character. She said she didn't know exactly. The character of the kind of take-charge woman. Like the taking-charge-of-her-life, modern woman, stepping out of those older roles into something new and different and free, and in doing so repudiating the old values of family and mother and patriarchy and all that. Which is a fine role in a movie, she said. But I don't want to do that in my actual life. I feel like I've traded one role for another or something, she said. He said that made sense and then asked her then what did she want to do instead. She said she didn't know. It wasn't as simple as some easy narrative arc, some clear character change. She was still herself. She was different and she wasn't different. There had been a change, but it wasn't some grandiose thing. But people treat us like it's some grandiose thing. He nodded and asked, How so? She said she'd noticed something strange with their friends. Our friends address us as though nothing has changed, though also with a certain distance, she said. And I know your relatives will do the same. Our friends treat us like nothing has happened. The one or two times I've tried to talk about it, they don't know what to say, she said. He said he knew what she was talking about and actually had heard something, that a friend of theirs had been in a conversation with one of their couple-friends, and he'd said they'd all talked about them and their last year. Not gossip exactly, is what this friend had said, he said. Don't tell me, it's too easy to imagine, she said. She pretended to enter character, and then performed it in the passenger seat. They had trouble, she said. She got depressed and went to someone else. He disappeared into his work and pushed her away, he said. They began articulating the imagined conversation together. Oh yes: they had some troubles a year ago, bad troubles, infidelity and lying and all kinds of ugliness, she kicked him out, kicked him right out of the house, and during Thanksgiving. He'd done nothing wrong, she continued. Their poor daughters. So hard on them. Children feel everything, and just the stress of being in that situation can rob a child of their childhood. And that's on her, that's the mother's job, really, to provide a stable environment. But you could see the cracks. She's hard on him, she said. Too hard. But he ignores her, he said. He disappears into his work, his art, and is unavailable, and I've seen him outright ignore her in public, like she barely exists, and who wouldn't react poorly to that. Think of being ignored in small, mundane ways over years, you'd begin to feel like you were invisible, he said. But yes, it's too bad what they did to their daughters, especially the youngest. How could they not have known that things weren't right before they had children? he said. They waited too long in the first place, she said. That was part of their problem, and with him being so focused on his art, it's no wonder she gets sick of dealing with him. But still, she's too hard on him, she said. I've seen her pick a fight with him in public, completely because of her jealousy. She can be a very jealous person, and so it's really ironic and just awful that she was the one who found someone else. That really says a lot.

There was a pause in the conversation as they came to one of the three tolls on the turnpike. He paid the woman two dollars, and they resumed talking, the car cutting smoothly through the mountains with the rest of the traffic. Is that about what you heard? she said, turning in the passenger seat. Pretty much, he said. He added that there was an attempt to temper the conversation with some kindness, like, everyone gets into trouble some of the time. Something like that, he said. One of our friends also stood up for us, is what my friend said. He told her that apparently one of the women had said that she thought it was all admirable. That we'd had dark times and worked through it, he said. That that says something about us. That makes sense, she said to him. She put a hand on his shoulder. He hadn't

shaved for a few days, and she ran a thumb along his
jawline. Are you going to shave? she said. He shrugged.
She said he looked different, and then said that she understood why people would feel strange. It wasn't as though
she thought anything bad about their friends. It's just that
she felt something now, a distance of some kind. She was
sure that was on her, too. I don't know, she said. I can't put
my finger on it. It's almost like because I don't know exactly
what I'm doing, that somehow gets communicated to them,
and they don't know where I stand on things. They were
always more your friends than mine, I was always the third
wheel, but it's definitely different now, like I think people
don't know how to handle me. Like I'm either broken or
something or that I no longer approve of committed relationships. He laughed a small laugh, then said he knew
what she meant. It was as though something was somehow
wrong with them now, and no one wanted to look at that.
They treat me differently now too, he said. At the same time,
they helped me a lot. Then he said that one of the things
he noticed after all this, and after counselling especially, is
how indirect everyone is. Everyone is indirect. Everyone's
constantly hiding what they really think and feel behind
a wall of either insecurity, insincerity or judgement. Occasionally there's a crisis point and someone has to say what
they really feel, but it's strange that it takes a crisis to get
there. She said that it wasn't so strange, that was American
life. People are so distracted from what they actually think
and feel, she said. Distracted by our jobs, in which we're
overworked, distracted by entertainment and technology,
which is everywhere, and distracted by our need for
distraction. Even when we begin feeling or thinking
something significant, we don't know how to deal with it.

So we distract ourselves and call it anxiety or stress, making us slightly meaner, more aggressive versions of ourselves, she said. Or else depressed and numb versions, he said. It's what happened to us, she said. She said that they were no better than anyone. At the same time, she said, this thing we've gone through, it has changed us and let us see differently.

She began to say something else, but behind them, in the rear-view mirror, he saw a police car with its blue lights on. He said hold on for just one moment, because, not to alarm her, but there was a police car with lights on in their lane. She immediately turned around and looked out the window. She saw the police car was far, far back, rounding up the mountain curve. We've been coasting along with the other cars, he said. So we should be okay. But they were both thinking of what was in the car, and though they had given it some consideration before now – they had discussed it before leaving – they hadn't thought about what they would do if they were pulled over. They each looked in a mirror – he in the rear view and she in the side view. The police car, still rounding a bend in the mountainside, still in the distance but gaining ground, still in their lane. In the trunk, in two duffel-like suitcases, they had brought shorts and T-shirts and socks and underwear, toys and clothes for their daughters as well, books, and in the backseat, in a cooler, there were sandwiches and water for the eight-hour drive from South Carolina to Ohio. There was a bag that contained tennis rackets, a Frisbee, a soccer ball and a puzzle. All of this would appear, to anyone who looked, like the exact approximation of a normal American family, and yet, in another bag, along with sandals and tennis shoes and hiking shoes, there was four or five grams of cannabis, about two grams of Orange Kush and another two grams or so of White Fire, which he had bought from a friend, along with all the associated paraphernalia – a glass one-hitter, a glass bowl, rolling papers, a lighter. In another bag there were meditation cushions and a meditation bell, which he used every day in their second bedroom, and 8 grams of *Psilocybe cubensis*, the strain the so-called Golden Teacher, which he had grown over the previous two or three months, which in the American South would be problematic to be caught with. In the passenger seat, he observed her gripping the side door as the police car's sirens now became apparent, and he inwardly told himself that if they were getting pulled over for speeding, they looked like a completely acceptable, normal, healthy, adjusted, together American family, that they were doing nothing suspicious, that there was no reason for their car to be searched, that, in all likelihood, he would get a speeding ticket, and at worst their daughters would wake from their nap early and would be cranky for a bit of the trip. He felt his heart beating faster as the police car approached. She told him to put on the indicator. Now? he said. One second, she said. Now. They laughed. She said, You're letting him know that you're sober and aware, that we're changing lanes, officer, and we're here only to comply. She said this in an approximation of an American male voice. He manoeuvred the car from the left-hand lane to the middle lane, then, calculatedly and safely, to the right-hand lane, where he told himself he would find a safe spot to pull over, all demonstrating sobriety and good citizenry. We'll use our daughters, she said. We'll say we were just trying to get a lot of miles in when they were asleep and ask him please to not wake them. That's good, he said. Turn it around on him.

Then he said that there was really nothing to worry about, but that his heart was beating fast in his chest. When he changed lanes, though, the police car sped past. Her hand released the door handle. Their oldest daughter squirmed a bit in the back seat, opened her eyes, and began eating a bag of pretzels. Slow down, she said to him, and he did.

The drive continued for another five hours, coming down from the green mountains that cut through West Virginia and into the rolling hills of Kentucky, then into Ohio, through Athens and Ohio University and Hocking Hills, where, in a few days, they planned to ingest the psilocybin. Their daughters wanted McDonald's and then sang songs, and as they drove out of Hocking Hills and the land flattened as they came into Columbus, the hot summer day slowly faded to a cool evening. They opened the windows. Cicadas began their drone, the sound filling the car, both passing by and not, distorted by the wind and the motion of the vehicle. They didn't speak much. Inwardly, he observed their approach to Columbus. He had lived there for half of his life, until he was eighteen, then had moved to Dayton to attend college, and he returned every summer with her, and now their daughters, to visit family and see it all again, feeling more and more distant from his younger self. When he was younger, summer meant certain things. When very young, it meant family and fireflies and endless nights, and when he got older it meant friends and games and ghosts in the graveyard, and when older still it meant long drives with high school friends and weed and albums from the past generation and albums from his generation that they felt were worthy, and then it meant waiting tables and drinking too much and girlfriends and sex, and there was a sense that the world, that summer itself, was there for him. It wasn't, he thought now. Summer was no longer the summer that it had been, and it was changing all the time.

Driving into Columbus, this place that she knew but was not hers, that was his, she saw the maples, not just the sugar maples of the South but the red and silver maples, the black oaks and pin oaks, which also grew in the South, but not as much as swamp oaks and water oaks. She watched the trees, knowing that in the following summer months their trunks, depending on the species, would widen one to four centimetres. Other trees, like aspens, could grow a couple of centimetres a day. She wondered what animals were out there. She picked up her phone and Googled animals in Ohio, but they didn't have service. She put her phone back down, glad. Why had she picked it up? she thought. Looking out on the landscape, the farmland surrounded by forest, she recognised that she had once felt about such a landscape that everything was set, permanent, just there, but it wasn't, it was wildly alive, especially now. Summer itself had once seemed like a static thing; yes, things were 'alive' again, but it didn't come into her consciousness to question how they were growing, how they were changing; but now that's what she saw and felt as the day greyed over the Columbus skyline, and they approached their destination.

They got in at eight in the evening. His parents had dinner ready for them. They all embraced, put their bags away, cleaned up. This was where he had come when she needed space, she thought. What did they think of her? He watched her and wondered if she was comfortable and hoped she was. They ate on the back porch, corn and hamburgers and salad, and their daughters chased the fireflies with their grandparents, collecting them in a jar with a sprig of a tree as a home, but then, once the jar had its lid on, with little holes poked in it, their youngest asked if they could let them all go, because they wouldn't get to be with their families, and so they all went into the backyard again and released the fireflies. They did this several nights in a row. They ate meals with his parents, they felt things out, they saw his relatives and she felt left out, and she was left out, and yet his parents were gracious and understanding and welcoming, and after three days of being with family, they went to the woods to see what they could see.

*

They drove from a cabin they had rented to a park, where they ate the mushrooms. The day before, they had scouted the place and there had been no other people. There were trails and a waterfall and picnic tables, and it had reminded him of places he had taken psilocybin before, isolated places in a natural setting, and he thought it was a good spot, and she agreed. They sat in the car a moment and he asked her if she was ready. She nodded, and they ate the psilocybin with crackers. After a moment, they grabbed their packs and then went on a walk. They said little, smiling at each other occasionally. They passed by the roaring waterfall, waiting for the psychedelic effects to begin. As they passed the falls, he told her he was beginning to feel something. Twenty minutes later, she said she was feeling it too. They discussed this: they both felt nauseated, their legs rubbery, their bodies unbalanced, and they felt as though they were passing through something as they walked on the forest trail. She said she felt as though she was being squeezed through a tube, and he said he felt the same way, like his consciousness was being reduced way, way down to only physical sensations, which were kind of awful. I don't feel good, she said. It'll pass, he said. It's okay. Let's keep walking.

The trees around them, the forest itself, seemed to shrink and narrow, the path in front of them the only thing that was real. Then, some short time later, things began to change. They settled into the trip. The nausea began to release. The forest, at first almost edited out of their consciousness, began to grow and swirl and breathe around them. They began to smile and laugh at it all. All the typical things people experience on psychedelics took place: he saw the trail undulating and moving before him, and he kept tripping as he walked; she saw the trees breathing and seemingly looking at her. Are you seeing this? she said. Yes, he said. But along with this, there was anxiety. He wanted them to have some moment, something that brought them together, but it wasn't happening. They kept encountering people on the trail, the trail that had been deserted the previous day, and he continually felt powerful waves of the drug that made him feel like he was going to vomit. His arms seemed longer than usual, his legs shorter, and he kept tripping on what appeared to be nothing at all. I can't walk, he said, but I'm also having interesting thoughts. For instance, I know that I'm not really who I believe I am. What? she said. He looked at her, thought a moment, the trees swirled and morphed behind her head, and he said, I can't remember. They laughed. He recognised that he was having small insights that were pleasant and interesting, but he also saw that these insights had nothing to do with them, and he couldn't tell why that was happening, why wasn't something happening between them? For her part, she continually said that she wanted only a place to sit down, to lie down in the sun or the shade, to sit, then she burped. Sorry, she said shyly, and thought that what she really wanted was to just allow whatever was happening to happen, to be alone and to be alone with him. As they walked, she thought that she wasn't getting a chance to speak to him because they had to hide what they were really doing from the people they were passing, and so she felt frustrated.

They had to sit often, feeling tired at times and nauseated at others. It felt better to sit, and whenever people passed by, she produced an orange from her pocket and held it up for people to see. Orange time, she said. Just taking a break for orange time. They both laughed about this, and something began to loosen. They continued after people had passed. After a good bit of walking, they stopped at an open field and lay down in the sun. More walkers passed and gave them suspicious looks, but neither of them cared. They closed their eyes and watched patterns on their eyelids. The sun was hot, there was no wind. They spent some time in the field completely engulfed in psychedelic imagery and experience, which they would later relate to each other. Visual patterns, seemingly meeting other beings, their thoughts about their lives contained in metaphor. It was unclear how long they had stayed in the field, but eventually they both decided to go back to the car, to leave the park. We can't just lie here all day, she said. They manoeuvred their way back to the parking lot along the trails, back to their car. The trail was populated with people now. Hilarious people, they thought, doing and saying hilarious things. One old man explained to them how he'd had to get down on all fours to get around a rocky, muddy part of the trail, and when they crossed easily, stepping through the mud, he and his group exclaimed, Whoa, a couple of experts. Later, a gnome-like boy hopped up the side of a steep hill. Another man exclaimed, And my first camera was a Minolta! These things both made sense and didn't, and they had to work to contain their laughter.

When they made it back to the car, they stood next to it, uncertain what to do. People at picnic tables were staring. He realised they were just standing next to the car. Just get in, he said. We'll decide inside. They sat for a moment and she said, Now what do we do? and he said that this probably sounded insane, but although he couldn't fully operate his body, he thought he could operate a car. She looked at him, feeling like her eyes were so wide and would continue widening forever. This is a bad idea, right? he said. Yes, she said, but if you feel like you can do it, I say let's do it. I can't stay here. What about our daughters? he said. What about them? she said. What if we get pulled over and jailed? What if I crash? She looked at him again. Okay, then don't drive, she said. I think I can do it, he said. Then do it, she said. He turned on the car and began backing out of the space. It felt like moving some giant beast, he could feel the weight of the car, all the metal, like his mind was propelling it on. He pulled it out of the space and then drove it towards the road. They went down a small hill and she said whoa, whoa as he went off the road a little. Then he righted the car and they were moving, and she said, You're doing well. Are you hallucinating? Not at all, he said. It sort of comes in waves. Okay, she said. If you need to stop, just stop. They drove, and at first she imagined they wouldn't speak at all so that he could concentrate, but then they were talking animatedly about what had happened on the trail, which now seemed to have lasted a long time: she said it was so funny when that park ranger asked them if he had any questions, and he'd stared at the person and said, About what? And then he'd said, Oh, like about trees and stuff. He laughed and said that he hadn't realised she was a park ranger. He'd thought it was just some random stranger asking if he had questions, and at that moment, he said, he had so many questions. She said it was pretty weird that they'd just decided to lie down in a field. I got some ugly looks, she said. I didn't even notice, he said. I was so engrossed in what was going on behind my eyelids. Which was what? she said. He said he seemed to meet a man, who showed him things. A sort of carnival, but the carnival was just a disguise, and the man was disguised too, as a sort of jester. Mainly, he said, it was terrifying. The visual hallucinations seemed to grow in size and I felt small, and this jester-like character, well, I began to question my sanity. And now? she said. Now I feel like he's a little shithead that I don't want to play with anymore. He asked what'd she seen in the field. She told him it was so lovely, not frightening at all. She'd entered a rose-coloured room and met a rose lady, who showed her her life. A train of images. She was on the train, then watching the train. It wasn't images so much as the emotions of my life, she said. It's very hard to describe. He said he'd really love to meet her, the rose lady, that sounded much better than his mushroom man. She said she wasn't sure that was how it worked, she couldn't just introduce him without getting to know her better. Then they both began laughing, smiling at each other while they were driving. Eyes on the road, she said. Right, he said.

When they arrived back at the cabin, she laid out a
blanket. He put their bag down next to it and they both col-
lapsed in the small yard, the forest all around them. A plane
passed in the sky and made the blue ripple, as though the
sky were made of water. They watched the clouds forming
different patterns. Insects flew around them, dragonflies
and bees and butterflies, and the cabin sat quietly in the
woods. Her hand touched his arm, and he moved his body
closer to hers. She touched his face, his chin, and turned
his head to hers and she looked into his eyes, green and
brown, the same green in their daughters' eyes, and he felt
her hand gently turn his chin to her and he looked into her
eyes, blue-grey, and she felt that there was nothing else,
only his eyes, and he felt that there was nothing else, only
her eyes, that all the universe was there, that something
had been cut off, some way of thinking had ended, the circles that had been there before were suddenly gone, and
a new circle formed. The trees made a rushing sound in the
wind, which was the wind inside them and outside them,
and she saw all the pain he was carrying and she felt it go
into her, through her, and then pass away, and he saw her
crying and knew all the pain he'd caused her, and he felt
it come into him and then move out of him on the breeze,
and he heard her voice say that she was scared, what was
happening right now, which were also his words, and then
something in each of them gave way fully and there were no
more words for some time, only smiling eyes, until, sometime later on the blanket, they said thank you to the other
for this, their last year. He pulled her to him and they closed
their eyes, body and minds melting together, slipping
gently into the ground, no distinction between them, not
between the ground or the trees or the sky or the sun, each

271

a part of each in the shaded lawn in front of the cabin, their breath in unison with the wind blowing their hearts beating together their bodies dissolving, no eyes, no ears, no nose, no tongue, no bodies, no minds, no consciousness, no earth no trees, everything rubbed out the sky fading away the clouds the sun the solar system the galaxy stars slipping away, gone, gone, falling away dripping away faster and faster towards a singularity which vanished into the pregnant void from which all things come and go, no coming and going at all, and they were no longer there, and then from that dark depthless place there was a sound like tinnitus, an almost imperceptible quiet high-pitched humming sound that turned into a louder whine that grew louder and louder into the buzz-like sound of the universe itself vibrating. They smiled when they opened their eyes. It was cicadas, beginning their afternoon singing.

The cabin looked pleasant set against the forest. Wind blew through the tulip trees and beeches and made the trunks rock gently. The forest appeared endless. It seemed to become bigger the more they looked into it. It felt like a stream pulling them along, they were it and it was them. The sun moved below the treeline, casting long shadows that seemed to ripple over their bodies. Insects flew in the slanting light. Dust motes. Ants on the ground. They could see emotions like palpable things inside them, which they handled with great care. Two deer flashed by between the trees. They watched it all without any understanding, completely engrossed in the recognition of a thing that could not be spoken but which felt like a long-forgotten home.

*

They slept through the late afternoon and woke in the evening. The world was aglow: a blazing orange sunset, lighting the blacktop road and making it a mirror; treetops tipped with orange; cicadas buzzing in the small town they went to for dinner; people, all of them strange, smiling or frowning or with no expression at all, all lost – punks and yuppies and hippies and millennials and children and parents – and them lost among them, enjoying being lost among them. They walked to dinner and called his parents to see how their daughters were. They had gone to the zoo, they had seen elephants, tigers, polar bears, penguins. The animals were behind glass, their youngest said. The animals were happy, their oldest said. It was a good zoo. But the youngest worried about the animals not being able to go home, to their real home. They agreed she was right. They listened on speakerphone. Their daughters had a lot to tell them, and they listened and then said they would see them tomorrow.

They arrived at a Mediterranean place. It was full of people, some in cut-off shorts and tank tops, some who looked like ageing golfers, a woman in a sari. When the waiter came, he seemed unnerved by them, though they hadn't said or done anything differently, and they laughed when he went away. Maybe our pupils are still big, he said. She leaned in and looked. No, she said. Then they ordered and laughed at what they had done, they couldn't believe they had done that, they couldn't believe he'd driven the car, they said they could've died, they said he shouldn't have done that, he said she was supposed to tell him that, she said she couldn't possibly have. He seemed utterly new to her, her eyes and hair, expressions and gestures. She saw that he couldn't stop touching her and smiling at her, and she felt herself there again with him, like it had been, it hadn't gone away, it had always been there, it was there again now, and then she realised she felt utterly new to herself. She seemed radiant to him while she ate her salad, elegant and clumsy at once, a piece of salad stuck in the corner of her mouth, laughing, talking, telling him what she'd felt and seen, and he felt he had taken so much for granted, taken her for granted, and he knew he would again, but it wouldn't be the same, he'd remember, he told himself to remember. He asked her for a favour and she said maybe, what? He told her that if he ever began to take her, or their life, for granted again, and she saw it, was able to see it, to let him know what he was doing. He said he was going to need help. She nodded quickly and said me too. She reached under the table and squeezed his hand. Then she said, Did we do that? I mean, did we make all of that happen this afternoon? And he said he thought so, he didn't know for sure. She said didn't it make sense that it wouldn't have happened that way if they hadn't wanted it to. If we hadn't both wanted it to? It was never just going to happen on its own, she said. He said he hadn't thought of that but that it sounded right to him. So it was a choice, then, she said. Which must mean that it's a choice every moment. Every moment had been, she said. We made it all. He looked at her.

After dinner they walked the streets, they drove back to the cabin, they slept, they made love in the morning, they drove back to their daughters and his parents and then they drove back to their home in the Blue Ridge Mountains. The summer went on. They said to themselves and the few they chose to share it with and who chose to listen that they had been reminded of something vitally important,

274

something about their relationship, yes, but also about a new kind of relationship, which they were just seeing. What was it? When they tried to wrap words around it, it couldn't be spoken. It was easily reduced to a cliché, they realised, so they kept it to themselves. It was theirs. It was everyone's, too, they said to each other, but this version of it was theirs.

the lover his wife had ~~faded~~ away too ~~tidily~~ & we don't get her interia experience of LOSS w/ that — failure of imagination & empathy b/c too painful for him, but its okay. still a really nice story.

For their support and encouragement, I am grateful to Seren Adams, Eric Kocher, Tao Lin, Mamie Morgan and Patrick Whitfill. Thank you to Jess Chandler for giving this book a home at Prototype and to Aimee Selby for all her hard work – thank you both for taking such good care. Most importantly, thank you to Emily Rossi, for living this life with me and for living this book with me – you wrote half.

( ) (   ) p   prototype

poetry / prose / interdisciplinary projects / anthologies

Creating new possibilities in the publishing of fiction and poetry through a flexible, interdisciplinary approach and the production of unique and beautiful books.

Prototype is an independent publisher working across genres and disciplines, committed to discovering and sharing work that exists outside the mainstream.

Each publication is unique in its form and presentation, and the aesthetic of each object is considered critical to its production.

Prototype strives to increase audiences for experimental writing, as the home for writers and artists whose work requires a creative vision not offered by mainstream literary publishers.

In its current, evolving form, Prototype consists of 4 strands of publications:

(type 1 – poetry)
(type 2 – prose)
(type 3 – interdisciplinary projects)
(type 4 – anthologies) including an annual anthology
of new work, *PROTOTYPE*.

Forthcoming

(type 2 – prose)
Vehicle by Jen Calleja (2023)
Lori & Joe by Amy Arnold (2023)
Pleasure Beach by Helen Palmer (2023)

Back Catalogue

(type 1 – poetry)
Plainspeak by Astrid Alben (2019)
Safe Metamorphosis by Otis Mensah (2020)
Republic Of Dogs/Republic Of Birds by Stephen Watts (2016/2020)
Home by Emily Critchley (2021)
Away From Me by Caleb Klaces (2021)
Path Through Wood by Sam Buchan-Watts (2021)
Two Twin Pipes Sprout Water by Lila Matsumoto (2021)
Deltas by Leonie Rushforth (2022)
Island mountain glacier by Anne Vegter, trans. Astrid Alben (2022)
Little Dead Rabbit by Astrid Alben (2022)
Twenty-Four Hours by Stephen Watts (2022)
Emblem by Lucy Mercer (2022)

(type 2 – prose)
Fatherhood by Caleb Klaces (2019)
I'm Afraid That's All We've Got Time For by Jen Calleja (2020)
The Boiled in Between by Helen Marten (2020)
Along the River Run by Paul Buck (2020)
Lorem Ipsum by Oli Hazzard (2021)
The Weak Spot by Lucie Elven (2021)
Deceit by Yuri Felsen, trans. Bryan Karetnyk (2022)

(type 3 – interdisciplinary projects)
alphabet poem: for kids! by Emily Critchley, Michael Kindellan
& Alison Honey Woods (2020)
The sea is spread and cleaved and furled by Ahren Warner (2020)
Songs for Ireland by Robert Herbert McClean (2020)
microbursts by Elizabeth Reeder & Amanda Thomson (2021)

(type 4 – anthologies)
Try To Be Better ed. Sam Buchan-Watts & Lavinia Singer (2019)
PROTOTYPE 1 (2019)
PROTOTYPE 2 (2020)
Intertitles: An anthology at the intersection of writing & visual art ed.
Jess Chandler, Aimee Selby, Hana Noorali & Lynton Talbot (2021)
PROTOTYPE 3 (2021)
PROTOTYPE 4 (2022)

Our Last Year by Alan Rossi
Published by Prototype in 2022

Design by Matthew Stuart & Andrew Walsh-Lister
(Traven T. Croves)
Typeset in Marist by Seb McLauchlan
Printed in the UK by TJ Books

ISBN 978-1-913513-26-9

(type 2 – prose)
www.prototypepublishing.co.uk
@prototypepubs

prototype publishing
71 oriel road
london e9 5sg
uk

( )

ISBN 1913513262

9 781913 513269